Nine Tol

By

Pamela Cartlidge

BOOKS BY PAMELA CARTLIDGE

Bluebells and tin hats
Rhubarb without Sugar
Restless Yew Tree Cottage
Text me from your Grave
Waltzing with Ghosts

Foreword

Nine tolls for murder is a fictitious novel. All the characters, their work places and addresses are creations of my imagination. Place names such as Saint Winefride's well, Saltney, Chester, Wrexham and other well-known towns and cities that surround the area, have been mentioned in a fictitious form. The lake referred to does not exist, I only wish it did! The town of Saltney actually encompasses the border of Wales and England.

For the purposes of the novel, I have also re-arranged the geographical area that surrounds the town of Holywell.

Any resemblance to actual persons living or deceased, or events such as the wedding is purely coincidental.

A bit about Holywell

The small market town of Holywell in North Wales is the central location for this novel. It is approximately twenty five miles away from Wrexham where I was born and grew up.

Being close to the Dee estuary and the North Wales coast, family day trips in the car to the beach invariably took us through Holywell, but without stopping! So I was aware of the myths, legends call it what you will about St. Winefride's well from an early age, although I actually didn't visit the place until many decades later.

The well and the small pool around it took my breath away, far exceeding my expectations. Whilst I hadn't intended to write a story about St. Winefride, somehow a little time after my first visit, I got the inspiration to write "Text me from your Grave" and then "Nine tolls for Murder."

This book was first drafted in 2020, and whilst I know Coronavirus is a much disliked word, I felt it would be unjust not to, at the very least, to mention it.

Pamela Cartlidge

Nine Tolls for Murder

CHAPTER ONE

Friday 28 February 2020

Phil waited until Emily had negotiated the car park barriers to leave Manchester airport before starting to chat.

'So how's the new job going?'

Emily took a few seconds to glance at her brother in the driver's mirror. His hazel brown eyes matched her own.

'Great! It's not as if I haven't been doing the job for the last two years. Now it's official at last and I'm being paid the appropriate salary. The school governors have actually got round to appointing my replacement. How's yours?'

Phil groaned. 'Actually, I'm not working at the moment. At least not for any real financial gain.' In the mirror, he saw his sister raise quizzical eyebrows. Before he could say anything further Clare intervened.

'As a matter of fact he is working hard, with research and other stuff but not at the university.'

'Oh!' Emily said. 'I take it the contract came to an end and wasn't renewed?'

'Yes,' Phil sighed. 'But there's a chance of something better, if things go according to plan.'

'Would it mean coming back to the UK to work? It would be great having you home again.'

'Hard to say,' he said lightly, choosing not to elaborate.

In the driver's mirror, Emily recognised a secretive glance pass between Phil and Clare and decided not to ask any more questions. She knew that look. It was a "we'll tell you when we're ready kind of look." She wanted to ask about her sister-in-law's work, but held back. There would be plenty of time for that conversation later. She pushed a stray, dark strand of hair behind her ear then changed the subject.

'It's good news about Gavin and Abigail getting married.'

Phil grinned. His eyes twinkled as he recalled the day when his friend met his future bride.

'They hit it off right from the start. Even though Gav wasn't at the best place in his life for romance,' he said.

Emily inclined her head slightly in a gesture of sympathy. 'Yes that was a terrible time for him and his dad, losing his mother so soon after Rachel's murder. By the way Sergeant Ward asked after you quite recently.' A smile edged Emily's lips. 'I think he always suspected that you had something to do with solving the case. He hinted broadly about séances, but I didn't enlighten him.' Emily's smile widened.

'Why were you talking to Sergeant Ward?' Phil asked.

'His wife Christine and her friend Susan come to my book club. Sometimes he picks them up, so that they can have a couple of glasses of wine. When he found out you and I are related, he hung around a while to talk to me. Usually he's in a hurry to get away.'

Phil nodded, remembering his conversation with the sergeant almost two years earlier.

'It was obvious he wanted to talk about you,' Emily went on. 'He did it in a covert sort of way, asking questions about Dad. He must have found out that Dad is a magistrate.'

Phil grinned. 'He's done some background checks on me.'

'Yes, and when Christine realised that you are my brother and the psychic who'd held the séance at the house of her friend Susan, well the conversation rocketed.' Emily's unrestrained laughter filled the car. 'I'm guessing that the sergeant - diligent and attentive as he is - doesn't want to accept that anything to do with the supernatural had solved the murder case.'

Clare smirked. 'And yet he asks questions about Phil?'

'Yep. It's like he can't help himself!'

Emily parked her Honda Jazz outside St. Winefride's hotel.

'I'm sorry I can't put you up in my house, the wedding has come at a bad time. For us I mean. We are still renovating the house, and the kids are sharing a room with a lot of our downstairs furniture.' She laughed. 'Fortunately they think it's funny.

They play hide and seek a lot under the dust covers. I didn't think you would be comfortable downstairs on the sofa bed with all the building materials stacked around you, though it's actually not too bad...once you get used to it. I mean if you were really stuck...'

Clare put a reassuring hand on her sister-in-law's shoulder. 'Don't worry. The hotel is fine.'

Phil got the cases out of the car.

'We'll see you later at your place. Thanks for the lift.' He put down the luggage and waved to his sister as she drove away. Turning towards the hotel entrance, he put his arms across Clare's shoulders. Together they gazed for a few seconds at the front of the hotel.

'Here we are again,' Clare whispered softly. 'Though this time it's for a happy event. A wedding.'

Phil bent down and kissed his wife lightly on the forehead.

'Ours was brilliant. Come on, let's check into our room. If we're lucky we'll have a view of the old cathedral.'

A few hours later after checking in, Clare picked up her swipe card, closed the bedroom door and followed her husband along the third floor corridor of the hotel towards the lift. At a corner of the passageway she stopped at the window to admire the view.

'You can see almost all of the lake from here.' She stood on tip toe, straining her neck in an attempt to see more.

Phil, three inches taller looked over her shoulder and supported her as she fell against him. 'Steady now.' He took in the vista below. 'I've never been this high up in the hotel.'

Through the falling dusk he gazed at the large expanse of water, noting the rowing boats at various spots on the lake. Some were clustered together, a few were at isolated positions. For a second, his eyes drifted from the water and took in the grey sky. A glance at his watch told him it was quarter to five.

'They'll be calling the rowers in very soon. The light is fading, though it isn't too bad, considering it's not yet March. Technically it would be tomorrow, if it wasn't for the fact that we have a leap year.'

'I'm not sure I like the idea of getting married on the twenty ninth of February,' remarked Clare, not for the first time since they received the invitation to the wedding. 'How do you celebrate your anniversary?'

'There's something exciting about it though, don't you think? Like changing the dynamics of life and death.'

'Are you suggesting there is something supernatural about a leap year?' Clare raised her eyebrows at her husband.

Phil shrugged. 'I don't dismiss the idea.' He turned to focus on the lake again, allowing his eyes to rove the glistening water. He frowned as he caught sight of two boats that seemed to be further out from the rest.

'There are a couple of strays over there. One of them seems to be struggling.

They'll need a strong arm to row back to the club before it gets dark. It might be a round up job for the wardens if they don't hurry.' As he spoke he watched one lone rower battling with the oars, and for the first time in many months, his thoughts returned to the last occasion he had visited the lake.

A familiar feeling disturbed him. Shockwaves shuddered through his body taking him by surprise. He shook himself out of his reverie turning to comment upon this unexpected sensation to his wife. But Clare was already walking away from him towards the stairs. She called to him over her shoulder.

'Come on, the lift is taking ages, let's walk.'

Phil pushed his thoughts to one side and followed his wife downstairs.

*

Emily lived in a hamlet known as Five Bells. Locals assumed it was so named because of the bells of a small and old church that stood in the middle of the village. It was frequently over looked by tourists, despite its history, most likely because of the close proximity of the ancient St. Winefride's Cathedral that dominated the town.

When they reached Bell Lane, after a twenty minute walk from the hotel, Phil knocked the door of Willow Cottage and waited for his sister to answer. Emily took them to the garden where she had placed her patio table under a gazebo. The table was laid ready for their meal.

'Thank goodness the weather is fine, though I know it isn't very warm.' She pointed to the crocheted blankets hanging over each chair. 'If you get cold these should warm you up. I'm lucky to have this outdoor space, seeing as the house is a construction site. I'm not sure how waterproof this shelter is, but the weather forecast said it will be dry. She poured them glasses of wine then pointed to the stacks of building materials pushed to one side. Under Emily's supervision, the builders had camouflaged the eyesore with tarpaulin. Bricks, and a concrete paving slab had been placed on top to keep it in place.

'I know the garden could be more attractive. I'm sorry about the mess, but one day soon it will look lovely.'

Phil grinned at his sister. 'The price you pay for alterations.' He watched as she stopped at various points in the garden to place a lantern containing a candle on top of the bricks. 'At least that makes it a bit better.'

She stepped back and sipped her drink. 'Cheers.' They raised their glasses in a toast. 'It's good to see you both again. I'm so pleased you're here.' Emily wiped a tear from her eye. 'Don't mind me, I'm getting emotional.' She put her drink down. 'Right I must leave you for a few minutes to give my attention to the food. She returned five minutes later accompanied by two more guests. Phil got up to greet them, a wide grin on his face.

'Gavin! How are you old mate?' The friends ignored their instincts to grab each other by the shoulders and slap backs. Instead, they nodded their heads and bumped elbows, with resigned sighs and shrugs.

'Good to see you again.'

'You too. So glad you could make it. I really appreciate you coming.' Gavin turned towards the woman beside him. 'You remember Abigail?'

'Of course. Congratulations to you both.' Phil imitated kissing Abigail on each of her cheeks and then introduced her to Clare. As they exchanged greetings, Phil observed wryly that Abigail's hair, which he recalled was blonde heavily streaked with purple last time he saw her, was now predominantly blonde. However, the shimmering strands that had been deftly woven through her golden tresses, which Phil perceived had entranced his friend, still remained. Gavin's usual shoulder length brown hair, looked well groomed; a testament, he supposed to Abi's good work as a stylist. He still wore the small gold sleeper in one ear.

'Sorry we couldn't put you up at home. Abi's parents' house is full of bridesmaids and dad's place is chocka with relatives. Some, I haven't seen for years!'

'No worries. It's a trip down memory lane for us staying at the hotel. It was the beginning of our honeymoon five years ago.' He glanced at Clare who returned his smile.

'Have you two sorted out a honeymoon?' Clare asked. She looked from first Gavin then to Abi. A shake of Gavin's head corresponded with his fiancé's.

'Sort of. We …' Gavin started to say.

Abi reached for his hand. 'It will be just fine,' she explained. 'Travel anywhere in the world is dicey what with this virus spreading everywhere. We don't want to worry about queues at airports for health checks and all that, so we've rented a cottage in Anglesey for a weekend and we'll have a big holiday next year.'

Gavin turned to Phil. 'Thanks for agreeing to be my best man and again for coming. Both of you.' He smiled at Clare as he added his last remark. 'I just hope you won't be too inconvenienced with this blasted Covid19, and you can get back to Transylvania without a problem.'

'Don't worry. There weren't any restrictions to get here. It's not like Italy and Spain. We had no problems coming out,' Clare assured him.

Abigail laughed nervously. 'At the moment there are no UK travel restrictions which is a relief, because we have guests coming from places all over the country, as well as some from abroad.'

'Fingers crossed,' Clare said. 'We're hoping to enjoy a few extra days here after the wedding.'

Despite the unusual warmth of the early evening, the nights were still chilly and they were glad of the blankets Emily had provided as they chatted into the night. They reluctantly relinquished them to put on their coats to leave.

'I hope the weather stays dry for tomorrow,' Clare commented on the short stroll back to the hotel. 'At least we haven't got far to walk from the hotel if it rains. No buses or taxis to get or worry about parking. I wonder how many guests there will be.'

'Thirty-six, I think Gavin said.' Phil smiled playfully at his wife. 'Living ones anyway. Who can say how many others there will be?'

CHAPTER TWO

The wedding was to take place in St. Winefride's Cathedral a ten minute walk from the hotel. Phil and Clare arrived with plenty of time to take up their places on the front pew next to the bridegroom and his father.

Nervously Gavin tugged at his ear as he scanned the high walls of the cathedral. He half expected, half hoped, to see something out of the ordinary beyond the strategically placed video cameras. Beside him his father breathed heavily. Catching sight of his son's eyes, Dan saw reflected there the same anticipation he was feeling. Laced with the excitement of waiting for the bride was a yearning for something extra.

They were not alone in their expectations. Phil casually surveyed the niches and pillars. He couldn't feel any exceptional supernatural presence, other than the aura he usually felt in churches, though like his friend he was hopeful for something special. He just didn't know what. He inhaled deeply relaxing his muscles, making himself accessible to a paranormal vibe.

At that precise moment, Gavin's late mother Anna placed herself outside the cathedral entrance to wait for the bride to arrive.

Rachel floated towards her along with three of their phantom buddies Margareta, Desmond and Stefan.

'I'm glad they decided to get married here,' Anna said giving Rachel an air kiss.

'I think they chose to get married in this cathedral on purpose Mum. Making Phil his best man was a good idea too. Do you think we will be able to make contact?'

Anna sighed. 'Now you have lost your special powers, it will be difficult, but Phil senses things. If we combine our efforts we may be able to make him aware of us.'

'Hmm. I had meant to hover around him when he came through the gates, but I was on the roof trying to catch a glimpse of Abigail. I concentrated hard on watching for the car to arrive with the bride and her father and so forgot Phil and Clare. When I spotted them by the door, I floated down to circulate them but they'd already gone inside. They're probably with Dad and Gav. I'll try to make contact as soon as the ceremony starts, I just want to see Abi arriving…'

'I thought you said you didn't like weddings,' Stefan grinned whilst Rachel pulled a face.

'I'll make an exception for my brother!'

'Look here she comes,' Margareta floated excitedly towards the lych-gate. Together the five spectres watched as Abigail stepped out of the beribboned limousine. Doors opened from a similar car behind her. Three young women and a child trod lightly on to the gravel outside the cemetery wall. Their satin shoes made no sound as they took their places behind the bride.

'Four bridesmaids! Blimey,' Rachel commented. 'That's a bit over the top.'

Anna gave her daughter a withering look. 'She could hardly not ask her sisters and best friend could she? I suppose the little girl is a relative of Abi's.'

Rachel shrugged. 'Well I wouldn't even bother to get married with all this fuss. Even before I was murdered, I always said, I wouldn't waste money on a wedding.'

Rachel's words were lost on her companions as they watched Abigail on her father's arm, walk sedately along the path towards the cathedral's arched doorway. The bridesmaids giggled behind her as they and the bride tried not to trip over their long gowns.

'They could be phantasms the way they glide in those clothes,' Stefan commented.

Rachel laughed then changed her expression after her mother sent her a silent rebuke.

Inside the cathedral, Anna and Rachel perched themselves in front of the first pew where Gavin, Dan, Phil and Clare waited. Both spectres concentrated hard on trying to make contact with Phil. Their own phantom allies along with other departed spirits lined the high recesses of the cathedral. They looked forward to the event to brighten up their dull, interminable routine.

As the bride approached the altar, the three waiting men and Clare stood up along with the rest of the congregation. It was then that Phil felt a familiar sensation swathe his body. He let out a small gasp and winked at Dan who'd turned to raise a querying eyebrow. He silently mouthed the question 'Anna?' Phil nodded and a satisfied smile curved Dan's lips.

Gavin, whose full attention beamed on Abigail missed the sign language between his father and best man. When Phil passed the rings to the anxious groom he whispered in his ear, 'they're here.'

The beam on Gavin's face broadened as he and Abigail exchanged rings. Softly he repeated the message to his bride. She raised astonished eyes to her new husband.

'Wow,' she murmured.

'They know,' Anna said triumphantly. She shared a grin of satisfaction with Rachel.

When the newlyweds left the congregation to sign the register, the bridesmaids were left behind whilst the congregation listened to a recorded version of the *"Flower Duet" by Leo Delibes*. Anna and Rachel remained hovering near the altar and became aware of the youngest bridesmaid staring at them.

'Do you think she can see us?' Anna asked.

'I don't know. Let's shift our position, see if she watches us.'

The two spirits floated towards the ceiling. The little girl raised her head, her eyes followed them. Anna and Rachel returned to the altar and the child turned to watch.

'Let's keep still for now. We don't want to cause a fuss,' Anna advised. *'When they go outside for photos let's see if we can distract her from the group.'*

'I agree to keep still, but how are we going to make contact with the child? She's only about five, maybe six. She'll be with her relatives.'

They were interrupted by Margareta enthusing about the bride's beautiful dress and those of the bridesmaids.

'Do you think Abi's dress is made of silk? I love the embroidered hearts decorated with pearls around the neckline.'

Anna and Rachel agreed with nods.

'I'm also glad to see Nicky so happy,' Margareta continued. *'After all that trouble she went through, this is such a joyous occasion. Almost like a reward. After all she might have died if it hadn't been for you Rachel.'* She moved away again to get a closer look.

Rachel shrugged and turned to Anna again. 'What shall we do, Mum? That little bridesmaid is so young. It's the first time a child has ever seen me. A man saw me once, but I managed to elude him.'

'I'm not sure yet. We don't want to frighten her.' Anna frowned trying to think what to do.

'I wonder if she thinks we're ghosts,' Rachel replied. *'She might just think we are real people who can float in the air?'*

Anna frowned. 'That's something I would very much like to know. Also, if she can hear us.'

The guests followed the bride and groom outside. There they gathered in groups for photographs whilst listening to the peal of the church bells.

Anna was relieved that they were in tune and that the bell ringers hadn't been put off their stride by Thomas who loved to try to disturb them at work. Anna had warned him that she would be very annoyed if he did anything to spoil her son's wedding day. Thomas had promised he wouldn't. Not even an old timer like Thomas was willing to invoke Anna's wrath. She was a formidable spirit. Within the two years of her death she had launched a successful campaign and got herself elected as an Assessor and was highly respected by the other seven Assessors.

The downside of that position, she often lamented, prevented her from lodging a request to be a full ghost. Such a wish granted, would give her permission to roam freely outside the confines of St. Winefride's Well and Cathedral.

An opportunity to distract the young bridesmaid came when the photographer arranged various groups with the bride and groom. The child fidgeted, evidently bored. Eventually, she managed to detach herself from her mother who was absorbed in the bonhomie of the wedding. The little girl ran up and down the paths singing songs to herself. Feeling sorry for her, Clare took her hand and led her to a side of the cathedral where it was quiet.

'I think that's Phil's wife,' Anna said. 'I didn't know her very well, I met her only a *few times after they were married. She's changed since then. Thinner I think, though she wasn't over weight to begin with, and her hair is shorter than I remember it. Still attractive though. She has a lovely amiable smile. Look how she reaches out to the child. I can see why Phil loves her.'*

'Do you think she is psychic like Phil?' Rachel asked.

'Let's find out. But first of all we'd better explain to Margareta what we're up to. She can tell Desmond and Stefan to stay back. They're hovering over there.'

'If the girl can see us, surely she can see all of the spirits? She seems calm anyway. Actually, if she can see all the dead, she might indeed think we are real,' Rachel said with a giggle. 'Even though there are some strange looking sights in the graveyard. Fortunately most of the decrepit ones are hanging around inside the cathedral or on the roof.'

Anna frowned impatiently. 'Come on. Clare might be able to help us.'

Clare held the bridesmaid's hand firmly and was explaining that after the photos, there would be lots of food and drink.

'Will we have burgers and chips?' The girl asked.

'Oh yes. How wonderful,' Rachel sighed. 'I haven't had a burger for ages. I suppose they'll be having a hot roast dinner. Or maybe a buffet with hot food.'

'What's a buffet?' The girl's eyes fixed on Rachel. Astonished that the child spoke

to her, she wafted a bit nearer. Anna watched in awe.

'Hello, can you hear me?' Rachel realised as soon as she said it, that this was a stupid question because it was obvious she could. 'What's your name?'

'Lucy. What's your name? How do you fly? I saw you in the church. Can you show me how to do it?'

'What are you talking about Lucy?' Clare was mystified. She looked from left to right then stared at the space where Lucy was pointing.

'Those ladies can fly. I saw them?'

'Quick tell her our names, so that Clare can tell Phil,' urged Anna.

'I like your orangutan Tee shirt. I want to grow my hair long like yours. You look like a fairy princess!' she giggled.

'Do you think so?' Rachel laughed. She'd never compared her streaky auborn hair with a fairy princess before.

'Is that lady in the blue dress your mummy?'

'Yes. Her name is Anna and I am Rachel.'

'Hello Rachel.'

'Who are you talking to Lucy?'

'Rachel and Anna. I want to fly like they can. Auntie Clare can I fly with them?'

Clare's face paled. 'Did you say Rachel and Anna?'

'Yes, I said,' the child answered impatiently.

'What should we do Mum?' Rachel asked. 'If we tell her we're ghosts she might *get frightened. Clare is already scared out of her wits.'*

Anna thought quickly. 'Let's use the experience to pass on our good wishes to the bride and groom. It's more than we hoped for. What else can we do? We can't risk giving the girl nightmares.'

Rachel bent down to the girl. 'Lucy we have to go now. Can you tell Auntie Clare to say congratulations to Gavin and Abi?'

'But I want to fly like you. Don't go Rachel.'

Clare felt her legs trembling and her heart racing. Despite having attended a few of her husband's séances, she'd never been able to overcome her fear of the supernatural. Guardedly she looked around her as if to see Rachel and Anna standing near. Without knowing why she felt scared or saying another word to Lucy she pulled the child away. The two spirits made an effort to move as if they were walking. They needn't have worried, Lucy's attention had been taken by the confetti that the guests were throwing over the married couple. One of the older bridesmaids handed Lucy a box of the stuff. Immediately distracted, the child joined in the conviviality as the entire entourage made their way out of St. Winefride's Cathedral grounds then walk the short distance to St. Winefride's hotel where the reception was to take place.

Phil and Clare strolled together accompanied by other guests who engaged them in light hearted chatter and complimentary comments about the ceremony. It was twenty minutes later before Clare was able to whisper to Phil what she had witnessed.

CHAPTER THREE

They didn't tell Gavin and Dan about Clare's experience in the graveyard until the newlyweds were getting ready to leave for their mini honeymoon. All five gathered in Phil and Clare's room at the hotel where the newly married couple had arranged to get changed.

Phil leaned against the bedroom door as he addressed his friends.

'We've got some news for you. You'd better sit down first, it might come as a bit of shock,' he advised. He turned to his wife.

'Over to you darling.'

Clare sat on one side of the bed and crossed her legs to face her audience. She unconsciously traced with a finger, the pattern of her embossed jacquard trousers. The matching green jacket lay discarded at the end of the bed. Gavin, ignoring the advice to sit down, remained standing, propped up against the wardrobe door. Abigail, still in her bridal dress leaned into him. She smoothed down the silken folds of her gown with her hands as she focused on Clare. Despite her bewilderment that she and Gavin were not alone in the room as planned; the excitement of the day still rippled through her leaving her content to gaze indulgently at those gathered around her. She examined her fingers, admiring the golden embellishments on her finger nails and how they set off her engagement and wedding rings. Dan sat in the only available armchair in the room, as equally puzzled as his son and daughter-in-law.

'Outside in the cathedral grounds, I looked after your youngest bridesmaid,' Clare began. She turned towards Abigail, who nodded.

'My cousin Lucy.'

'She started saying the weirdest things, staring at things that I couldn't see and then she spoke Rachel's name as well as Anna's.'

'What? You're joking!' Abigail's blue eyes widened and a hesitant smile edged her face as she glanced at her new husband.

Gavin and his father shot each other an astonished glance. Yet neither were surprised to recognise a glimmer of excitement mingled with shock in their respective faces.

'But how? Are you sure?' Dan asked. He wanted to believe it, but why would his late wife and daughter communicate with an unknown five year old girl?

Clare took in a deep breath. 'I know you're shocked, I was too. I still am. But, there's more. Lucy could see them!'

Gavin blinked. 'What?'

Dan's body moved forward, his hands gripped the sides of his chair. 'Lucy saw them did you say?' he asked hoarsely.

Abigail's complexion matched the white of her gown. She turned to face Gavin clutching his hand then wheeled round again to speak to Clare.

'But Anna and Rachel don't know Lucy. My cousin and her family live in Harrogate, we only see them about twice a year.'

Phil intervened. 'I have heard of this kind of phenomena before. Some young children are able to see ghosts, but they don't realise that's what they are. I'm not saying all children can, there has to be some kind of sixth sense present for it to happen.'

'But how do you know the child saw them?' Dan asked. He pulled out a handkerchief from his shirt pocket and mopped his forehead. Trembling fingers unbuttoned the top button of his shirt then loosened his tie. His son copied him.

'Lucy said she admired Rachel's "Tee" shirt. She said something about an orangutan?' Clare spoke gently.

Open mouthed Dan nodded. He checked his son's bewildered expression before speaking again. Gavin tightened his grip on Abigail's hand. She rested her free hand on top of his.

'Oh!..Yes! My late wife Anna insisted upon dressing Rachel's body in it for the coffin.'

'Lucy also mentioned the woman in the blue dress. Would that be Anna?' Again Dan nodded. 'She referred to it as her turquoise outfit. We buried her in it.'

Gavin breathed out slowly. 'This is amazing. Hard to take in.'

Disregarding social distancing advice, Phil put a reassuring hand on his friend's shoulder. All day the wedding party guests had tried not to get too close to each other, many of them forgetting the government guidance on Coronavirus. Several guests had worn a face mask, whereas others had mingled freely, enjoying the social event, regardless of what the consequences may be. Most people believed that such a horrible disease wouldn't infect them.

Up until this moment Phil had maintained a decent distance, even in the church. But now, on this special day, Gavin needed some extra support.

'Look upon it as an extra wedding gift. I felt them breeze in when we were at the altar. I told you that,' Phil turned to face Dan. 'You were both half expecting, half hoping anyway weren't you?'

The men nodded.

'There's something else,' Clare said smiling. 'Lucy said, that Anna had told her to pass on their congratulations.'

'Oh so that's what she meant,' Abigail laughed nervously. 'She kept coming to me and saying, "The lady said congratulations." I wondered what lady she meant, but forgot about it. Lucy ran off and of course I got distracted, talking to the other guests.'

'After I heard Lucy talking, I felt I ought to take her away in case she realised they were ghosts. But in any case she was already saying goodbye to them,' Clare said.

Dan breathed heavily. 'Well I don't know what to say. This is the icing on the…wedding cake!' He smiled at his new daughter-in-law. 'What family have you married into Abi?'

Abigail stepped towards him to give him a hug. 'A wonderful one.'

Phil turned to Clare, 'Didn't I say that unexpected things can happen on the twenty ninth of February?'

*

A few hours later, Phil and Clare shared a bottle of wine with Emily in the hotel lounge. After waving goodbye to the married couple enroute to their mini honeymoon, she'd gone home to change. Taking advantage of her husband being home to look after the children; she'd returned to join her brother and sister-in-law for a chat.

Emily produced from her shoulder bag a copy of the evening newspaper and showed Phil and Clare a disturbing article.

'I'm so glad that this news didn't get out earlier. It would have thrown a cloud over the wedding. Though I'm sorry for the man who is missing,' Emily admitted. 'He may have drowned. I don't know him. Have you ever heard of him?'

They shook their heads. Phil felt uneasy. He recalled the night before when he had seen a pair of boats on the lake that seemed to be too far away from the boathouse. He got out of his chair to lean over Clare's shoulder to read the headline and the rest of the article:

"**Man missing on St. Winefride's lake. An empty** boat was found last night by boathouse staff. Police believe he may have fallen overboard. A life jacket and a small rucksack believed to contain the missing man's possessions were still in the boat. His wallet revealed the owner to be **Ben Sloan**. Police are appealing for witnesses. Meanwhile a search for a body in the lake has begun."

A contact telephone number was printed at the bottom of the article.

'Ben Sloan. Where are you?' Phil muttered.

*

At that moment Ben Sloan's spirit was drifting towards the grounds of St. Winefride's graveyard. It hovered just inside the cemetery boundary wall where Rachel, Anna and their friends were gathered. They'd clustered as close to the graveyard walls as they could get, hoping for a last glimpse of any of the wedding guests. Seeing the small group, Ben glided towards them. Distracted by the newcomer they turned quizzical bony faces towards him.

'Hello, what happened to you?' Stefan asked, taking in Ben's dripping wet clothes.

'Hi. Well to get to the point - I was murdered - over there on that bloody lake. In a boat actually. Yesterday. My body is still in the water.' He looked down at his transparent silhouette, mesmerised how it dipped and tilted in the air. His saturated clothes, leaked droplets of water. 'I still can't believe it.'

'Yesterday?' Anna commented. She curiously examined his drenched shape. Her companions echoed her incredulity.

'So how come you managed to get here? You haven't got a grave. You would need to be buried here to have permission to roam around this zone.'

Anna assumed an authoritative air. As a member of the Board of Assessors she took her role seriously.

Margareta who had seen this kind of thing before, explained to Anna. 'If his body hasn't been discovered, he is a free spirit and can roam around anywhere. When he's been found and taken to the morgue, his spirit will automatically be pulled to his corpse.'

'So that's why I didn't get to come here when I was murdered,' Rachel said. 'I was dying in my rescuers arms.'

'What's your name?' Stefan asked, ignoring Rachel's outburst.

'Ben… Ben Sloan. I don't, or rather I didn't, live around here. I'm from Saltney, almost in Chester really, so I suppose when my dear wife buries me or cremates me I will end up somewhere in Cheshire. Funny we've never discussed it. I wasn't expecting to die so soon…'

'Do you know who murdered you?' Stefan asked. He focused his patched up face on the newcomer's, trying to work out how he had been killed.

Ben nodded. 'Yes, I know who killed me alright. His name is Dean Roper, a bloody psychopath! He thought I was shagging his wife. Sorry about the language.' He looked shamefaced when he saw Anna's put out expression.

'And were you?' Anna asked.

'No, I bloody wasn't! The man's crazy.'

'But why did he think you were?' Rachel asked. 'You must have given him some reason. And how did he manage to kill you when you were in a boat?'

'He stabbed me. Well actually he hit me first with the oar. When I tried to get my balance, I was dazed, you see, he took advantage of that and stabbed me here. Twice!' Ben pointed to his heart and the blood stained shirt.'

The spirits looked on sympathetically. They'd seen worse.

'But why did he stab you?' Stefan took up Rachel's line of questioning. Why did he think you were shagging his wife?' He ignored Anna's condemnation of the use of the word.

'We were friends, that's all. Not Dean, I mean his wife. I've known Tracey for years. Nothing was going on. I didn't think I was in danger, even though he sent me texts to keep away from his wife. He didn't mention Tracey but I guessed he meant her because apart from my wife I didn't have any female friends. Then he started calling me.'

'So what did you do?' Rachel asked.

'I told him to fuck off. Sorry. I'm mad about this.' Ben tried to compose himself. 'I said that I wasn't having an affair, and that I'd known his wife a long time. I also told him I knew she wasn't interested in me sexually.'

'She might have been,' Margareta observed. She trailed off after catching Ben's glare. 'Just a thought...' she added.

'So what did Tracey say about all this? Did you tell her what was happening?' Rachel probed.

'I don't think she knew he'd threatened me. I never told her about it. Anyway, I didn't see her that often.'

'So he came looking for you,' Stefan said slowly.

Ben nodded.

'So how come he was in the boat with you?' Margareta queried. 'Surely you weren't having a tete a tete with him?'

'No. I wanted to get away for a while. He followed me.'

'What do you mean he followed you?' Stefan asked. He studied the spectre in front of him closely. He seemed to be telling the truth but there were gaps in his story.

'What I mean is I hired a boat and soon after that, he must have hired one, then rowed out to threaten me. I didn't see him approaching. Before I knew what was happening he'd climbed aboard and clacked me with the oar. When I looked up I saw the knife and his face as he plunged it into my chest and then he did it again. I felt the life seeping out of me as he rocked the boat and pushed me in to the water.'

'I take it you weren't wearing a life jacket?' Stefan asked. 'It might have saved you from the stabbing.'

'I'm a good swimmer, or at least I was. I'd taken it off. Besides, I don't think it would have made any difference.'

'Well look, this is all very well, and I'm sorry this happened, but why did you go to the lake in the first place?' Anna attempted to fold her arms and put on her Assessor's interrogative expression.

'Yes, good point Mum,' Rachel said. 'It all sounds a tad dodgy to me.'

Ben's exasperated countenance intensified, simultaneously, his outline started to fade. His damp hair and clothes clung to his clammy corpse that shimmered eerily in the dim light. 'It's like I said, he's been hounding me for weeks leaving short, stupid threatening messages. He's been hanging outside my house too. I got fed up and told him I was going to call the police to say he was stalking me.'

'Did you do that?' Margareta asked.

'No. I thought about it, and probably would have done. I just needed to think. So I took the day off work and came here with my wife to talk things through with her. She knew Tracey, and I wanted to make sure that she understood what was going on.'

'Or not going on,' Rachel added.

'Yes. Poor Olive, she must be worried sick.' Ben's woeful voice dropped to a whisper. Relentlessly, Rachel persisted with her questioning. She and the spirits hovered closer towards him to catch his words.

'So how do you know Tracey?'

'Wait a minute, Rachel, we're bombarding him with questions and not *getting the full picture. It's like putting together a jigsaw. Let's find out first where Olive is,' Anna interrupted. She turned to Ben. 'Obviously you're distraught and disorientated and worrying about your wife. You said you and Olive came to the lake together. So wasn't she in the boat with you?'*

Ben sighed. 'No. She changed her mind when we got here. She said she would stroll around the town, have a look at the famous well, then wait for me in the St. Winefride's café. She'd brought a book with her.' His voice softened to a whisper forcing the spirits to hover closer to him as he carried on in a low tone. His outline diminished with each second. 'So I thought I would have a row on the lake on my own. Give me time to go over things in my mind. I like boats.'

Anna frowned. 'Did you tell Olive about Tracey?'

'No. I was going to, but then this happened. But she knew I had something on my mind.'

'What made you come to Holywell?' Margareta was curious.

'I hadn't intended to come here. When we got in the car my intention was to drive to the North Wales coast, stop for supper somewhere, perhaps in Llandudno. Like I said, I hadn't thought it through. Then my wife saw the road sign for Holywell and said she'd never been to St. Winefride's well, so I took a diversion…' His bitter sigh was barely audible, 'and ended up dead!'

'So Dean Roper must have been outside your house watching and decided to follow,' Stefan stated. *'Clearly a dangerous man. Do you think his wife is in danger?'*

Ben shook his head. 'I don't know. I don't think so. Tracey has never mentioned he was violent. She always looked happy.'

At that remark the sceptical spirits tutted in unison. They began to speak all at once but Rachel spoke above them, 'How often did you see her?'

'I actually saw her every week. She works for a recycling company. She hasn't been there long, about six or seven months I think. She's based in the charity shop at street level across the road from the building where I work, so I waved to her sometimes as I walked past.'

'Aha!'

This exclamation was echoed amongst the listening spirits.

'What do you mean, 'Aha?' Ben frowned.

'Nothing. I just assumed you saw Tracey less frequently,' Rachel said quickly. Her companions grunted a similar response.

'You said you didn't see her often!' Margareta glared.

'I meant I didn't see her often to talk to!' He stared at the spirits who surrounded him. Each were trying to make sense of the fragments of information that Ben had given them. He tried again to explain.

'I hadn't seen her for years, and because we were in school together, it seemed natural to want to catch up.

Sometimes on the days she worked alone, I'd get takeaway coffees and we'd drink them in the charity shop. But I didn't actually arrange to meet her. I just saw her…in the distance when I passed by. Like I said, all innocent.'

'Then one day, her husband got suspicious?' Stefan suggested.

'I think so. About five weeks ago. That's when the texts started. I took no notice at first. I didn't know who he was.'

'Presumably you sent texts to Tracey and she left her mobile lying around. He picked it up and saw them?' Rachel asked.

'No, nothing like that. I didn't have her mobile number. I just popped into the charity shop now and again to see her. I don't know how he got mine unless he found my business card in Tracey's bag. She asked for it!' He spoke his last words defensively as he caught the suspicious expressions on the faces of the spectres surrounding him.

'I didn't know what her husband looked like, until a few weeks ago when I saw her with him. He'd picked her up after work. After that I noticed him hanging outside my house. Not every day, but at least twice a week.'

'So yesterday you decided to take a day off work and unfortunately it was the same day Dean decided to kill you,' Stefan observed.

The little light afforded to them from the night sky disappeared completely. Whilst the spirits were used to seeing one another's shimmering shapes in the dark, they were concerned that Ben was becoming less and less visible. His form glided backwards as if he had been dragged away by a superior force. The spirits coasted along with him skirting the cemetery boundary wall.

'It seems that way. I didn't think he'd kill me though. Even when I saw him in the boat alongside me. I thought he just wanted to intimidate me. It happened so …'

'Ben, are you there?' Anna called. There was no response.

'Seems like his body's been found,' Margareta sighed. 'We won't see him again. His family will take him to Chester or Hawarden cemetery and we can't visit him without permission. Bugger.'

'Can't they bury him here?' Stefan frowned. His patchwork eye wrinkled eerily.

'Why would they want to?' Rachel asked.

'It's convenient and a nice place…'

'It would be convenient for us if he was buried here because we haven't got the full picture,' Margareta interrupted.

'Not everything is clear,' Anna agreed. Stefan shrugged. 'Well, it's not as if we can do anything about it. As it stands we know who killed him but we can't tell the police, no matter how much more information we get.'

I wonder if they will find his mobile,' Rachel pondered. 'The police would be able to check his texts.'

'It'll be soaking wet, if they do find it, so it won't be much use,' Anna retorted.

'I'm not so sure Mum. I've heard that if you put a wet mobile in a bag of rice for a

few days, the rice absorbs the moisture and you can use it again.'

Anna was astonished, especially when she saw Stefan nod his agreement with Rachel.

Margareta who had been dead several years had never possessed a mobile phone. The first time she'd come into contact with a mobile was when she saw the ones that had been buried in both Anna's and Rachel's coffins.

Rachel bubbled with enthusiasm. 'If Ben usually wore his mobile in his back pocket like most men, then the police will find it on him.'

Stefan laughed. 'If they do, the odds are that they have better technology than a bag of rice.' He slowly glided away, turning round to add, 'There's nothing we can do about it in any case. It's getting late, I'm off to my coffin for some rest. See you lot tomorrow.'

'He's right. There's absolutely nothing we can do,' Margareta echoed. She glanced from Anna's thoughtful expression and then to Rachel's glittering eyes as they focused on her mothers, 'or is there?'

CHAPTER FOUR

In the kitchen making toast for his breakfast, Dan cheerfully hummed along to an old fifties Rhythm and Blues song on the local radio station. It was by a group called the *Spaniels*. Relishing the happy and unusual events of the wedding day before, influenced his jovial mood. His cousins had left early to avoid heavy traffic on the way back to Cornwall. He'd appreciated their company, but now, after a few hectic, though enjoyable days, the house was peaceful again and he could relax. When a news bulletin on the radio announced that the body of a man had been found in Saint Winefride's lake, he stopped buttering his toast, knife poised as he listened intently for more details. It seemed that the police suspected, though not confirmed that the body was the missing man Ben Sloan from Saltney.

Dan breathed heavily, he wondered if it had been a suicide. It distressed him to think that a person had died in the vicinity of the lake. He speculated on who the unfortunate man had been and rolled the surname around in his head. Dan knew no-one locally with that name, and after living over thirty years in Holywell, he knew a lot of people. He and his late wife Anna had been members of many local groups and societies. He still attended most of them. He supposed that the man may have had family living nearby. He felt the pain for their loss. Sighing, he picked up his food and carried it to the dining room table. Leo, wagging his tail followed him and lay down under the window.

Phil and Clare received the news of the discovery of a body in the lake at the same time as Dan. They were listening to the radio as they were getting ready to go down to the hotel restaurant for their breakfast.

'There's something odd about this,' Phil said as he laced up his shoes. 'It seems too much of a coincidence that a corpse is found in the lake, just two days after I noticed those boats the other night. Do you remember? I said that it struck me as unusual to see them so far away from the boathouse especially as the light was fading. The occupants would have had a lot of hard rowing to do to get back to the jetty. I assumed they were experienced rowers. Now I'm wondering whether that missing man had been in one of those boats. I dismissed it at the time, because we had other things to think about, but now…' He stood up and stroked his chin whilst recalling the scene he had witnessed.

'Are you suggesting it wasn't an accident?'

Phil nodded. 'I'm afraid so.' He turned towards her noting her frown.

'But the body they found may not have any connection with those boats you saw.' Clare pulled on a thick woollen jumper then brushed her short dark hair into place. She faced her husband.

'I know you can sense these things, but what with the wedding and the delays we had at the airport, plus this damn virus that seems to be spreading, do you think that your senses may have somehow been, how can I put it, clouded?' She shrugged helplessly, 'I don't know, but I think you know what I'm trying to say? What you felt may have been an old and sad connection with the lake? I admit, you sensed something was wrong; and as a body has been found, you were right. But it might have been an unfortunate accident involving a different boat. Do you see what I'm saying?'

Phil nodded. 'Even so, I still think something sinister has happened.' He paused and with a pretence of being offended by his wife's remark added, 'and just for the record, I've had more stressful times in my life than last Friday and my psychic senses have never "clouded up" as you put it, before. Still there's always a first time, I suppose.'

He folded his arms and watched his wife pull on her boots. 'I don't think I'm mistaken though and I very much doubt it's a coincidence,' he repeated stubbornly.' He reached for his jacket.

'Come on let's get something to eat. I'm looking forward to a fried breakfast to soak up that red wine I had last night. Perhaps we could go for a stroll later.'

'Yes, but not like that though.' Clare leaned forward and unbuttoned his shirt. 'You've missed a button, you have one side longer than the other.'

'Thank you.' He kissed the top of her head.

*

An array of vases filled with daffodils decorated the restaurant tables.

'There's a cheerful sight, after hearing that news flash,' Clare commented. She leaned over and gently lifted a stem to her nose appreciating their delicate scent. They chose a table close to a window that gave them a view of Holywell town square. Alongside the arched doorway two council employees placed a ladder against the wall where upon one worker climbed to reach the pulley on the flag pole that secured the halyard of the Welsh flag.

'I forgot, it's Saint David's day today,' Phil said before knocking back his orange juice. He poured himself another glass and gave a satisfied sigh.

'Hmm so it'll be leek soup on the hotel lunch menu today then,' Clare replied. She bit into her croissant.

'We'll never know seeing that we're going round to Emily's. She's bound to do a Sunday roast of some kind.'

Their morning stroll took them in the direction of the lake. Half way along the lakeside path they stopped. 'Looks like we can't go much further,' Phil said pointing towards the hazard tape sectioning off part of the way to the boathouse.

'Looks like this area is the designated crime scene,' Phil commented.

Two police constables and a plain clothed man in a padded jacket who they assumed to be a detective, were assessing the area.

'How long do you think it will be closed to the public?' Clare asked.

'Difficult to say. Depends where they found the body, and what they've discovered. But no matter how he died, it just makes it hard to take in, especially after what happened here only three years ago.' He sighed. 'This will be bad news for Dan and Gavin.'

'Yes, it will bring back memories of Rachel's death.'

Phil nodded. 'Rachel's body was found at the edge of the lake just over there.' He pointed towards the cathedral. 'The spot wasn't far from the rear entrance to St. Winefride's. It was where she'd been waiting for her friends.' He sighed. 'At the moment we don't know where the body of that dead man was found. If it's anywhere near where I saw those boats it will be far away on the opposite side of the lake from where we are standing. It's a huge expanse of water, there's a lot to consider.'

'You really think he was murdered don't you?'

Phil nodded. 'I admit, I could be wrong. Like you said earlier, it might have been a terrible accident; it's possible he had a heart attack and fell in. I have to say I'm inclined to think something more disturbing happened.'

Clare turned to her husband, a worried expression on her face. Without speaking, she changed her focus to the boathouse. Phil followed her glance and tried to reassure her.

'It doesn't necessarily mean that anyone employed at the boathouse is the murderer. If, of course it is established that he has been murdered.'

'Even so. This incident won't be good for their reputation,' Clare reflected, 'bearing in mind what happened in the not so distant past. Not that I don't care about the unlucky man who died of course. It's very sad.'

'I wouldn't be too worried about the boathouse. You'd be surprised how events such as this actually entices people to a place. The public seem to be fascinated by the macabre. I mean look over there at the little crowd gathering on the railway bridge? I can also see spectators hanging around the hazard tapes on the other side of the foot path. All of them craning their necks trying to see what's going on.'

Phil turned to gaze across the wide, gleaming stretch of St. Winefride's lake. He shielded his eyes with his hand to block out the bright, late winter sunlight. He could just make out clusters of walkers, their figures matchstick like in the distance. Other solitary individuals, periodically stopped to stare as they strolled along the path that circled the edge of the lake. All along the opposite lakeside path, more curious on-lookers stopped every now and again to gawp at the police activities.

Clare shuddered. 'We're no better. Look at us.'

Phil feigned an injured expression. 'I'm here to try to establish something. It matters to me that my extra sensory skills are intact. Despite the stresses of last Friday, I don't want to think that my radar has been affected.'

'Your radar? That's what you call it now,' she teased.

'Alright then, my psychic powers.'

'Right.'

'What do you mean "right?" First you suggest I'm losing my touch and now you're being ambivalent about my psychic powers. What's going on?' Concern traced his smile as he gently took hold of her by the shoulders to look into her eyes. 'You're the one who wanted us to go and live in bloody Transylvania to track down vampires!' he teased.

'You know it was more to do with my interest in Romanian history and culture!' she replied hotly. 'How was I to know when I fell in love with you that you had supernatural powers?'

'So what's troubling you? I can see you have something on your mind.'

She forced a smile. 'I think that incident yesterday in the graveyard has really got to me. I was scared, yet I don't know why. Now there's this unknown dead man and you believing there is something amiss.' She stopped then started again. 'You seem to be able to cope with it easily, and I can see you getting involved in this murder case, that's if it is a murder case.'

'Oh so you're the psychic now.'

She smiled reluctantly at his joke.

Phil grinned and put his arm around her and dropped a kiss on her forehead.

'Come on, let's go and see if we can find somewhere open for a coffee. I think the bakery on the square opens on Sundays. We could have one of those Portuguese custard tart things.'

'We only had breakfast an hour ago! Honestly I don't know where you put it.' She glanced admiringly at his lean though muscular body.

'I feed the fat to the vampires.'

Despite her anxiety Clare laughed though quickly returned to the subject that bothered her. She linked her hand with his as they retraced their steps to the town centre.

'It's strange about what happened yesterday with that cousin of Abi's,' she said.

Phil squeezed her hand. 'Yes, I admit it was uncanny. I'm sorry I should've realised what a shock it would have been for you. I would have been delighted if I'd witnessed it.'

'Have you ever experienced that kind of thing yourself?'

'Actually, now you mention it, yes.' Phil took a deep breath before continuing. 'When I was young - about the same age as Lucy I suppose, I actually saw ghosts. I also saw some shadowy images of - spectres or spirits - for want of a better word to describe them. I've even had a conversation with ghosts, if you know what I mean, just as Lucy did. I knew they were ghosts because when I tried to touch them, they vanished.'

'Were you scared?'

'No. If anything, I was annoyed that they didn't come back! As I've aged, I see ghosts less frequently. However I've been lucky to see an apparition of some kind several times over the years. Each occasion was during a séance. Apart from séances, I've conversed with what I can only describe as an aura. What happened to Lucy is rare. I've read about it though. It's a gift, if you want to call it that. It may develop as the child grows older. On the other hand it might just be a one off. Sometimes it can happen on just one occasion, like yesterday and never again. I suppose if the elements are right it could re-occur.'

'Or if the moon is in the right place?'

'Don't mock.'

'I'm not actually. I'm deadly serious.'

'Since you mention it, yes it could be a question of the moon. Like I said to you yesterday, it was the twenty ninth of February. Anything could happen.'

'And it certainly did.'

'I'm glad you told me how you felt. I really am sorry. I should have realised.'

Clare smiled. 'It's alright. I feel better now we've talked about it. I'm annoyed with myself for feeling like that.'

Phil hugged her. 'Don't beat yourself up. It's a reasonable response. At least you didn't faint or scream. Imagine what would have happened if you'd screamed all over the graveyard just as the photographer was clicking her camera!'

Clare laughed good-naturedly. Over their coffees, she broached the subject they'd both been avoiding. 'Do you think we should tell Emily today about our long term plans?'

Phil nodded, his mouth full of pastel de nata.

Clare cradled her coffee cup in her hands as she spoke to her husband over the rim. She felt calmer and in control of her feelings after confiding in him. 'She'll be disappointed that we're not coming back here to live - at least not for a while.'

Phil swallowed the last crumb of his pastry. 'Probably, but she'll understand. Whether my mum and dad will, is another story. I was thinking of borrowing Emily's car and driving over to Hawarden to tell them. I'm not sure when. Will you come too? They'll be expecting us.'

'Of course. I like your mum and dad. I take it you didn't give them an exact day or time when we'd visit?'

Phil shook his head and sipped his coffee.

'At least I haven't got parents to upset,' Clare remarked bitterly. She'd been adopted at the age of three, and then both her adoptive parents passed away within a few years of each other during Clare's late teens. After they died, she traced her natural mother and was sorry she'd bothered. She'd been in and out of prison many times for petty crimes. On the one occasion when they had met it soon became obvious that she was only interested in Clare if she was rich.

Her natural father had disappeared soon after Clare was born. When she managed to trace his whereabouts she discovered he'd died of heart failure several years earlier, in his forties. She was grateful that she'd had a happy upbringing with her adoptive parents, though sad she'd had no siblings.

Phil grasped her hands. 'Come on, let's walk over to the cathedral and have a look at the old well.'

Stepping around the rectangular pool set below the well, they weren't surprised to see visitors casting coins in the water for luck. Some sat alongside the pool allowing their feet to dangle in the water.

Clare laughed. 'I can't vouch for the healing properties of the water but bathing your feet is relaxing even though it is chilly today. However, I'm not going to do it.' She led the way into the cathedral to get a second peek at the flowers left over from the previous day's wedding. She breathed in the scent of the white roses.

'They still smell beautiful. It seems a shame to leave them here.'

'I expect the churchgoers will appreciate them, then perhaps someone will take them down. Maybe Abi's mother and her sisters.' Phil glanced at his watch just as some members of the congregation entered the cathedral. 'It's twenty past eleven, it looks like some worshippers are already coming in.

It said outside on the notice board that there would be a service at eleven thirty. We'd better go, unless you want to stay?'

'No thanks. I just wanted to see the flowers again before they wilt. I've just taken some photos. I didn't like to do it yesterday. It didn't seem appropriate.'

Phil smiled at his wife. He knew she was remembering their own special day. 'Come on.'

After a backward wistful glance, Clare followed him out of the cathedral.

Shall we amble around to see Rachel's and Anna's graves?' Phil suggested.

'If you like. Are you hoping to pick up some kind of a vibe?'

'Something like that.'

The graves weren't far apart, and they could see fresh flowers on each of them. Clare recognised the assorted blooms from Abigail's bouquet. She'd obviously split it into two and put half on each grave.

'That's a nice touch. Especially now we know they witnessed the marriage. It's a shame that Abigail never met either of them before they died. It's funny, I feel as if I have a new connection with them after that experience yesterday with Lucy. I can't get over it. I'm so glad I was with her, otherwise we may never have got the message. Lucy may have forgotten to pass it on. She got it muddled up anyway. Gavin and Dan were so chuffed.'

'Abigail was emotional too you know,' Phil said. 'It was a phenomenal thing to have happened on such a special day. When she met Gavin she didn't know what she was getting herself into. She got involved with everything in the end, even though she never met Anna or Rachel. It all got somewhat messy before the investigation wound-up, especially with her friend Nicky. Without their help I doubt we'd have tracked down Rachel's killers.'

'Not forgetting that bizarre mobile message Gavin got from Rachel,' Clare added. 'You were with him weren't you?'

'The first message yes, but I was on my way to Bucharest back to you when he got the message to say Nicky was in hospital. I often wondered how Rachel managed to communicate with him from her grave.'

Rachel and Anna laughed. They were perched on the cemetery wall watching them.

'That's something we'll never be able to tell him,' Anna sighed.

Rachel agreed. 'I doubt we'll ever be able to pull that stunt again. Saint Winefride avoids us even more than she did before!' She giggled. 'I wonder if Gavin has still got his mobile, or whether he bought a new one. I think he'd had the one with the number I used at least three years even then.' As she spoke she sashayed towards Phil.

'Shall we see if we can get him to sense us again? I'm hoping yesterday wasn't a fluke.'

Anna glided towards her daughter. Each spirit positioned themselves either side of Phil.

'I'm game for anything. But some of the spirits told me that he picked up a vibe from us because of all the wedding excitement and that yesterday was a leap year. Concentrate.'

'Are you getting anything?' Clare asked. She trembled anxiously as she watched Phil's agitated expression. He nodded.

'I think I am. I can feel something like a kind of a light cape enveloping me. The sensation isn't unpleasant. It's like threads or strands of soft yarn, it's hard to describe, but I know it's not normal. It's no-where near as strong as yesterday. Can you feel anything?'

'No of course not. The air is completely still around me. Clare swished her arms around as if she could see something. 'Nothing there.'

'What's she doing?' Rachel grinned.

'She thinks she's helping,' Anna chuckled. *She was pleased that at last she was able to make some kind of contact with Phil despite it being small.*

'This feeling is nothing like when I got involved with the investigation. I experienced a terrible pain, usually in my stomach, like as if a bus had driven through me. This is more like an awareness of a gentle breeze swirling around my body. Still, she is obviously trying to communicate. I wonder if Anna is around.'

'Maybe the strong whack you got when you stayed with Gavin, was because Rachel had some urgency about finding out who murdered her. Now those thugs are behind bars, she is at peace,' Clare suggested.

'You could be right. And yet, I can't help thinking that this hit is different. When she made contact before it was usually at a séance or somewhere away from the grave yard. The only time we were aware of her presence in the cemetery was because Leo could see her. Or at least we guessed he could because of the dog's strange behaviour.' Phil frowned.

'Perhaps she just wants to make contact because of the events of yesterday,' Clare suggested. 'That reminds me.' She faced her husband eagerly, 'I was wondering if there may be an image of Rachel and Anna on the wedding video? I believe a friend of Abigail's did it. She told me when we chatted at the reception.'

'That would be interesting. We'll have to wait until they get back from Anglesey tomorrow to ask them.'

'If we do show up on that video, it would be good if we could see it,' Anna said wistfully.

'No such luck,' Rachel said.

'They didn't mention anything about that chap Ben Sloan. Maybe they don't know that his body has been found,' Anna commented. 'Do you think Phil can find out who killed him?'

'I don't know. He hasn't really got anything to go on, nor has he any connection with him,' Rachel replied. 'I wish I could find Ben's murderer. It would be good to work with Phil again.'

'You'd have to have a very good reason to ask the Assessors to grant you permission. I must admit I'm sympathetic and I would probably give you my vote, but I'm not sure what the rest of the Assessors would say.'

'Even if Ben's wife doesn't decide to bury him here, she might want to try to use a psychic like Phil to get justice. I could provide the necessary link,' Rachel said.

'It's a pity we can't get in touch with him,' Anna agreed. 'With regard to burying him here, she would have to get special permission. Local authorities get a bit possessive of their grave yards. Apparently it's all to do with space. I think she'd have to take him to Hawarden. It depends which side of the boundary lane in Saltney where he lived.

'Cremation is the most sensible way to dispose of cadavers. I did some research when we arranged your funeral. Actually I considered cremation for myself then changed my mind. As you know I was never a believer in the afterlife, but I decided in the end that if there was a chance of seeing you again, I would be buried here instead.'

'And of course now you know it makes no difference to the afterlife whether you are cremated or buried,' Margareta interjected. She'd floated up to talk to them after she'd seen Phil and Clare near her friends' graves.

'Even so, I would have been at the crematorium miles away from here,' retorted Anna.

Rachel had heard all this before and steered the conversation back to Ben Sloan. 'Listen, I think they know about Ben!'

'Do you think she might have some information about that dead man they found in the lake?' Clare asked.

'I don't think so. We don't know the man or his family, and as far as I'm aware she is not related to him. So there's no way she could make any connection between him and me.'

'Ask her now. See if you can get some kind of a sign. She might have seen something from the roof tops of the cathedral. If they can float around like Lucy described, it might be possible.'

'Alright I'll give it a go.' He stood still, closed his eyes and said, 'Rachel, Anna, hello it's Phil. Do you know anything about the dead man in the lake?'

'Quick Mum, he's trying to find out something about Ben Sloan. He knows about him after all. What can we do?' Frantically the spirits moved closer to Phil, Margareta joined them too and together tried to make a link, but other than the same ripple Phil felt before there was nothing more.

'Anything?' Clare asked hopefully despite herself.

'No, nothing other than like the sensation I had a few minutes ago, but I feel they are close.'

'Pity. Come on let's stroll to Emily's and see what kind of a Sunday lunch she's concocting. I suppose we'll be eating outside again, with blankets wrapped around us or with our coats on.'

CHAPTER FIVE

Emily had re-organised her kitchen so that her guests could sit inside the house. She'd set up a small camping table in another room for her children where they happily sat on the floor with cushions underneath them. Despite the limited space the adults sat in relative comfort enjoying the heat from the oven.

Jack stooped over the table to offer wine, deftly dodging the wind chimes that hung above him from the ceiling. He laughed when Phil hesitated for a second before nodding his consent to his brother-in-law.

'Hair of the dog, as they say,' Phil said sniffing the wine appreciatively.

'This is a good one. You can't afford to say no to this. A full bodied Rioja, yet surprisingly not too expensive.'

Jack passed Phil the bottle so he could read the label.
Phil took a sip whilst studying the description of the wine. He knew Jack prided himself on searching and getting good quality wines at economical prices. Phil believed he also knew a thing or two about wine, and the pair often compared notes on their choices.

'Yes. I agree, a good find,' Phil announced. He took another sip. Clare nodded her agreement.

Emily put the roast lamb on the table, skilfully avoiding the wind chimes. She handed around the dishes of assorted vegetables.

'I suppose you heard the news this morning that the police have found Ben Sloan - the missing man?' Emily turned to her brother as she spoke, simultaneously squeezing herself into the chair beside her husband, her back a few inches away from the kitchen sink.

'Yes a nasty business. They haven't reported how he died yet though. It might have been an accident,' Clare said.

'Actually they have. He was murdered. Stabbed. It was on the mid-day news today.' Emily pulled a face as she picked up a large knife to carve the joint of meat.

'We've been out walking, so missed the day time news. The last we heard about it was at breakfast time,' Phil said. 'So, the ill-fated chap was killed.' He caught Clare's eye and she shrugged, her expression sad.

'But how come no-one saw what happened?' Jack paused to take a sip of wine. 'Could the police be mistaken about murder and not considered that he stabbed himself, taking his weapon into the water with him? It's not impossible.' He searched the faces of his companions before adding, 'is it?' He handed a dish of vegetables to Clare then poured some mint sauce over his meat before passing the jug to Emily. Without saying anything she held the jug in front of her brother who shook his head then turned to address his brother-in-law.

'I'm not sure Jack, I know it's possible to take your own life with a knife, such as cutting your own throat or stabbing yourself but why go to the trouble of hiring a boat to do it? It sounds strange to me. The police must have their reasons for believing it's a murder case.' His thoughts returned to the two crafts he'd seen close together on the lake on Friday night. As if reading his mind, Clare pressed her hand on his knee under the table. He covered her hand with his own gently caressing it.

'The only logical explanation I can think of; if of course it *is* murder, and that's what the police reckon; is for someone to jump into his boat, kill him, dump his body in the water and then jump back into a different boat,' Emily suggested.

'Yes, but what kind of a man or woman for that matter would be able to do it?' Clare asked. 'You'd have to be fit. I'm pretty athletic myself, but I doubt if I could do it quickly. And surely someone would notice?'

'If the killer attacked him from behind first, perhaps hit him to render him unconscious, or at least make him dazed, it would be easy to knife him, that would work,' Phil said slowly.

Jack grunted, his fork held high loaded with food. Before putting it into his mouth he offered another scenario… 'I think it would be more effective for the murderer to jump onto the boat and rock it vigorously to make the man fall out, then when he tried to get back in, the assailant would be waiting with a knife to stab him, so that he fell dead into the water.'

'It's plausible,' Phil agreed. 'All of it.'

'No matter how it was done, who did it and why?' Clare asked. Where did the dead man and his murderer come from? Why did they come to the lake? None of it makes sense.'

'Let's change the subject. We'll just have to wait for the police to find out. There's nothing we can do. Now who wants apple pie and custard?' Emily asked. She manoeuvred herself out of her chair to take portions of the dessert to the children in the other room, giving the wind chimes a swish with the back of her hands.

'Why don't you take that thing down until you've finished building the extension?' Phil asked standing up to straighten it.'

Jack groaned. 'Too much hassle. It's just one of those things we put up with. Anyway it's safer there than anywhere else. It could get lost amongst all the other debris.'

'When are you going to see Mum and Dad?' Emily asked on her return to the kitchen.

'I was going to ask you if I could borrow your car to go and see them later on,' Phil replied sheepishly. Emily eyed him as she busied herself putting portions of apple pie on to dishes. Meanwhile Jack offered to top up the wine glasses and Phil shrugged his consent, curling up his lips into a rueful smile. 'But as I've been drinking, I won't be able to drive.' He glanced at his wife who screwed up her face in mock apology as she took another sip of her wine, 'and neither can Clare.'

'I'm sorry Love, I didn't know that was what you were planning to do today. When you mentioned it earlier, you didn't say when. I would've reminded you not to drink.'

'I'm sorry too, it was just a vague plan I had.'

'Did you tell them you were going to visit them today? Cream or custard?' Emily leaned towards him a jug in each hand.

Phil shook his head. 'Custard please.'

'We can go tomorrow,' Clare said quickly. 'We can get the train. Custard for me too, please.'

'If you take me to work in the morning, you can have my car for the day. Just pick me up later,' Emily offered.

'Thanks.' Phil glanced at his wife, as if to ask her another question. He read in her eyes that she was in agreement that they should tell Emily about their future plans.

'The thing is Em, tomorrow morning I have an interview for a job, so I won't be able to borrow your car. Thanks anyway. After the interview, we'll get a bus or taxi to Flint and then get a train to Hawarden. It makes things easier now they've moved from Connah's Quay.'

'It's what we were going to do anyway,' Clare added.

'An interview? Where? So is this for the job you hinted at and you might be coming back to UK? What about you Clare, are you both going to get jobs here?'

Phil held up his hands feigning protest. 'So many questions. The fact is Em, the job is in Bucharest, but will possibly mean… and I'm hoping… coming to UK every now and again. The interview is by Skype. Clare is going to carry on with her work at the university. Neither of us will be coming back to live here in this country permanently, for quite some time. But we will see more of each other nevertheless, if things work out as I hope.' He exhaled heavily, relieved to get things out in the open.

Emily's face fell. 'I thought you meant you would be home for good. The two of you.'

Phil sighed. 'Home is where your work is these days. Despite having Zoom and Skype I still need to be based in Bucharest.'

'What is this job you are going for?' Jack asked.

'It's a brilliant opportunity to put my PhD in Romanian culture to good use. If everything goes well I would be promoting it in Wales and eventually in the rest of UK. Nothing has been set up properly. I would be instrumental in getting the organisation off the ground and would be the link for Wales. So I could spend large chunks of time here in Wales, though not necessarily in Holywell.' He added this last sentence apologetically.

'But there would be opportunities for you guys to meet up more often,' Clare chipped in. 'It's a big task which, anyway, may not be funded by the Transylvanian government. All of it is just a proposal, it's a huge project.'

'It has so many possibilities,' Phil enthused.

'So what you're saying really is that at the moment there is no concrete job, but there might be one, and you might be the one to get it off the ground?' Emily frowned as she spoke. She cradled her chin between her thumb and fingers focusing her eyes on her brother's.

'Yes.'

'So who is behind this scheme?' Jack asked. 'And where is the interview?'

'I'll answer the easy question first. The interview is by Skype on my lap top in the hotel. The organisation is a cross party group of politicians from various political backgrounds in Romania who are keen to make an impact on the rest of Europe about their culture. Transylvania is not just about vampires. The region as well as the whole of Romania has a lot to offer. I know Dracula brings in a lot of tourism, but these people who I am associated with want to project another image. Nature, wildlife, history, their traditions.'

'But now the UK is limping out of the European Union why would the Transylvanian government want to start things off with Wales and the like?' Jack persisted.

Phil smiled. 'I think I happened to be in the right place at the right time, when Avram – my colleague at the university came up with his proposition. We were just having a casual pint in a pub when he mentioned it. He has a lot of contacts with people in Romania. And as you know, I'm interested in old languages and of course Welsh.

Romania has roots in many ancient dialects. But it isn't just the language, it's the way of life, now and in the past which I'm interested in. Just as Clare is interested in the arts, music and literature. In fact because of the nature of her job our paths may cross in this.'

Clare nodded. She sipped her wine and glanced at her sister-in-law. 'If this takes off, and I really hope it will, then the contract for Phil could last for a good few years. He would have far more job security than he's ever had in the past.'

Emily turned to her brother. 'I don't know what to say.'

Phil grinned. 'It's a unique chance Emmy. Something that I really want to do.'

'I have to say, it sounds like it's the kind of thing that's up your street. But,' she bit her lip and managed a grudging smile, 'I was looking forward to having my brother close by. And you of course, Clare.' She extended her smile towards her sister-in-law.

Clare chuckled, 'Actually, I have just signed a contract for another three years at the university. That means I won't be back for a while. Sorry to disappoint.' She put on an apologetic smile.

Emily opened another bottle of wine. 'If that's what you want, then I'll keep my fingers crossed for you. Good luck to you both.'

'Maybe you can come and visit us with the children, once this Coronavirus thing has burnt itself out. Surely it can't last much longer! In any case, if I get the job it could take some time before we launch a big tourism campaign. At the moment there are no restrictions on travel. Let's hope it stays that way.'

'You don't think you'll have problems going back do you?' Emily frowned.

Phil shook his head. 'We might have to go in to quarantine for fourteen days, but it won't be a problem for us as we can work from home with our laptops.'

'It's a good job you didn't have to go in to quarantine when you arrived in Manchester airport. The government hasn't taken any measures in UK. All we ever get is news bulletins saying we should wash our hands,' Jack commented. He scratched his head. 'It's really worrying though, what's happening across Europe, especially in Spain and Italy. Portugal too, I think.'

On the way back to the hotel Clare confided in Phil that she worried about whether they would be able to fly home without any difficulty.

'As long as we follow the measures put in place, I think we'll be ok,' Phil assured her. 'It's not as if we have been to Italy or Spain. It's like Jack said, other governments seem to have put in place more severe restrictions for people leaving and entering those countries. We might have to take some kind of health test when we get back, but we can live with that. The only other problem will be if Boris Johnson suddenly decides to put the country into some kind of a lockdown. It might stop us leaving the UK.'

Clare pulled a face. 'Surely that's not going to happen. And if it does, let's hope, for our sakes, it's after the sixth of March.'

*

After breakfast the next day, Clare got ready to go out for a stroll leaving Phil in their hotel room to prepare for his interview. He hugged her before giving her a lingering kiss. 'Thanks for your support.'

She smiled. 'Good luck.'

'Where will you go?'

'I was thinking of popping around to see Dan. He might be upset when he hears about the body in the lake. He might appreciate some company.'

Phil nodded. 'Good plan.'

Outside, the ground was dry though the air was cold. Clare buttoned up her herringbone patterned coat and set off for a brisk walk to Dan's place. She felt a country walk would be more interesting than following the road. She knew of a network of pathways behind the hotel well used by locals. Some led out of the town and joined nature trails leading towards the coast. Clare chose a well-trodden track that weaved itself around the hotel, passing St. Winefride's Cathedral. Eventually it would merge on to the lane near Dan's house. He'd given her and Phil an open invitation to call for a coffee, and that morning seemed the perfect opportunity. If he was out then she'd call some other time. Meanwhile she would enjoy the scenery.

The path on her selected route undulated gently before it swelled to a grassy hillock. From the top she enjoyed breathtaking views of the lake. Turning her back on the water she was rewarded with the magnificent sight of St. Winefride's Cathedral. She paused for a few minutes to admire, not for the first time the striking Gothic architecture. She never tired of gazing at the structure.

To the right of the building, she could see the coloured tents that surrounded the famous well. These were setup for pilgrims to conveniently change their clothes. Clare knew that visitors from all over the world came to plunge into the small pool below the well. Even now in early March there were a small group of brave individuals stepping into the water.

She shivered at the thought of cold wet feet and moved on. After walking on a little further she stopped again to view the lake. This time to appreciate from a different angle, the length and width of it. She knew that to walk all around it, the distance would be approximately three miles.

That morning the water looked tranquil, despite a few ripples stirred up by the light prevailing wind. She speculated over the many secrets that lay beneath it. With a heavy sigh, she increased her pace towards Dan's house.

Leo's barking even before she knocked on the back door and the sound of his paws scratching against it gave her away. Dan opened it slowly, dressed as if to go out. The dog's lead hung loosely over his shoulder. He held Leo away from the door by his collar.

'Is this a bad time to call?'

Dan shook his head and waved her in. 'No, of course not. We've actually just got back from our walk. I was about to hang up the lead on the hook. Come in, I'll make us some coffee to warm us up. I'll just sort out Leo. I expect he wants a drink of water. I'm not sure if he remembers you. It's a few years since you were last here.'
Dan gently released the pressure of his hold on Leo's collar allowing him to sniff around Clare's outstretched hand. She held it gingerly.

'He won't bite. The fact that I have invited you in, has reassured him. He just wants to be friendly.'

Finally Dan let the dog go, and Clare stroked his head. She relaxed when Leo wagged his tail and licked her hand. Satisfied, she sat down at the kitchen table.

'Right, I'll wash my hands and make the coffee.' He handed a wet cloth to Clare. 'Here, take this for your own hands. Can't be too careful these days.'

She wiped her hands and handed the cloth back to Dan who tossed it into the sink. She watched him fill the kettle and then plug it into the wall socket.

'Didn't Phil want to come for a walk?'

'He's working on his laptop. So I left him in peace.' Clare kept her tone light.

'I thought you two were having a few days holiday. I didn't think he would bring work with him.' Dan filled a tray laden with a cafetière; jug of milk; some sugar and a plate of biscuits. 'Come on, let's go into the sitting room, it's more comfortable in there.'

Taking off her coat she carried it over her arm as she followed him through the hallway. They passed the dining room and then he ushered her into the warm lounge where she made herself comfortable on an armchair. She watched him put the tray down on a coffee table in front of an open fire. Drawn to the blaze, she put her hands up to the flames to warm them, turning her head to face Dan.

'We are on holiday. He just had something to sort out. This afternoon we're going to Hawarden to see his parents.'

'Hmm, it's a shame he didn't come with you. Now that the wedding is over, I was hoping to have a few words with him and you about what happened with that little girl. I forget her name.'

'You mean Lucy the youngest bridesmaid.'

'Yes that's the one. It was uncanny wasn't it? Mind you, I think I've got used to strange things happening when Phil is around. I had to come to terms with a lot when he arrived here last time. That was Gavin's idea to invite him, not mine but I'll always be grateful to him. Phil I mean.'

Dan poured out the coffees. 'Help yourself to these chocolate Florentines. They were a gift from one of my cousins and his wife. They were staying here over the week end. They've gone back to Cornwall now.'

'I heard you had a house full of visitors.'

'Yes, I had my two teen-age nieces and their boyfriends here too. They went back to Manchester straight after the reception. It's been a hectic few days. Weeks actually, with one thing and another.' He smiled. 'But worth it. Abigail has been wonderful.'

Clare took a biscuit. Looking up she saw the hesitation on Dan's face.

'I was worrying about Lucy,' he said. 'Whether talking to ghosts might have upset her.'

'There's no need to worry about Lucy. She forgot about the incident straight away. I have to say that it was a shock for me!'

'Yes I suppose it must have been! Are you alright?'

Clare laughed. 'Yes of course I'm fine now. And like I said, so is Lucy. I'm certain she didn't know they were ghosts. She was talking to them as if they were guests at the wedding!' Clare chuckled. 'Actually they were.'

Dan managed a doleful smile. 'It's the sort of thing Anna would do. She would be determined to see her son getting married. It's incredible that it happened. So although I'm sad she couldn't be here in person and help with all the arrangements, it's good to know that she was there in spirit. Literally.'

'Yes and of course Rachel was there too.'

Inwardly Clare pondered how Anna and Abigail would have got on with the wedding preparations. She knew that Anna, though generous had been a strong minded and forceful woman. She imagined her having some heated arguments with Abigail's mother, and possibly with Abigail too. She hid her smile behind another biscuit.'

In an attempt to avoid raking up the unhappy past, Clare changed the subject.

'Do you know what time Gavin and Abigail will get back from Anglesey?'

'About four o'clock. I'm going to pick them up from Chester railway station and take them to their new house.'

'Oh, of course, I forgot. They've bought a place somewhere in the town haven't they?'

'It's not far from where Abigail works. She got offered a job at the same salon where she trained. It hadn't been her original plan, but things didn't work out because of what happened to her friend Nicky. Anyway, the salon is set into a terrace of shops just past the old railway bridge. If you walk to the top of the terrace, turn right past the salon and then go down the hill there is another terrace of four houses. They've got the first end one. It's quite small and has just two bedrooms, but they've done it up nicely. I expect they'll invite you to see it before you go back to Transylvania.'

'I'll look forward to it.' She drained her coffee and got ready to leave. 'I'm sure we'll see you again before we go back. Tell Gavin to text Phil when he's ready to meet up for a drink or whatever.' She bent down to pick up the tray of crockery but Dan stopped her.

'Leave that. I'll clear it up. Don't worry. Come on, let me help you with your coat.' He walked her to the back kitchen door, where she patted Leo on his head before stepping on to the garden path. Outside she turned to wave to Dan who, in Clare's opinion looked somewhat frail. She hoped he wouldn't be too lonely now that Gavin had moved out. She was relieved he hadn't mentioned the body in the lake. She'd felt reluctant to bring up the subject herself, thinking it would be better if he broached the incident first. There was no doubt in her mind that he was aware of the murder, because she knew he listened to the local radio practically all day, preferring it to the television.

Back at the hotel, Phil had changed into his casual clothes ready for the visit to see his parents.

'How did it go?' Clare asked.

'Not bad. Quite well, I think. At least, I hope so.' He grinned. 'I have to wait for their decision now. It could be a couple of days. Still it's a relief to get it over and done with.'

Clare kissed him. 'Yes, onwards and upwards now as they say. Come on let's get to the train station. Did you ring your mother?'

'Yes, she's making a late lunch. Dad's picking us up from the station.'

*

After their visit to Phil's parents in Hawarden, Emily dropped them off outside the hotel. She'd 'phoned them ahead to say, that if they waited until seven o clock when Jack would be home to look after the children, she would be able to pick them up. In any case she saw it as an excuse for a mini family reunion.

Outside the hotel, they saw a parked police car. As Emily waited for her brother and his wife to get out of her vehicle, they could see a pair of police officers knocking on the doors of the houses that lay on the immediate outskirts of the town.

'I suppose they're looking for witnesses because of what happened to that man,' Emily said. She put her head out of the open car window to peer down the road.

'I wonder if they'll come to the hotel,' Clare whispered. She glanced at Phil. He hadn't mentioned seeing the two boats to his sister.

'They might. It's on their route,' Phil muttered with a shrug.

Emily said goodnight and wound up the window. Phil and Clare stood together to watch her reverse the car in the tiny space, then drive off home.

An hour later, the manager of the hotel telephoned them in their room to ask them if they were willing to answer some questions from the police.

In the reception area, they were conducted to a small storage room which the manager had allocated for the use of the police officers. She'd placed a few folding chairs for their convenience.

'Thank you for coming down at this late hour,' Police Constable Kath Morris said after introducing herself and her colleague Detective Constable Robert Ellis.

'You are probably aware by now that we are investigating the murder of Ben Sloan. The man whose body was found in the lake.'

'Yes we are. Sad thing to happen,' Phil said as he caught Clare's eye.
The two police officers murmured their agreement.

'We know it's a long shot, but we're wondering if you saw anything unusual round about early evening last Friday?' DC Robert Ellis asked. 'We're asking everyone in the hotel the same question.'

'Friday evening was when my wife and I had just arrived from Bucharest. We were here to attend a wedding the following day.'

'Yes I understand that from the manager,' the officer smiled. 'I suppose you were distracted by all the excitement and didn't see anything. We had to ask you see.' He made as if to go until Phil spoke again.

'Actually I did see something odd. It might not be anything, and it probably won't help, but I had a strange feeling something was wrong when I looked through the window at the lake. I, that is... we,' he gestured towards Clare.

The police officer nodded. 'Go on.'
'We were on the landing admiring the view around five o'clock ish on that day.'

Both officers focused on Phil now, and he wished he hadn't spoken. After all he didn't actually see the murder.

'It's hard to describe, but when we were walking along the corridor of the hotel I looked out through the landing window and saw a pair of rowing boats at the furthest point of the lake. They were only just distinguishable because the lake is vast and the light was fading. I remember thinking they were too far out considering the time of day and how long it would take to row back to the boathouse.'

'Could you see the people in the boats?' PC Kath Morris asked. Her eyes brightened. This was the first speck of a possible lead they'd had all day.

'Unfortunately, from that distance it was impossible to make out anything clearly other than the outline of the crafts. I saw one rower struggling, but I didn't see the other. Yet something made me feel uneasy.' There, Phil had said it and wished he hadn't shared that feeling. He'd seen nothing else that was helpful. It wounded him to see the interest fade from the eyes of each constable.

'Perhaps if we show you the landing in the hotel, you will see what my husband means,' Clare suggested.

The officers shrugged. 'We may as well since we're here,' PC Kath Morris said. They followed Phil and Clare up three flights of stairs to the landing. Phil switched off the light so that they could see through the window.

'Obviously you can't see much from here now it's late, but you'll be able to gauge the immense size of the lake up here, and understand my concern that the boats were a long distance away from the boatshed,' Phil explained.

'I get your point,' DC Robert Ellis said. 'The fact that you saw two and no-one in one of them suggests that the murder was about to be committed, or perhaps already done. The killer might have hired his own craft and swam to the outer side of the victim's boat so you wouldn't have seen him.

Phil frowned trying to think. 'Possibly. They were too far away for me to make out anyone actually in the water... Sorry.'

'No, don't apologise. This is very helpful information. It would be useful if we could come back tomorrow and look again in daylight, if that's alright with you? It's a great view. '

'Yes not a problem, though obviously I can't speak for the manager.' Phil shrugged. 'She might not like the police trailing through the hotel again.'

'Of course, we will observe the niceties,' DC Ellis replied. His colleague nodded.

'Do you know the time of death?' Phil asked. Both officers looked uncomfortable. 'We're waiting for the forensic report,' DC Ellis replied avoiding Phil's eyes.

The officers followed them back down to reception, where they murmured thanks to the receptionist and then left.

As soon as they'd gone, Clare excitedly confided in her husband. 'They know the time of death! You were right. It was when you had that funny experience.' Phil nodded, his attention drawn to the entrance to the hotel bar. He checked his mobile for the time.

'I'm not going to be able to sleep now. Time for a quick nightcap. What do you think?'

'Sounds like a good idea.' She followed him to the bar and chuckled when he said,

'By the way darling, I wouldn't describe it as a 'funny experience!'

CHAPTER SIX

The police officers returned at nine thirty the following morning. Through the open glass reception doors that led to the restaurant, Phil and Clare saw them chatting to a receptionist. Phil gulped down the last of his coffee and got up to greet them. They had just finished eating their breakfast.

'You drink your tea and I'll get them to wait for you. A few more minutes won't harm,' he whispered to Clare.

In the short time it took Phil to engage with the police officers, the hotel manager arrived. She cheerfully gave her consent for Phil to conduct them to the landing, to see the view of the lake in daylight. This time the officers produced a pair of binoculars.

'We came prepared,' DC Robert Ellis said. He turned to greet Clare who joined the small party. Together they climbed the stairs to the third floor. DC Ellis stepped closer to the window and stretched his neck to view the lake through the binoculars.

'It's a good walk along the bankside to the boathouse from where you saw the boats; about two or three miles I'd say, and I don't think the cameras would have picked him up. The CCTV system is designed to survey the water, and sometimes even that can sometimes be unreliable.' He passed the binoculars to his colleague. 'Even If the assailant escaped by swimming from one boat to another, you probably wouldn't have seen him bearing in mind the time of day,' DC Robert Ellis observed. He nodded, apparently agreeing with himself.

'Are you assuming it really *was* a man and not a woman?' Clare asked. 'If, as you suggest, someone knifed the man, pushed him in the water then swam away, it could just as easily have been a woman?'

'I'm sorry we can't discuss this case, but I think the murderer is likely to be a man,' DC Ellis advised guardedly.

'Have you spoken to the dead man's wife, or partner?' Phil ignored the detective constable's statement.

'Clearly Detective Inspector Barker will have informed the next of kin,' DC Ellis replied. He straightened his back and looked Phil in the eye, his lips tightly pressed.

'But did they say he had any enemies?' Clare persisted.

'Evidently someone wanted him dead,' PC Kath Morris avoided answering the direct question. 'In my experience the wife or husband is usually the last to know of any enemies. Almost as if the victim was leading a double life. Sometimes they are.'

'Did you get any clues from his mobile phone? I assume he would have had one.'

The officers regarded Phil warily, reluctant to give away any more information.
'We retrieved one from the water. It may not be the victim's. As you would expect, it will take some drying out,' PC Kath Morris

volunteered the information. After a nudge from her colleague, she refused to be drawn into divulging any more intelligence. Phil's question about how long it would take to get the mobile serviceable again was unanswered.

'Anyway we're done here. Thank you. We appreciate your co-operation. I hope you have a safe journey back to Bucharest,' DC Ellis said.

Phil and Clare accompanied the officers down to reception. As they watched them pass through the hotel swing doors, Gavin and Abigail entered the lobby.

'I've been trying to contact you, to see if you wanted to come for a coffee,' Gavin said. He grinned, pleased to see his friend again.

Phil slapped the pocket in his trousers looking for his mobile. 'Sorry, I didn't get your call, I must have left it upstairs. Coffee sounds good. What do you think Clare?'

'Yes, but we need our coats. You stay here and I'll get them. I'll get your mobile too.'

'Have you been helping the police with their inquiries?' Abigail flashed a wry smile at Phil.

He caught her expression and smiled sheepishly. 'Something like that. Though I don't think I was much use.'

'I suppose this is about that dead man they found in the lake over the week end?' Gavin asked. 'We heard about it when we were in Anglesey.'

'Yep.'

'So how come the police are asking you questions? Are they asking all the hotel guests?'

'Apparently. Look, here's Clare. Let's get away from here and I'll tell you all about it. How was the honeymoon?'

Their response to Phil's question was spoken simultaneously. 'Great!'

A few minutes stroll from the hotel took them to the town square.

'It's too cold to sit out here.' Gavin pointed to the Baker's takeaway coffee shop where he and Phil had often sat to drink coffee and pastries. 'A new café has opened just further up next to the Post Office, we can sit in there for a chat.

'When my dad picked us up at the train station yesterday, he told us that the police were treating the incident as murder, so what's your view on it?' Gavin asked when they had been served with drinks. He took off his coat to drape over a chair and helped Abigail with hers.

Clare noted how Gavin caressed one of Abigail's hands with one of his own as he spoke and sipped his coffee with his free hand. His wife's eyes sparkled as she hung on to every word Gavin said. They looked very much in love. She studied their faces as they listened avidly to Phil's account of what he'd observed on Friday evening.
'That's it,' Phil finished off.' I didn't see anything else.'

'So you can't help the police?' Abigail lifted an amused eyebrow almost as if she suspected Phil was holding something back. He put his hands up faking surrender.

'I've told you everything I know.'

'It's true,' Clare leaned forward as she spoke. 'In any case we haven't time to get involved even if we did have more information. We're flying back on Friday. We've really only got two more days,' she added.

Phil agreed. 'Besides, I've got nothing to go on. I don't know the dead man's wife's name; I don't know where she lives and I don't know his friends or family. I would need some kind of link to get me started.'

'So not a séance then?' Abi asked.

'No.' Phil shook his head. 'Not possible unless there are people present connected to the dead man.'

'Do you think my little cousin could help?' Abi asked. 'Second cousin actually,' she amended.

Again, Phil shook his head. 'There's all sorts of reasons not to involve Lucy. She's too young for a start, she wouldn't understand what was happening. Asking her to make contact with a murdered victim wouldn't be fair. She'd never sleep at night. It's unethical, I wouldn't put a child through that.'

Abigail bit her lip. 'I'm sorry, I wasn't thinking. You're quite right. I wouldn't want to give little Lucy nightmares. In any case she and my cousins are back home in Harrogate.'

Phil smiled. 'By the way, there's every chance that what she experienced on the day of your wedding was a fluke.'

'A good fluke, all the same,' Gavin laughed. 'I might have known that those two characters, my mum and sister would find some way to make contact. Strong women you see. I must be attracted to them.' He squeezed Abi's hand and then kissed her lightly on the lips.

'If you don't mind. I know you are newly-weds, but you're putting me off my cake,' Phil teased.

'Nothing seems to put you off cake,' Clare laughed. She watched her husband stuff another piece of fudge cake into his mouth then turned to Gavin.

'I'm glad to see you two happy. I said as much to your dad yesterday.'

'Yes he said you'd called. He appreciated it. Thanks for making the effort.'

Gavin's mobile bleeped. He gave Abi an apologetic smile as he let hold of her hand to get it out of his pocket to read a text.

'Hell. I've just had a message from a colleague from the Art College, he's on holiday in Spain. It seems he's struggling to get a flight back home to Manchester next week. They're being urged to come home earlier. There's a rumour that Spain will start closing down places.'

'That doesn't sound good. I'm glad we decided not to go out of the country for our honeymoon,' Abi said. 'But will you two be able to get back home?'

'I really hope so. Not much we can do about it. We haven't heard anything from our airline and I've been keeping track with the Transylvanian news,' Phil replied.

'So have I. It seems the Romanian government want to keep the borders between Italy and Romania closed. So far, they are allowing returning citizens and workers back from other parts of Europe as long as they go into quarantine,' Clare sighed.

'Let's hope the situation doesn't get any worse,' Abi said.

'Abi, I've been meaning to ask you about the video. Have you had it back yet?'

'My friend is sending it later today. Do you want to come and see it?' Her eyes flicked from Phil and then back to Clare.

'We'd love to. I must warn you we have a special interest.' Clare hesitated, before casting a glance at her husband. 'You see we are hoping that we might see an image of Anna and Rachel.'

'We are too!' Gavin's face broke into a wide smile. 'After we discovered what happened with Lucy, we were wondering if some kind of spectral image had been caught by the camera. Why don't you both come round to our house later and we can watch it together. What time do you think would be best Abi?'

'About four o'clock? Is that ok? We've got a couple of bottles of champagne left over from the reception. We can drink it while we watch.'

'If there's champagne in the mix, how could we refuse?' Phil laughed. 'At the moment though I could do with another coffee. Anyone else?'

*

An hour later, back at the hotel, Clare and Phil were surprised to see DC Robert Ellis in the reception area. He was accompanied with another uniformed officer who had his back turned away from them. When the officer spun round after being tipped off by his colleague, Phil recognised the features of Sergeant Ward.

'Phil Redwood? I believe we've met before,' Sergeant Ward began.

'Yes we have.' Phil's lips curled in a wry smile. 'This is my wife.'

The sergeant politely held out his hand to Clare. She hesitated before shaking it and gave herself a mental note to make sure she washed her hands as soon as she got to her bedroom.

'How can I help you Sergeant?' Phil asked. He already had an inkling why the officer was there.

Sergeant Ward scratched his head and looked uncomfortable. 'My colleague here tells me that you had a feeling something was wrong, when you looked out on the lake on Friday evening.' He glanced at DC Ellis, who nodded.

'I did. What of it?'

'And you are absolutely sure you saw nothing untoward other than the two boats a great distance away?'

'For the time of evening and the fact the light was fading, yes, I am,' Phil confirmed.

The sergeant was silent for a few seconds. He stood stroking his chin with his thumb as if unable to make his mind up about something. All the time his eyes flicked from Phil and then to his colleague. Phil waited, sensing the sergeant's reluctance to talk to him. Then as if coming to a decision, he asked Phil and Clare if he could have a private word with them. He signalled to DC Robert Ellis to remain where he was standing, then led them to a quiet corner of the hotel lounge.

'I won't beat about the bush, Mr. Redwood.' The officer took a deep breath before continuing. 'I recall that you were instrumental in solving the murder of Rachel Bellis by using your psychic powers. Though it beats me how you did it.'

'I like to think I was of use.' Phil smiled and allowed his smile to widen as he caught his wife's amused expression.

'The thing is, as you've had this, "feeling," the officer laboured over the word, 'I wondered if you may be able to help us find Ben Sloan's killer?' The last sentence came out hurriedly, as if he was forcing himself to speak before he changed his mind. 'I know it's a long shot and I don't know what skills you have, but...'

'Sergeant, I would love to help. My problem is I have no link with your victim nor his family. Furthermore, my wife and I are leaving in a couple of days.'

'Anything at all would be appreciated. The dead man's wife hasn't given us any clues. Too distraught I suppose. Maybe if you could talk to her you might get something like a...a... sensation? I don't know how these things work, but my wife Christine speaks highly of you.'

Phil laughed. 'That's gratifying. I understand your wife is in the same book club as my sister Emily.'

'That's right.'

'Is the victim's wife willing to speak to Phil?' Clare asked.

The sergeant shifted from one foot to the other. He avoided Clare's eyes. 'As yet neither she nor the DI know anything about my proposal to you. It's just an idea I have. I need to clear things with the DI first before we ask Mrs. Sloan. I think he'll agree though.'

'What makes you so sure?' Phil asked.

'Suffice to say something he mentioned to me in the past and that I know he likes to think outside the box.'

'Interesting,' Phil replied genuinely intrigued by the sergeant's explanation.

'Anyway, even if he wants to go ahead with my proposal, we will have to get agreement from Mrs. Sloan that she is willing to talk to you. If so, I can arrange for her to come to the station, so that it would be more convenient for you.'

Phil felt torn between wanting to help and refusing to get involved on the grounds that he had little information. Yet, part of him acknowledged that if the wife of Ben Sloan was prepared to talk to him, then he should do what he could. He promised he would attend a meeting at the station.

'Thank you. I'm sorry to ask, but since Rachel's murderers were locked up, and what with Christine's beliefs, I'm also learning to think outside the box, in many ways. I'll be in touch.' He made to leave then turned back. 'Do you have a mobile number?'

Folding the note with Phil's contact details on it, he straightened his uniform jacket, shook Phil's hand and with shoulders back marched out of the hotel triumphantly, a hopeful expression on his face. DC Ellis followed, taking time to nod goodbye.

'What do you make of that?' Clare turned to Phil as they mounted the stairs to their room.

He shrugged. 'It sounds like they're clutching at straws if they're coming to me. If Sergeant Ward really does clear this idea of his with the lead detective, I hope that his team are informed too. They won't be happy to see me getting involved in their murder case. It's still hot.'

'Surely he will.'
'Hmm.'

*

Sergeant Ward mulled over his proposal for several hours before deciding to mention to DI Barker that he had always suspected that somehow or other Phil had been involved in solving Rachel's murder. He couldn't explain it, but after listening to his wife Christine go on about séances and such like, he'd dared to think there might be some substance in it.

The detective inspector, fifteen years younger than the sergeant had a different approach to his cases. He was well respected and known to have an open mind. To the sergeant's immense relief, the senior officer listened and agreed they should enlist Phil's help. Sergeant Ward had never confided in any one about his unanswered questions about Rachel's murder. He could never figure out how her father and brother as well as Phil had been able to come up with the names of the murderers.

That particular case had also puzzled DI Barker. He had been the investigating detective. The events that led to locking up the killers had been extraordinary. At some point the DI had even suspected witchcraft, but had dismissed the thought as soon as it entered his mind. Neither sergeant nor detective ever confided in each other over those events prior to making an arrest.

When the sergeant suggested, somewhat apologetically, that they should utilise the help of a psychic, Detective Barker stroked his moustache, hiding a smile as he observed the officer's anxious expression. He enjoyed seeing the relief spread on Ward's face when he'd agreed. The proposal was something new, and he had nothing else to go on. The wife of the victim gave him no clues and questioning Ben Sloan's few relatives who didn't live locally also proved fruitless. His only other line of inquiry was to interview the victim's workmates and his friends. He hoped he might get something useful from them.

CHAPTER SEVEN

At four o clock, Dan greeted Phil and Clare into the newlyweds' home with a grin.

'They are experiencing a slight, "technical hitch," as they say in the trade.'
He ushered them along a narrow hallway into a small room where Abi was sprawled on the floor surrounded by information papers, boxes, cables and plugs. She was putting together a new television.

'Hi. Sorry about the mess. We bought this the week before we got married and haven't had time to install it properly. Gav's sorting out the drinks. I think my IT skills are marginally better than his,' she grinned.

'Follow me,' Dan said. 'I'll take you to the kitchen. I'm no good with this sort of thing either.' Phil cast his eyes over the clutter on the floor and decided to take the easy way out. He stepped in the direction Dan indicated. Clare hung back and offered to help Abi.

'I can probably sort this. I've had to do a lot of this kind of thing at work, plus Phil and I recently bought a new Smart TV that does almost everything. I managed to get that working when he was conveniently out.' She shrugged and made a wry smile.

'Great. Thanks.' Abi pulled herself to a sitting position. 'With a bit of luck I think I've got it fixed up now. It was something to do with setting crystals. All these bits and pieces on the floor is just spare stuff from the old TV we were using.'

'Ah yes, I remember something about crystals. It reminded me of crystal balls and such stuff. Now that kind of thing would definitely be up Phil's street. Though this isn't!' They both sniggered. 'Despite the computer course he took with Gavin a long time ago, his knowledge hasn't increased. I think he learned enough for his immediate needs such as emails and writing and saving documents. The behind the scenes technical stuff he leaves to me.'

Abigail chuckled and re-positioned herself. She sat cross legged on the floor and reached for the remote. 'Let's see. Fingers crossed.' She switched on the TV.

'Hey presto.'

A newsflash appeared on the screen warning the public to wash their hands and to avoid crowds.

'This Coronavirus is really worrying isn't it?' Abi said. She changed the channel not waiting for a response.

Clare nodded. 'It is.' She kept her tone light though secretly she worried about the Transavia airlines. She changed the subject with a smile.

'Did your friend send you the *video* of the wedding?'

Abi nodded enthusiastically. 'Yes I got the email an hour ago. All I need to do is down-load it on to this screen here. I'm looking forward to seeing it. I was so nervous on the day, I scarcely noticed what was happening. It'll be fantastic to be able to watch it properly.' She blushed. 'I was thinking of wearing my bridal dress to watch it but I changed my mind.' She giggled. 'Silly really.'

'It was a beautiful dress. I loved your train and the hearts and pearls around the neckline. I noticed the pattern was repeated in pink on the bridesmaids' dresses.'

'And she looked beautiful too,' Gavin said as he came into the room with a tray of glasses. Behind him Phil carried another tray with crisps and other nibbles. Dan produced the promised bottle of champagne.

'Should I draw the curtains? It's getting dark outside.' Abigail stared out through the window as vehicles passed the street outside. Flashing headlights streamed through the panes of glass, lighting up the near dark room. Getting up from the floor, she closed the curtains and then clapped her hands. Immediately a lamp in the corner of the room switched itself on providing just enough light to see each other. They focused on the television screen.

As they sat together and watched Abigail walk down the aisle on the arm of her father, all eyes covertly searched St. Winefride's Cathedral for anything unusual. It was as the bride reached the spot where Gavin and Phil stood waiting, when simultaneously they caught their breath. A shimmering outline hovered in front of the first pew.

'There, stop!' Gavin shouted. 'Can you see anything just at the side of where Phil's standing?'

Phil nodded. 'Yes, that's when I had a paranormal sensation. Do you remember I whispered to you that I felt something?'

Gavin inclined his head, his attention still on the screen. Abigail turned to agree with her husband. 'Yes you indicated with your eyes that something was up.'

Dan's mouth fell open. Speechlessly he stared at the frozen screen. Eventually he shook himself and asked quietly, 'Do you think that's your mother?'

'It's likely,' Phil answered for his friend. 'I think Rachel was lurking about on the other side of her. I got a stronger awareness just when we went to the vestry to sign the register. I was at the back of you, if you remember.'

'Can you start the film again Darling?' Gavin said.

Try as they might they couldn't see another shape near the vestry.

'Maybe it's a trick of the light,' Dan mused.

'I'm convinced they were both there,' Phil said stubbornly. 'I know I felt more than one presence. There was something extra. One aura stronger than the other.'

'Sorry, I didn't mean that you didn't feel anything,' Dan said quickly. 'What I meant was, the natural light on that side of the aisle exposed some kind of a shape - a spirit or ghost or something, call it what you will, but the light on the other side of the aisle wasn't so bright?'

'Do you think the shape we can see is Rachel and Anna merged together?' Clare suggested. 'Although you can sense ghosts you don't know what image will actually be visible to you or us? Besides you can sense other spirits besides them. There may have been more inside the church and they've all clustered together? You might have been picking up a lot of vibes at the same time.'

Phil mulled this over, as Gavin re-filled their glasses. 'I get what you're saying, and I think you're right. It could explain why I felt such a strong aura around me. It's the kind of sensation I get when a spirit wants to make contact with me. This time, I felt it was Anna who wanted to communicate. I don't know why, but it's like as if a message in my head told me it was her. I know that sounds weird.'

Abigail stared at him, a look of fascination on her face. Until Gavin had told her about Phil's exceptional psychic skills, she'd never in her life known anyone who could talk to the dead. She felt she should feel afraid but strangely she wasn't.

'I've never witnessed anything like this before. I can't believe it's happening.' She wriggled comfortably against Gavin as they sat together on one armchair. Her denim clad legs hung over the arm of the chair. 'How do you cope with these sensations?'

Phil grinned. 'It's like a kind of normal thing for me. Some sensations are weaker than others, maybe just a trace of something strange. Other times it's very strong, persuasive. When it's like that, I know a spirit is trying to tell me something.'

Abigail sat up quickly, her hair flicked the side of Gavin's face as she turned. He blinked and gently pushed it back on to her shoulder. 'I've got an idea,' she said. 'Why don't we switch off the lamp and run it again? If it is something to do with the angle of the light, the camera may have picked something up that isn't visible in this setting. We may see something extra if we're completely in the dark.'

'I'm not sure that will work, but it's worth a try,' Gavin said. 'What do you think Phil?'

'Who knows? Let's give it a go.'
Abigail clapped her hands to turn off the lamp then ran the film again. 'I'll stop it as soon as you shout,' she said excitedly.

'Always supposing we see anything,' Gavin said. 'I don't want to dampen your spirits. Oh hell! No pun intended.' He cast a look at his father hoping he hadn't offended him. He was relieved to see that Dan was amused. Gavin's remark had softened the mood.

In some ways, Dan had hoped not to see anything; he wanted to enjoy the film for what it was. A happy occasion. His emotions were all at odds. Memories of the unusual events on the wedding day still lingered in his mind. Still, he admitted to himself, it was pleasing to know that there had been a connection of sorts with his wife and daughter on that special day. Two members of his family who he'd loved and lost too soon. They would have loved to have been able to see Gavin get married. For a few moments he immersed himself in his thoughts, thinking about how they would have behaved. He jolted out of his reverie by Clare's excited shout.

'Look, there on the left, behind the first shape,' she pointed, just as Abi dropped the remote and so the moment was lost.

'Sorry, I'll play it back.'

'Before you do, let me go and get the other bottle of champagne,' Gavin said. He gently lifted Abigail from his knee and got up from the armchair. He returned within seconds and refilled their glasses.

'What did you see Clare?' Abigail asked when she started the video again.

'It seemed to me that the first shape we saw was actually two in one. For a second it splits apart. There, look! You see how it separates and then merges again? I don't know about you but when I first saw that shape I focused on other parts of the aisle not realising that the shape was changing in size.'

'You're right. I see it now,' Phil said. He paused before continuing, 'and another thing, all around the church there seems to be flashing lights. Did you organise special lighting Gav? Abi?'

They shook their heads.

'What is it?' Gavin asked.

'Well if you are certain there was no extra illumination in place other than the cameras; and I know that the sun wasn't shining through the stained glass; because it was a cloudy day;' he took a breath then continued, 'there is a possibility that other phantoms witnessed your marriage!'

'Are you sure?' Clare asked.

'It makes sense doesn't it? You yourself suggested there could be other phantoms present. There are a lot of dead bodies resting in that cemetery. If the departed can move around like Rachel and Anna, what's to stop others? An event such as a marriage is going to appeal to them too. Think about it. People love a wedding. Complete strangers will stop and gawk so why not wandering spirits? It would explain why I was experiencing unusually strong vibes.'

A heavy rush of mixed sentiments suffused the room as Phil's words sank in.

'Perhaps your mother invited them,' Dan tittered nervously. 'It would be just like her.' Despite his shock, he couldn't disguise his amusement with the notion. He could imagine his dearly departed wife, who had been so efficient in life, organising dead spirits. This thought oddly comforted him and he allowed a smile to play on his lips as he glanced at his bewildered son.

'I'm not going to tell my mum and dad when they watch this,' Abigail said. 'They'll have the willies if I tell them ghosts were at the wedding.'

'What will you say to your friend who made the video? Wouldn't she have noticed something odd?' Clare asked.

'If she'd noticed anything odd, she would have said, I'm sure. If later on, she mentions to me that she saw something peculiar, I'll just tell her it's a trick of the light from the stained glass windows in the cathedral. To be honest, I doubt she would even consider that the shapes might be spirits or ghosts.'

'I take it your family don't know about the séances that helped the investigation to find Rachel's attackers? Not forgetting the physical effects Phil felt when trying to communicate with Rachel?'

Abigail shook her head. 'No, I've never told them. It would spook them out, my mum especially. She's quite fragile. But I knew what I was getting into the night Nicky was attacked. After we'd left the hospital when it was more or less all over for Rachel's killers, I met up with Gavin again and he explained as best he could without frightening me that Phil was a psychic and that he'd been helping him investigate Rachel's murder. I was frightened though. At first, I thought he was winding me up. Yet it all made sense, you know, why he and Phil kept asking me questions. But I never thought the paranormal had anything to do with things until much later. I believed him but I have to say I was shocked. I've never come across anything like it before. And as for my little cousin Lucy, that was amazing.'

'It's more than likely a one off,' Phil tried to comfort her. 'A combination of her young age; the twenty ninth of February and the fact that Anna and Rachel were determined characters.'

'Still, I don't want my parents nor Lucy's ever to know about it. Not even my sisters. I hope they don't notice anything in the video when they see it.'

'They probably won't. And if they do, they'll dismiss it as a fault on the film,' Gavin reassured her.

The others agreed. Dan heaved himself out of his chair and reached for the empty bottles of champagne that had been left beside him on the parquet floor. He put them with the glasses on the tray that was on the coffee table in the centre of the room. Abigail slithered off the armchair to help him. 'Here, I can do that.'

'It's no trouble. You bring the rest of the things. I won't break them, I know they were a present from Gavin's art students.' Abigail giggled, picked up the empty snack bowls and followed him into the kitchen. When they were out of earshot Phil confided in his friend.

'By the way, do you remember Sergeant Ward from Holywell police station?'

Gavin nodded and inhaled deeply. 'How could I forget?' His forehead creased as he painfully recalled the conversation with the sergeant regarding his murdered sister.

'He's asked me to assist the detectives to solve the case of that man they found in the lake over the week-end.'

'So are you going to?'

Phil caught Clare's look of approval before answering. 'I explained I have limited time, but will do what I can. It's going to be difficult as I have little information. It was different with Rachel. We already had a connection because I knew her.'

Abigail returned from the kitchen to collect plates and soiled paper serviettes. Clare asked her about Nicky.

'She's doing ok. When she came out of hospital she went to live with her mum and step dad in Chester. She missed her exams unfortunately, but she can do them again. We were going to start a salon of our own together, but we'll have to postpone that now.'

'So you're still working at the place where you cut my hair?' Phil asked with a twinkle in his eye as he recalled the incident.

Abigail grinned. 'Yes, they offered me a permanent job there when I qualified. Nicky is coming back again soon to complete her training.'

'Did you tell Nicky about the paranormal occurrences that put Rachel's murderers in gaol?'

'No. I've never told her. I think she had enough to contend with. She's lucky to be alive.'

'She looked happy at the church,' Phil remarked. He leaned back on the sofa with his arm around Clare.

'Where's Dad? Have you left him washing up?' Gavin grinned at his wife.

'He insisted.' Abigail blew him a kiss and stepped towards the kitchen. 'I'm going to make some coffee. Does everybody want some?'

CHAPTER EIGHT

On their way back to the hotel, Phil suggested a stroll around St. Winefride's well. 'It always looks ethereal with the moonlight shining on it and there is a smidgeon of it nudging through the clouds tonight. So many secrets lie in its depths.'

'You're very poetic tonight darling.' Clare hooked her arm through his. 'Come on let's do it then walk across to Rachel's grave, I know that's what you really want to do. You are hoping to connect with her. You can't resist.'

In response Phil squeezed her arm.
From her perch on the cathedral's boundary wall Rachel watched them as they approached her grave. In the dim light afforded by the moon she could see anyone or anything that approached her resting place. Sometimes she saw squirrels burying their nuts beneath the headstone, but she didn't mind. Hovering around her as usual were her mother, Stefan, Margareta, Tom and Desmond. The little group were surprised to see Phil and Clare in the graveyard. Though not late, at seven o clock, visitors to the graveyard rarely came in the dark. It would be another four weeks before

the clocks went forward and the nights would be lighter. The spirits were glad of any diversion and watched the couple stand close to Rachel's head- stone.

Clare picked up the fading flowers from Abigail's bouquet. Automatically she sniffed them for any lingering scent, even though she knew there would be nothing.

Phil spoke to the gravestone. 'Rachel if you can hear me, it would be useful to get your assistance again. I have little time and yet the police want me to collaborate with them to solve a murder. Tragically, a body has recently been found not far from here, in St. Winefride's lake. I'm hoping you can help me with solving this crime. I think we worked well together previously to find your killers. Please can you give me a sign if you can? Though I must admit, I didn't enjoy the whacks to my stomach!' He grinned to himself in the dark, hoping that Rachel would be amused.

His wife was not surprised to hear Phil talking to a granite head stone. Over the years she had accompanied him to many places reputed to have been haunted. Some had been hoaxes, whereas at others, she knew he had experienced extraordinary supernatural vibes. She admired him though at the same time it unnerved her.

Nearby the fragile leaves of an Aspen tree quivered and whispered as a gentle breeze sidled through the foliage. Clare shivered, whilst an uneasy sensation crawled along her spine. She moved closer to her husband.

'It sounds like the police haven't got any leads to solve Ben's case?' Rachel commented. *'I wish there was something we could do to co-operate. It's a nuisance not being allowed out of this graveyard, and even worse, I no longer have power to communicate with Phil.'*
The others agreed.

'Even if we spirits could travel further afield we still wouldn't be of any use to Phil. It's not like we would be proper ghosts,' Stefan remarked. *'And from what you said last time, when you had authorisation to roam, it wasn't easy to develop your powers even when you were given full ghost status! Remember how you struggled to channel your energies as soon as you wandered away from this graveyard?'*

'I've been thinking about that,' Anna said.' *'Not about the power thing, I mean the permission to roam thing.* *'Maybe in this particular case, and because Rachel has worked with Phil on her own murder investigation; there may be a special contingency to allow her to assist with Ben Sloan's case, especially as Phil has made an appeal specifically asking for Rachel's co-operation.'*

The spirits focused on Anna with interest. In the moonlight their skeletal faces sparkled. Despite the spectral glow neither Phil nor Clare were able to witness anything of the phenomenon.

'How do you mean Mum? Do you think the Assessor's would let me roam outside the walls again? Cool! That would

be great. I could get to Phil and tell him straight away who the murderer is.'

'No you couldn't. You can't talk to him,' Stefan reminded her.

Anna frowned at them both. 'Wait a bit. Let me explain what I intend to do. You know I am newly appointed as an Assessor? Mind you I still have to convince the other seven that I have every right to be on the committee and that I have a lot to offer. Some of them are ancient. We need to modernise' – she sighed – 'Sebastian is like a dinosaur, so sexist, though he is susceptible to a bit of charm. Still I will have to summon up all my negotiating skills to persuade him and the rest to help Phil. It would be unfair not to respond to his request. Seeing as we know already the identity of Ben Sloan's killer, it might sway them.'

'The trouble with that Anna, even if you do persuade them to your way of thinking; you know the rule,' Margareta reminded her. 'Rachel would need three people to propose her and they would have to attend a special meeting.' Margareta shifted position as she spoke. Shafts of light picked out small rents in her fraying, lilac, burial dress. It flapped in the breeze, tangling itself with her glistening, golden hair that emphasized the wraithlike image she had become.

Rachel groaned. 'That could take ages. By the time the Assessors make up their mind, Phil will be on his way back to bloody Transylvania!'

'Not if I have anything to do with it,' Anna replied. *'I'm going to use the emergency rule.'*

'How does that work?' Stefan asked. *'And whilst we're on the subject, I wouldn't mind going with Rachel to offer some assistance. I used to know Phil a long time ago. He's a good sort.'*

Anna contemplated Stefan's earnest expression. She took in all the tiny break lines in his skull where he'd been pieced together again after his accident. Before she spoke she turned to Margareta and Tom, 'I suppose you two want to go too?'

Margareta shook her head. 'No, not me. From what Rachel and Stefan have said, the world has changed a lot since I walked the streets as a living being. I've been resting here too long to consider leaving now.'

Tom shook his head. 'That goes for me too. What about you Anna?'
Anna shrugged, putting on a resigned expression to face her companions. 'Much though I would like to go out and develop some tricks as a ghost, it would be too much to ask the Assessors to sanction. I will need all my persuasive skills to get them to agree to let these two go.'

Rachel grinned at Stefan. 'It will be good if we could. What do we need to do Mum?'

'Let's see. We need six spirits as proposers. Three for each of you. Who can we ask besides Margareta and Tom?'

'Big Steve and Desmond for a start,' Stefan suggested. 'Big Steve has quietened down since he went back as a ghost to find that hit and run killer. He understands the rules. He's been hanging around with Sylvia and Janice. They seem very sociable. Let's ask them to support us too.'

'Time is of the essence. Let's go and find them. Then I can fix up an emergency meeting with the Assessors,' Anna declared with a determined expression.

At that moment Phil's mobile rang. He pulled it out of his pocket.

'Yes, Phil Redwood speaking. He turned to Clare and mouthed "police." She leaned forward to listen to the conversation.

'Hello Detective Inspector Barker.'

The spirits gathered around them creating a spectral ring. Phil shivered, sensing a change of atmosphere. He put his free arm around Clare's waist.

'I understand from Sergeant Ward that you are able to help us with our inquiries into the death of Ben Sloan,' the DI said.

'That's correct. Though I did mention to Sergeant Ward that I have limited time. My flight back to Bucharest is on the sixth of March that only gives me two days. But I'm happy to do what I can.'

'I quite understand that, and I know that you are on holiday.'

'Yes.' Phil moved his head closer to Clare's so that she could hear.

'Can you catch what they're saying?' Rachel asked her mother. Anna had drifted closer

than the rest of her companions to the couple on the mobile.

'Just about. Though it's very faint.'

'We've been in touch with Mrs. Sloan and she has agreed to come to the station tomorrow morning to answer some more questions. Could you be here for nine-thirty? Do you have transport? If not, I'll send a car round for you.'

'Nine-thirty is fine and a lift to the station would be good, thanks. But Inspector, I'm not expecting to get a lot of information. I don't know this woman and if as you say she has not given you any clues, I won't have anything to go on.'

'Mr. Redwood, to be honest I'm not expecting a lot either. But it's worth a try. I like to keep an open mind. We're hoping we might get more information from the victim's mobile, when it's dried out. At the moment it is useless.'

'Fine.'

'Thank you. See you tomorrow.'

Phil replaced his mobile in his pocket. He felt a breeze surround him though fairly faint. He turned around as if half expecting to see something.

'Any vibes?' Clare asked.

'I sensed something very slightly when I was talking to the detective. But it wasn't anything like the kind of communication I would normally get from Rachel. It might have been just the breeze, though there did seem to be something extra about it.'

'Yes I felt a breeze too and so did those Aspen trees, it felt quite creepy.'

Phil laughed. 'Legend has it that Aspen trees tremble in the wind because it's their way of communicating between two worlds. The dead and the living.'

'They are in the right place here then.'

'It doesn't look like I'm going to get any assistance from Rachel. Maybe her mission was complete after we solved her own case.'

Putting his arm around Clare again they walked slowly to the lych-gate and out of the graveyard. 'Well that's taken care of tomorrow morning. What will you do when I'm out with the detective?'

'Oh I'm sure I'll find something to do. It depends on the weather. It's getting quite misty. If it persists or if it rains I'll stay in the hotel lobby and read.'

'This is definitely an emergency,' Anna declared. 'I will summon the Assessors for a meeting tonight. We're not scheduled until another three weeks but due to the circumstances we can't waste a minute.'

'What do you want us to do Anna?' Stefan asked.

'You can round up all those spirits we mentioned to act as proposers.'

'I'll get Big Steve, Sylvia and Janice. They'll probably be in the crypt. That's where they usually hang out,' Tom said. He drifted off without waiting to hear Anna's reply.

'I'll get Desmond,' Margareta offered.

'Fine.' Anna said. 'When you get them, ask them all to meet here so I can brief them before we go to "the tomb" for the

emergency meeting.' She turned to Rachel and Stefan.

'Come with me to track down the Assessors. You can back me up if any of them try to stall.'

'They wouldn't dare refuse you Anna,' Stefan said. He shared a smile with Rachel. She was used to her mother taking control. A retired head teacher before her untimely death, taking charge of situations came naturally to her.

'Believe me there will be a bit of reticence. Some of these spirits go back to the days before the Bow Street Runners. They've never even heard of Scotland Yard. They're unaccustomed to the Police Force as we know it.'

'Ok Mum, we're right behind you.'

Of the seven Assessors, only two proved difficult to convince that an emergency had arisen and they needed to meet to discuss it. Anna had anticipated their obstinacy. Both died in the seventeenth century and had only recently been voted on to the Council of Assessors. Neither knew of fellow spirits helping the authorities with their inquiries; in their day, policing was done by parish constables who weren't even paid a wage for their efforts. In some areas across England and Wales a local watchman had been given a very low salary for the job.

A reluctance to meet more than once a month by some of the older Assessors, added to Anna's challenges of getting a hearing. They didn't like to act out of routine. She finally managed to get five on her side.

She then employed all her persuasive skills to convince the brace of her remaining recalcitrant colleagues.

'You may recall that almost two years ago, my daughter Rachel, successfully assisted the police and an old family friend of ours to capture her murderers.' Anna indicated that Rachel should put herself forward. Both tenacious Assessors of the panel took in Rachel's twenty-first century clothing with amusement. Her "Save the Orangutan" Tee shirt and jeans had caused a stir amongst the older generations resting in the graveyard.

'Say something Rachel,' Anna hissed.

'What my Mum said is true. I was given a week's grace to roam with full powers of a ghost.' In an aside she muttered, 'Though I had to develop the blasted powers as I went along.'

'Rachel!' Anna pressured. She glanced at Stefan who was trying not to laugh at Rachel's murmuring.

'Phil is an excellent psychic, and I feel it is my duty to help him find the killer of that poor man found dead in the lake,' Rachel said formally, hoping to win her mother's approval. 'Furthermore, Stefan knows Phil Redwood too.'

She was about to add that Phil and Stefan had been on the same computer course but she realised that these two seventeenth century Assessors wouldn't have a clue about what she was talking about. She decided to keep her reasons as simple as possible.

'What I mean is, Stefan used to know him before his fatal accident. They were good friends and he was also instrumental in helping Phil to track down my killers. With Stefan's co-operation we managed to stop another young girl being murdered.'

This explanation seemed to appease the stubborn Assessors.

'Friendship is important,' one of them observed. The other inclined his head. 'Yes it is an honourable thing to aid a friend.' After a few tense minutes that caused Anna to turn towards her companions to roll her eyes in exasperation, she whirled around again when she heard them agree to attend the emergency meeting. Anna was triumphant.

'Come on let's get back to the others. I must explain to them what they must do to support you and Stefan to help Phil.'

'She's in her element,' Rachel whispered to Stefan.

'At least we might get to go and work with Phil,' he whispered back. 'I just hope that the full council of Assessors agree to Anna's proposal.'

'I don't think they'll refuse. Mum is only going to ask for two days, seeing as Phil hasn't much time before he goes back to Transylvania. Besides my mum can argue a case very convincingly.'

'You can say that again,' he sighed. 'I wish we could go to Transylvania,' he added with a whimsical smile. Rachel gazed at Stefan's patchwork countenance. His quirky expression enhanced the thin, neatly

interwoven lines of the bones that held his face together.

'Maybe one day we will get the chance. Who knows?'

*

The little group met in one of Anna's favourite parts of the old cathedral. It was a quiet area behind Saint Margaret Beaufort's chapel. Few spirits hung around that remote corner of the graveyard. Surrounded by high stone walls and set apart from the rest of the cathedral, it was ideal for a secret meeting. Anna took charge of those spirits that Margareta and Tom had collected. She didn't waste time before explaining what she wanted them to do.

'Most of you will have heard that a man has been found dead nearby and I know that some of you met his spirit a few days ago. His name is Ben Sloan. I think we should try to help find his killer. Agreed?'

The spirits nodded their support.

'Some of you know the procedure, at least Big Steve does. We have to convince the Assessors that we should send two spirits out to work with Phil. They will need full ghost status. Rachel and Stefan have offered to shadow Phil with his investigation and they need three proposers each to allow them to roam outside our zone. They will then have to develop their powers as ghosts in any way they see fit. Except of course anything evil.'

Anna paused to observe her audience, prepared for dissent, however the little group appeared compliant. Heartened *by their willingness to comply with her wishes, she continued.*

'Last time Rachel went out of our zone one of her proposers was Margareta, so I suggest this time she speaks in favour of Stefan. Just to be clear, Margareta, Big Steve and Tom should support Stefan.'
As Anna spoke, the spirits glided behind Stefan as if they were forming a team. Rachel thought this was amusing and giggled.

'You other three, Desmond, Janice and Sylvia, I would like you to recommend Rachel.'
With nothing better to do with their time banked over decades and in many cases for some spirits, several centuries, they were always pleased to have a diversion. They followed Anna to the Assessors meeting place - a grassy knoll that bore the tomb of St. Winefride. Set apart in a corner of the cemetery the saint's resting place was enclosed by eight straggly overgrown yew trees. It was a convenient place to meet though the saint herself never took part in the meetings. Her death had taken place many centuries earlier and her resting place a solitary one for several centuries more. As a result her unique dialect died with her. Few spirits in that cemetery shared her exact same vernacular.

On the first day of every month, the eight Assessors assembled themselves around the tomb. Each of them took up a position in front of a yew tree. This meant that all the Assessors faced each other.

Anna made her request then encouraged the others to speak. One by one the proposers spoke in support of Rachel and Stefan. After the last spirit had spoken, Anna concluded the emergency meeting, repeating her appeal for full support.

To her delight despite a little shuffling and the anticipated slow deliberation from the most ancient members of the panel, a unanimous decision gave consent. The longest serving Assessor emphasized that the decision was extraordinary, and that they would allow only two days. Stefan and Rachel must return to the graveyard by midnight on the fifth of March.

'That's a good outcome', Anna said. She turned to Margareta, 'I think that information you told me about Sebastian having been stabbed to death, added weight to our cause. Thanks for the tip off. I could see he was moved when we explained what had happened to Ben.'

'Yes, it happened in the street near his home three hundred and thirty four years ago, so I was told,' Margareta reported.

'When can we start?' Rachel asked.

'I suggest nine o clock in the morning,' Anna advised. 'Go to the hotel and wait with Phil for the police car to take you to the station. Listen to the interview with Ben Sloan's wife. Somehow you have to get Phil to find Dean. It might be easier to track down Tracey first in the charity shop. She would lead you to that horrible husband of hers. You'll have to figure out a way of communicating with Phil.'

'Maybe we should get to the hotel a bit earlier than necessary in the morning, so you can show me how to develop some useful moves, seeing as you've done it before Rachel,' Stefan suggested.

'I'll help you of course. I'm not sure if I will have to start from the beginning again. It's been a while. It took Laticia and me a couple of days to make headway with utilising our strength. I really hope we will be able to make a difference in the little time we have.'

'You'll just have to keep practising. At least you know what to expect from yourself, so you should be able to guide Stefan,' Anna said, always the optimist.

'I'm looking forward to it,' Stefan grinned. 'We could practise in the hotel reception area whilst we're waiting for Phil. Have a bit of fun.' He winked at Rachel. She stared at him incredulously.

'We don't want to cause alarm.'

'Only joking.'

Rachel wasn't sure if he really was joking. She hoped his new found freedom wasn't going to get them into trouble. This playful side of Stefan was amusing but also out of character. Or at least she thought it was. He'd always appeared to be a very serious sort of man.

During the investigation of her own murder, he had co-operated with her mother and their spirit friends extremely well. He had even charmed the famous St. Winefride herself to come to their aid.

Rachel shook her doubts from her mind, telling herself to put her trust in him as she had in the past. She was glad to have him as a partner. Over the past two years they had developed a close relationship. Yet as he hovered in front of her grinning like a Cheshire cat, and even whilst she returned his grin, she kept thinking she'd have to keep her eye on him.

The group of spirits drifted en masse towards the graveyard boundary wall. As a thick mist settled around them, they gazed towards the location of the hotel.

'It's a long time since I've been in that hotel,' Anna said wistfully. 'You must let me know if there have been any changes.'

'I wouldn't know Mum, I've only ever been there once. I can't remember much about it.'

'I can,' Stefan commented. 'That hotel was the venue for my mother's sixtieth birthday. It was a year before my accident. I remember the décor very well. It was pretty out of date. Actually, Anna in my opinion it was due for a make-over. I'd be surprised if they haven't re-decorated.'

'Fine, take notes and let me know.'

CHAPTER NINE

Over breakfast Phil checked that Clare was sure she didn't mind him going to help at the police station.

'I'll tell them I've changed my mind if you like? After all, we came here for a break besides attending the wedding.'

'Don't worry about me. I'll be fine for a few hours. The weather forecast said that the mist will lift soon and that it will be a nice dry day. I might go for a walk. I think it's a good thing that you are collaborating with the detectives. It's about time your psychic powers were recognised here. You've done so much to help the police in Transylvania.'

'Considering we live in Romania is that no surprise? People there are used to hearing tales about the paranormal.' He drained his coffee cup and got up to leave.

Clare smiled. 'Do your best and I'll see you back here for lunch.' She finished her own coffee and signalled the waiter for a top up. 'I'm tempted to stay in reception for a while to read and drink more coffee. They're using an excellent brand. In any case, I want to wave to you cheerfully from the entrance door when you get into the police car. I don't want any of the guests to think that you've been arrested.'

'That would be amusing,' Phil grinned, his hazel brown eyes sparkled at the notion. 'Actually now you mention it, I'd better alert the manager and her staff. We can't let them get any wrong ideas either.'

As Phil sauntered to the reception desk, he glanced at the clock over the main entrance door. In the split second that he noted the time was ten past nine, Rachel and Stefan drifted in to the hotel lobby. The closed entrance doors presented no obstacle for the ghosts, they easily glided through them. Immediately, Phil sensed a shift in the atmosphere. He turned raised eyebrows towards Clare to convey something was up, but she was intent on talking to the waiter about her coffee.

'There he is,' Rachel said. On her instruction, the two ghosts glided towards the desk to listen to Phil's explanation about the police car. They swirled around his body, gratified that Phil instantly responded with a twist of his head as if looking for something over his shoulder.

'He suspects we are here,' Rachel said.

'What do we do now?' Stefan asked as he took in his surroundings. Before she could answer he commented upon the room.

'I was right about a makeover. It looks like they've knocked through one of the walls to combine this reception area with the lounge. It looks good too, all open plan. Very modern yet comfortable looking chairs.'

'I like it. You must remember to give the details to my mum. She likes to know what's going on in the real world. But let's concentrate on Phil.'

Clare chose that moment to take her coffee away from her breakfast table and settle into one of the leather arm chairs near the entrance doors.

'Isn't that Phil's wife who just sat down over there?'

Rachel swivelled her head round to look. 'Yes. It looks like she's going to stay in the reception area. She's got a book in front of her. When Phil re-joins her, let's see if we can make contact with him. But remember, don't try too hard. We don't want him to be in pain, especially when he has to concentrate at the station.'

'Fine, I remember what you said. Use just enough energy to let him sense our presence but without hurting him.'

'I'll try first. I might not be able to do it straight away. It's been a while, and last time I had to practise to get it right.' Nevertheless Rachel was excited about using her power.

Phil returned from the reception desk and sat down next to Clare. 'All sorted. Just have to wait now for the cops.'

'Do you think you might get help from Rachel?' As soon as she asked the question she saw Phil's expression change as if he was in pain. 'Are you alright?'

He managed a grin as the spasm subsided. 'To answer your questions, yes! She's here, or at least someone is. I've just had a paranormal thump in my back.' He relaxed as the pain disappeared as quickly as it arrived.

'We've made contact. I think I was just a tad too energetic. It's good that I can still do it.'

'Yes let me have a go.'

'Take care, concentrate, but not too hard,' Rachel warned. Stefan nodded and focused on Phil's shoulder.

At that moment DC Ellis arrived in the hotel doorway and signalled to Phil with a raise of his hand. Phil got up and stooped down to kiss Clare goodbye. His affectionate gesture caused Stefan's efforts to result in only shoving a beer coaster on to the floor.

'That's a shame. Still, at least you managed to move something. You'll soon get the hang of it,' Rachel encouraged. 'The important thing is, that Phil knows we are going to help him.'

Clare bent down to retrieve the beer mat. When she looked up Phil was grinning.

'That wasn't me.' His grin widened when he saw Clare's surprised expression. 'You mean...?'

Phil nodded. He backed away, turning at the same time to raise his hand to acknowledge the constable. 'I have to go, can't keep the cops waiting.'

Despite being momentarily unnerved that a ghost had just been in her presence, Clare undertook her promise to smile and wave to her husband as she watched him leave the hotel, accompanied by a uniformed police officer.

Stefan looked disappointed. 'I guess it isn't as easy as I thought it would be. I *thought the energy would automatically swirl around Phil.'*

'You have to control and direct it yourself. But not bad for the first time. At least you didn't punch Phil in the stomach really hard like Laticia did, on more than one occasion I might add.'

'Ah yes. I remember Laticia. She was rather boisterous,' Stefan grinned. 'I wonder what she's doing now.'

'Probably infuriating people in the graveyard at Barbados,' Rachel retorted with a whimsical expression. 'Come on we need to get in that car with Phil, or we will miss our lift.'

'I've never been to Barbados. I wish I could go.'

'Yesterday you wanted to go to Transylvania.'

'I know I did. I still do. I learned Romanian languages just like Phil. I never got the chance to put my linguistic skills in to a career.'

'I thought you told me you trained to be a solicitor?'

'Yes, I did, but I kept my options open.'

Rachel sighed. 'I had aspirations too, you know. We died before our time. Still at least we're amongst friends at the graveyard. I'm happy enough really.'

'So am I. It's just being here in this hotel....'

'Which we'd better get out of pretty fast.'

Both ghosts sidled effortlessly through the closed hotel door and composed themselves as best they could on the back seat of the police vehicle parked outside. They watched Phil fasten his seat belt before DC Ellis drove off.

'I wonder what would happen if, after two days we didn't return to St. Winefride's graveyard?' Stefan mused.

'I don't know, but I'm not going to try it. We'd lose our powers, and probably end up as wandering spirits unable to communicate with neither the living nor the dead.'

Rachel turned to Stefan with a worried expression.

'You aren't thinking of absconding are you?'

Stefan smiled and shook his patchwork head. 'Don't worry I'm not about to abandon you. I'm really a trustworthy sort of bloke. I guess I'm over excited about being here and I started thinking about what I might have been. I know that it must have been horrible for you, the way you were murdered.'

Rachel nodded refusing to think about the past. 'And your terrible accident getting blown to bits. But here we are helping the police again. This time you are on the outside with me. Let's make the most of it.'

'Agreed,' Stefan said. 'You can trust me.'

'That's a great relief. I don't want the responsibility of keeping you on the straight and narrow.'

The police station occupied the rear of a hub that also housed the local library. Phil was conducted to a small interview room. A long narrow window that stretched across the exterior wall, provided a view of the rear of the station. Outside he could see the vehicle he had arrived in some minutes earlier, parked in one of the four spaces allocated to the police. The room was similar to the one he had sat in almost two years earlier with Gavin and Dan. He recalled how difficult it had been to convey their findings to Sergeant Ward. It was ironic that this time, the police were prepared to listen to him, even though he had no information to give.

Detective Inspector Barker shook hands with Phil and introduced him to Detective Sergeant Chloe Watson. As they seated themselves, Sergeant Ward led into the room a tall, dark haired woman, Phil presumed to be the widow of Ben Sloan. DI Barker got up to greet her.

'Good morning Mrs. Sloan thank you for coming. As I explained on the phone, Phil Redwood here is assisting us with our inquiries. We would like to go over things again please, to put him in the picture.'

The woman sat down and sighed as she adjusted her stylish, deep green puffer coat to make herself comfortable.

'Yes, I understand Inspector, but as I said before, I haven't anything to add. I have told you all I know.'

The DI had heard people say this so many times in interview rooms. He nodded abstractedly and proceeded to get down to business.

Phil took the opportunity to analyse the woman in front of him. She was nothing like he'd imagined. For some reason he'd expected a frail woman, a kind of shrinking violet, dressed in black. She was none of those things.

Over her fashionable coat, Mrs. Olive Sloan wore a green plaid woollen scarf at her neck. The colour enhanced her translucent complexion which was topped by a heavy fringe. She entered the room confidently, displaying no trace of intimidation by her unfamiliar environment. There didn't seem to be any sorrow in her demeanour either. Now and again she sniffed and put a tissue to her eyes. It seemed to Phil that the tissue was more for effect than a real need.

Rachel and Stefan were having similar viewpoints.

'It seems Ben wasn't telling us everything,' Stefan said. 'I got the impression from his brief chat with us that he and his wife were devoted to each other.'

'Me too. Maybe she is holding her grief back and she will breakdown later. It's only a few days since he died. Some people take longer to show their feelings,' Rachel suggested.

'I'm not convinced that's the case with her but let's give her the benefit of the doubt.'

'So Mrs. Sloan, you say you and your husband Ben were happy and had no enemies.'

'That's right Inspector. None that I know of.' She pressed the tissue to her eyes again as she answered.

'Can you think of anyone who would want to harm your husband?'

'No of course not. Like I said we had no enemies.'

'What about people at work? He was an engineer. Is that right?'

'Yes. As far as I know he got on well with his colleagues. You would have to ask them.'

'And at this moment we have people compiling a report on their inquiries at your husband's place of employment. Rest assured Mrs. Sloan we will find the person who killed your husband.'

Olive's unfathomable eyes stared at the DI.

'Tell me again about your husband's friends. Did he see any of them regularly after work?'

'A few. I don't know who they are. I didn't socialise with them. He rarely mentioned their names. He used to play pool and darts with them at the local pub, "The Greyhound". I never go there. It's not my kind of place.'

'Can you think of anyone else, Mrs. Sloan, besides his mates at the pub?'

Olive Sloan shook her head and dabbed her face with the tissue.

'I thought Ben told us that he had a friend who he used to have coffee with every now and again. The one that works in a charity shop,' Rachel said.

Stefan nodded. 'Yes he told us her name was Tracey Roper, and that his wife knew her too.'

'So why doesn't she tell them that?' Rachel asked.

Stefan shrugged. 'Maybe she didn't know that Ben used to meet her for coffee.'

Rachel frowned in an attempt to recall their conversation with Ben Sloan in the grave yard.

'I thought Ben said he'd told her about Tracey, but hadn't told her about Dean making threats. Damn I wish I could remember everything he said. I wonder where he is and if Olive's arranged his funeral yet.'

'I'm pretty sure Ben said he hadn't told her he had re-acquainted himself with Tracey, but intended to tell her the day he died.'

'Maybe you're right. We bombarded him with questions the other night, maybe I didn't hear him say that,' Rachel conceded.

'In any case it doesn't matter really if we can't remember everything Ben told us,' Stefan comforted her. 'We know who killed him. Our task is to make sure Phil makes contact with Tracey at the charity shop.'

Phil shifted in his chair ready to try to glean more information.

'If I may ask a question Inspector?'

'Go ahead.'

'What about family Mrs. Sloan. Did he have any relatives living nearby?'

'I've already answered that question. His parents live with his sister Rhona in Warrington. He has a niece who also lives in Warrington, but he doesn't see any of them very often. Didn't… see them, I mean.'

Again the tissue was pressed against her eyes.

'Do you have children?'

'I have a son. He's not Ben's. Keith - my son lives in Shrewsbury.'

'And his father?'

Olive sighed. 'A mistake. We were too young. We didn't stay together, he left before Keith was born. He is married now and lives in Hereford with his other children. Keith's birth father I mean – Derek.'

'Do you ever see him?'

'Not since Keith was born twenty-seven years ago. They meet from time to time, but aren't close.'

'How old was your son when you married Ben Sloan?'

Olive sighed. 'He was five.'

'Did your son get on with your husband?'

'Yes of course. Ben looked upon him as his own. We don't see him often, even though he doesn't live so far away. He moved out a few years ago to live with his girlfriend in Shrewsbury.'

'Not exactly local though,' Phil observed. 'So he wouldn't have some kind of grudge against your husband?'

'Certainly not! I've told the police that.' She glared at the inspector, who confirmed her statement with a nod. He turned to Phil, 'we've interviewed him.'

'Keith wouldn't have killed Ben!' Olive's eyes glittered. Phil sensed a surge of energy in the woman's bearing. Her concern for her son contrasted with her ostensible grief for her husband.

'We're just doing our job,' the inspector said.

'What about your own friends Mrs. Sloan? Did Ben get on with them?' Phil asked.

Olive Sloan looked surprised at the question. 'My friends wouldn't kill Ben. Why would they?' She snapped.

Taken aback by the woman's aggression, Phil continued with his line of inquiry. 'But did he get along with them?' His repeated question alerted the DI who also seemed interested in her reaction to Phil's probing. He followed it up with a suggestion.

'Perhaps if you could tell us the names of your friends, we could eliminate them from our inquiries. It's routine, we can't overlook anything if we're going to find your husband's killer.'

Olive Sloan sighed and took a deep breath as if she'd reached a decision. She assumed a grief stricken pose again.

'Of course, I understand. There's Helen Seaton, Elizabeth Murphy and Menna Jones. They are all married and they live near me. They've always liked Ben.'

'Perhaps you could write their names and addresses down and we will go and see them. Like I say it's just routine.'

DS Watson passed her a sheet of paper and a pen.

'She could have mentioned Tracey. Ben said they both knew her,' Rachel

persisted. She felt frustrated that the woman wasn't co-operating as well as she might.'

'It's likely these are the friends Olive Sloan sees regularly. She probably hasn't mentioned Tracey because she hasn't seen her for years.'

Rachel shrugged. 'I suppose so. But I still think she is behaving oddly, as if she is holding something back.'

'I agree she doesn't appear to care who killed Ben,' Stefan agreed. 'Maybe she's in shock still and doesn't want to think about it.'

'No male friends?' Phil ventured. He studied Olive's face keenly as she looked up from writing down the names. 'Of course not!' she responded sourly. 'What do you take me for?'

'Just asking,' Phil responded.

'What about the neighbours? Did he get on with them?' Phil asked. He turned to the inspector. I take it you've interviewed the neighbours DI Barker?'

'Of course.'

'They don't know us,' Olive said quickly. 'Ben spoke to them now and again. I ignored them. One of them is nosey,' Olive said bitterly. Abruptly, she stopped as if about to say something else then sniffed and made a show of wiping her eyes again.

'Do you work Mrs. Sloan?

'Yes. I'm a fashion buyer.'

'I see, that must keep you very busy,' Phil replied.

'It's part time. I don't travel much these days.'

'That'll explain her stylish clothes,' Rachel commented.

'So do your work colleagues know your husband?'

'He's never met them,' Olive Sloan said sourly.

The DI interrupted. 'We've interviewed them.'

'Was your husband acting unusually before he was killed?' Phil asked. He focused on her body language as she shook her head. 'Anything different in his behaviour to make you feel there was something wrong?'

Again a shake of the head.

'So why was your husband rowing a boat on the lake by himself?' Phil asked. Did you not want to go with him?'

'Good question Phil.'

Stefan agreed.

Olive blinked at the unexpected change in direction of the interview. Taking a deep breath she dabbed at her eyes avoiding Phil's inquiring ones.

'I intended to, but changed my mind. I had a headache and I decided to have a look around St. Winefride's well. Besides I don't like the water much. He wasn't interested in the well, said he'd have a walk around the lake and hire a rowing boat. He told me the exercise would be good for stress.'

'Oh so he was feeling stressed?' Phil asked.

'Yes. He was! Rachel said, with more energy than she meant. She was hovering just behind Phil and he experienced a blow to his back that made him double up with

pain. He covered his discomposure by bending over the file in front of him as if studying his notes. Rachel realised she'd used too much energy and withdrew.

Phil straightened up again. Although the piercing pain had been a shock, he was pleased. Rachel was going to co-operate.

'Did you do that?' Stefan asked. 'I'm impressed. But I think you hurt him.'

'I know. I over reacted. I didn't think I'd get my energy flow so quickly. At least Phil knows we're here.'

'He knows you are here. I wonder if he can tell the difference if various ghosts contact him like that.'

Rachel grinned. 'He always guessed that Laticia was around. She was less subtle. Sadly he never knew who she was.'

'Maybe later when he is alone, I will try to make contact.'

Olive bit her lip as if regretting having mentioned stress. 'No, he wasn't stressed. It was just a remark he said, an observation, that's all.' Olive fidgeted with a loose strand of her tartan scarf. It had slipped from around her neck and was caught on the zipper of her coat.

'What about messages or texts on his mobile. Did you ever read them?'

'No of course not. I wouldn't do that.' She still avoided eye contact with Phil and busied herself with untangling her zipper.

'I suppose his mobile phone is ruined? Poor Ben. I hope you find the man who killed him.'

She looked up with an expression Phil couldn't read but something didn't seem right to him. Boldly he risked a personal question.

'Was your husband having an affair?'

'Certainly not. Ben wouldn't do that. I've already told the police officers that. Why are you asking again? What are you suggesting?'

The DI intervened. 'I'm sorry we're upsetting you. We have to ask these questions. As you know Mr. Redwood here is trying to help.'

'Did you say he's a psychic?' Olive asked. 'Do you tell fortunes?'

Phil smiled. 'No nothing like that. Occasionally I get a vibe from people.'

Olive frowned. 'Vibe, what do you mean by that?'

Phil didn't want to go into detail about his experiences. He doubted the DI would want him to either. He took the easy way out to explain. 'Some people call it a sixth sense.'

'You mean like you can sense ghosts and things?'

'Yes, if you like.'

'Is this some kind of a séance?'

Phil forced a smile. 'No, I can assure you, it's nothing like that.'

Olive gave a furtive look around the room as if expecting to see a ghost. 'I don't see how that sixth sense of yours is going to find Ben's murderer.' Her lips twitched. In a brusque movement she stood up. 'I think I've had enough now Inspector. I've got things to do.'

The detective inspector got up too and Phil followed his example.

'Thanks for coming Mrs. Sloan,' the DI said. 'You've been very helpful. I will arrange for someone to take you home.' He ushered her into the corridor and down to the front desk of the station. DS Watson followed him leaving Phil alone.

Closing the door behind them Phil ventured to whisper Rachel's name. 'If you're here Rachel can you give me a sign?'

'Here's an opportunity for you Stefan. 'See if you can move that piece of paper off the desk. The one with the names and addresses.'
Delighted with the possibility of being able to communicate with his old friend, Stefan concentrated hard on the paper. At first nothing happened, then the paper began to slide across the desk very slowly.

'That's good,' Rachel cried, 'keep going.'
The paper slid towards the edge of the desk then fluttered to the floor just as the DI returned. He saw it and picked it up whilst Phil looked on smiling.

'We mustn't lose this piece of paper. We need to contact these people, they could be valuable leads.'

Phil nodded, then watched the paper again move off the desk. This time rapidly.

'I'm not so sure,' he said as the note soared away towards the window. The DI leaned forward to try to catch it but he was the wrong side of the desk.

'It's a waste of time. Let's get rid of it,' Rachel said. *'Quick I'll do it.'* She concentrated on getting the note on to the windowsill. *The narrow gap through the open window had been purposefully left, to let in some fresh air. Rachel managed to force the sheet of paper through it.*

Phil and the horrified DI watched as it soared outside. It landed in a puddle on the hub car park.

The DI with a frown directed at Phil ran out of the room to try to retrieve it. Convinced this was a sign from Rachel, Phil reluctantly followed the police officer outside.

'Drat, it's smudged. I can't read any of it. This is useless.' Barker balled it up in his hand and shoved it in his pocket. 'I didn't think it was draughty in that room. Must have caused it when I came back in and closed the door. I'll get someone to call her and get those names and addresses again.'

Phil felt the man's frustrations and tried to diffuse the situation. 'I know this may sound ridiculous, but I don't think those contacts are going to be of any use. You would be wasting valuable time. I think she's wasting our time too. She knows something, but she either won't tell us or she's too frightened.'

DI Barker ran his fingers over his moustache, breathed hard and relaxed. He stopped glaring at Phil. 'Did you get a vibe or something?'

'Yes, a very strong one.' Phil didn't explain that he'd got a physical strong vibe of the paranormal kind. 'I think her husband was stressed about something and she knows it. She may not know what he was stressed about, but has probably got an inkling of what it might be and doesn't want to tell us.'

'Do you think he was having an affair and she was too ashamed to admit it?'

Phil shrugged. 'I wouldn't rule it out. Though I sense something else, perhaps it's fear - someone could be threatening her. I would be interested to know what her husband's colleagues at work say about him.'

'Not much I'm afraid. If you like, you can read the notes from our inquiries at his workplace. I read them only an hour or so before you arrived. We didn't take any statements. I saw no reason to tell his wife that. If you've got time I'll get the file. It's very thin.'

Within seconds, the DI returned with DS Watson and the file. Barker explained that his officers had also interviewed Ben's mates at the "Greyhound" pub and none of them had given the detectives a lead. 'There is just one man we have been unable to locate because he's away on holiday in Scotland. He's due back sometime today I believe. Is that correct DS Watson?'

'Yes Sir. I'm planning to visit him later.' She folded her arms and leaned her back against the door. 'If you don't mind Sir, I need to get on.'

'Yes, of course. So do I.'

Alone in the room with the file a few seconds later, Phil was aware of an aura surrounding him.

'Rachel is that you?'

A page in the file turned over seemingly on its own accord.

'I take that as a yes. Is someone with you?'

The page turned back again.

'Is Anna with you?'

The file comprised of three pages, and nothing moved after his next question. It soon became clear to Phil that this was the only method Rachel could use to communicate with him. To give a negative reply she'd decided best to leave the papers still.

Phil frowned. 'Not Anna, but someone else?' He nodded when the first page turned over to confirm.

'Laticia?'

The papers stayed still.

'Not Anna, nor Laticia but someone else?'

Rachel forced the page over.

'I wish I could tell him your name, especially as you knew him so well.'

'Don't worry about it. We've established that I'm not Anna nor Laticia. He accepts we're trying to help. So let's read the notes with him. See if there's any mention of Tracey Roper. Didn't Ben say she worked in a charity shop a couple of doors down from a café?'

Phil found nothing to go on. He learned that though Ben was liked he hadn't formed any close relationships with his colleagues. Occasionally he would eat with them in the canteen, though sometimes like the rest of the employees, they had their lunch in the café across the road from their workplace. Two of the assistants at the café had revealed that Ben was always polite and courteous. Sometimes if he finished early he would call on the way home for takeaway coffees.

'That must be the coffee shop Ben told us about which is in the same street as the charity shop. There's no mention in the file of Tracey meeting him there or of the charity shop though,' Stefan observed.

'Maybe the workers in the coffee shop didn't know that Ben and Tracey knew each other.' Rachel spoke slowly, trying to analyse the scanty report. 'In that case, I suppose they wouldn't mention her nor the charity shop.'

'If the police think something fishy was going on they'll go back. But that report doesn't suggest they suspect anything suspicious. It seems to me it was just a routine inquiry,' Stefan said.

Rachel gazed at Stefan with new respect. Her doubts about his seriousness had vanished. He was now the sensible Stefan she had come to regard as an intelligent and respected friend.

'I suppose so,' she said. 'Tracey and Ben only met every now and again. Maybe they took it in turns to get coffee takeaways. That way the counter staff wouldn't connect them.'

Phil closed the file. He checked to see if he was still alone and then whispered.

'Rachel if you and whoever is with you have managed to read this file, what do you think I should do? I have a mind to try the coffee shop. Do you think that's a good idea?' Phil realised from old that a ghost wouldn't be able to have a long conversation with him, so after his initial question, he'd added another which required an affirmative or a negative answer.

'If he goes to the café, he will see the charity shop. We have to make him go in to look for Tracey,' Rachel said.

Stefan managed to open the file again and flip to the second page which contained the sentence referring to the café. Rachel was impressed. 'You did that well.'

'I took your advice. I concentrated hard on what I wanted.'

'I'll take that as a yes.' Phil smiled smugly and closed the file again. He got up taking the folder with him to the front desk of the station and handed it to Sergeant Ward, who looked up from his paperwork as Phil appeared.

'What do you think? Anything to go on?'

Making sure no-one was listening, Phil nodded. 'I definitely felt Olive Sloan is holding something back. I'm not sure what it is, yet. I need to think.'

Sergeant Ward's eyes gleamed. Phil got the impression he shared his sentiments about the bereaved wife but chose not to voice them. 'Very often it's the nearest and dearest who hold the key in these murder cases,' he offered. 'So what now? Do you need anything?'

'I would like DS Watson to contact me when she visits Rob Taylor, the guy who is returning from Scotland. If possible I would like to accompany her.'

'Right you are. I will remind her. Meanwhile I'll get someone to take you back to the hotel.' He picked up the phone and Phil sat down to wait for his lift. *Rachel and Stefan hovered near the door.*

CHAPTER TEN

Phil arrived back at the hotel at quarter to twelve. There was no sign of Clare in the lobby nor in their room. He went downstairs again and decided to study his notes in the spacious lounge whilst he waited for her.

'Now what do we do?' Rachel asked peering over Phil's shoulder. 'I guess he's waiting for Clare and they'll go for lunch somewhere.'

'We could go back to the graveyard and tell Anna and the others what's happened so far,' Stefan suggested.

'It's tempting, but if we do that, we might miss what Phil tells Clare and what he intends to do next. We ought to keep an eye on him.'

'I suppose you're right. I'll just have a good look around this hotel whilst we're waiting. I can give a full report to your mother.' He winked with his good eye causing his patchwork face to crinkle whilst Rachel effected a raised and exasperated eyebrow. She draped herself over a chair to keep watch.

At ten past twelve Clare returned, accompanied by Gavin and Abigail.

'Hi Darling, look who I bumped into just as I was on my way here?' She lightly kissed her husband's cheek. He got up to greet his friends. 'I didn't expect to see you two lovebirds again so soon.'

Abi grabbed a stool from a nearby table and sat down to face him as he sank back into his armchair.

Gavin grinned and pulled out another stool to sit next to Abi. 'We're wondering if you feel like having lunch with us at "The Raven."'

Phil glanced at his wife. 'Is that alright with you?'

Clare nodded. 'Sounds like a good idea to me. I haven't been to that pub before, and I remember you telling me about it after your last visit. I'd like to freshen up before we go. I've been walking a lot. But first, tell us how you got on with the murder investigation.'

Phil related the events of the morning and finished up by telling them about experiencing paranormal vibes. 'The thing is Gavin, Rachel is helping me again.'

Gavin stared open mouthed at Phil. Breathing heavily, he ran a hand through his hair. 'You're kidding?'

Phil shook his head, concern for his friend etched his face. Abigail squeezed her husband's free hand sympathetically as he faced Phil. 'Really? Are you sure?'

'Absolutely. She's working with someone else too.'

'Oh… I remember, wasn't it some woman called Lucrezia or something like that?' Gavin swallowed hard.

'Yes, her name was Laticia actually, but it isn't her. This other person is more subtle. At least I'm not getting violent stomach punches like I used to get.'

'Maybe Rachel knew you were suffering, and chose a different partner.'

Phil shrugged. 'Who knows?'

Clare got up. 'This all sounds amazing. I'll just go upstairs. I won't be long.'

Rachel smirked at Stefan who had drifted across just in time to hear Phil's comments.

'You've won some admiration from Phil. He did suffer a lot when Laticia barged into him. She couldn't help it though. And without her, I would never have found those evil men.'

'She did get over excited on occasion but was determined to find your murderer,' Stefan smiled graciously.

'It's early days yet, you might get overwhelmed yourself, if things develop with our investigations. I must admit, last time, when things started to unravel, I got so enraged that my energy levels soared out of control and poor Phil's stomach had to deal with the consequences.' She laughed.

Clare returned, buttoning up her coat again. She handed Phil his own. 'Ready?'

They got up to walk the short distance across town to "The Raven."

The ghosts followed.

'This place hasn't changed,' Phil commented as they walked into the lounge area. 'Same green leather furniture and wooden floor. I'm glad. I like it this way.'

'So what do you guys want to drink?' He reached the bar first where he picked up a menu. 'The food has changed though. I don't recall tapas. They do a deal too. Four for the price of three. I wouldn't mind giving them a try?' He raised an enquiring eyebrow at Clare.' He handed the menu to her and picked up a couple more for his companions.

'Yes, I'd like to have some tapas too. Shall we get a bottle of wine to share?' Clare suggested.

'You go ahead, I would prefer a fruit juice. It's too early for me,' Abigail smiled. 'I drank too much champagne last night.'

Once settled at a table with their drinks, and their food choices ordered, Gavin asked Phil what he intended to do with the flimsy information he'd picked up about the dead man.

'That depends on Clare,' Phil turned to his wife. She took a sip of her drink and met his gaze over the rim of her wine glass.

'What do you mean?'

'We're here on holiday, so if you don't want me to use up any more time on this investigation I won't.'

'I told you this morning, I don't mind if you feel you can be of any use to the police. Don't worry about me. But please be careful.' She examined his face. 'I have a feeling that the reason you've said that, is because you've thought of what you would like to do next. Am I right?'

Phil nodded sheepishly.

'Is there anything we can do?' Gavin asked. He tugged at his ear nervously. A quick glance at Abigail told him she was willing to help too.

'You are on your honeymoon, sort of. Surely you don't want to get mixed up with this?'

Abigail put her hand on Phil's arm. 'You were good enough to come to the wedding and be Gavin's best man. The least we can do is lend a hand. That's if we can. Besides if Gavin's sister is helping you, beyond the grave as it were, then it seems right that we should too. I hope that makes sense.'

'What are you planning to do this afternoon?' Clare asked. She popped an olive in her mouth.

Phil took a breath. 'Actually I would like to visit the café where Ben Sloan occasionally had lunch. According to the file notes, the police spoke to two members of the café's staff. One full time and the other part-time. I have a hunch one of them may have remembered something worth mentioning.'

'A lot of those places have a few part-time workers and so it's likely somebody was absent when inquiries were being made. One of them might be there today,' Clare suggested.

'There was no mention of missing part-time staff in the report I read. Besides, the police have limited resources and making return visits on the chance of interviewing all the staff is time consuming, especially if they didn't have a strong suspicion in the first place. I think they were making routine inquiries. If they suspected something dodgy going on, or if they had a lead, they would have followed it up. It would be difficult to keep any shady business secret in a small café.'

'Why do you want to go?' Clare frowned.

'Because I get the impression Rachel wants me to go. Maybe she wants to show me something.'

'Right. I see. So Rachel knows something that the police don't?'

Phil shrugged as he looked squarely at his wife's worried face. 'I don't know. It might be a link to something else. Rachel has limited means of communicating with me. It's possible I misunderstood what she was trying to tell me. But I feel I should check it out anyway.' He glanced at Gavin who was keenly following the conversation.

'This is uncanny. Who would have thought my sister has turned ghost detective?' He laughed.

Rachel and Stefan hovering nearby exchanged grins.

'At least he's going in the right direction. We'll have to make sure he gets to the charity shop though,' Stefan said.

'Right. How do we get there?' Clare asked.

'We?' Phil frowned at his wife. 'If there is some evil at work I don't want you involved.'

'We'll take you.' Abigail intervened quickly as she saw Clare about to protest. She put down her orange juice. 'It will take you too long by public transport and you may not be able to get all the way to the actual café. Didn't you say it was on a small industrial estate? You would lose valuable time walking from the bus stop. I'm the only one who hasn't been drinking.'

Gavin agreed. 'I'm in. What do you say?'

'Alright,' Phil sighed reluctantly. 'I just don't want any of you to get caught up with this investigation. There could be something sinister waiting for us at the other end.'

'He's got a point you know. But now there won't be room for all of us in the car,' Rachel said. *'It's uncomfortable hanging in a small space.'*

'Good of your brother and his wife to involve themselves in this. Perhaps we could follow them in another car,' Stefan suggested.

Rachel sighed. *'I suppose so, but it might mean car hopping. I've done it before. Let's see how big Abi's car is, we might be able to float above their heads. I just hope it isn't a mini.'*

'Darling I don't think you have much choice,' Clare smiled. 'Abigail's right. It would take ages to go by bus. You'd probably need to change twice. There isn't a train station near that place, and a taxi there and back would be ruinously expensive. Let's take up Abi's offer. If it makes you feel better, we can park the car a little distance from the café, and you can go in by yourself. If you need us you can phone.'

'It would save time too, especially if you want to be able to talk to that mate of Ben Sloan's that's travelling down from

Scotland. Did you say that the sergeant was going to call you?' Gavin asked.

'Good point.' Rachel approved.

Phil knew that everything his companions said made sense and he gratefully thanked Abigail, just as their food arrived.

'Do you want to go as soon as we've eaten this?' Abi suggested. 'We could get there around half three.'

'Fine.'

'That gives us about half an hour to report back at the graveyard, then come back here to get a lift,' Rachel said gleefully. 'It should make my mother happy,' she grinned. 'Keeping her informed!'

'That's OK with me. The other spirits might have some thoughts on what to do.'

'I wouldn't put it past my mother to have a few suggestions.'

The graveyard perimeter wall wasn't far from 'The Raven" pub.

Stefan and Rachel glided there easily as they weren't encumbered by gates and traffic lights. It took them just five minutes to find Anna. She was accompanied as usual by Margareta and Tom hovering around their usual niche in the cathedral. It was one of their favourite meeting places for them and their spirit comrades Desmond and Big Steve. The older spirits preferred to assemble on the roof tops of the tower or areas above the altar. The cathedral and its two ancient chapels provided plenty of nooks and crannies.

'Ah ha so here you are, with some news I hope,' Anna greeted them enthusiastically.

As Rachel and Stefan wafted towards the niche, Big Steve followed with his new acquaintances, Olga and Kay following closely behind. The deaths of all three occurred the year before Rachel's. Big Steve had been killed in a hit and run when he was in his forties. Olga passed away in her sleep when she was eighty-four. A heart attack had taken Kay at the age of seventy one.

That Big Steve hung around with the recently departed was due to Anna's encouragement. She maintained that it was a good way of keeping up to date with what was happening in the modern world.

'First of all tell me how my son is enjoying married life!'

Rachel laughed. 'He's fine Mum. They are very much in love.'

'Stefan nodded his agreement.

Anna smiled with satisfaction. 'So how's the investigation going?' Her quizzical eyes shifted from Rachel's to Stefan's then back again to her daughter's.

'We've made contact with Phil and he is on the right track, but progress is slow really because he has very little to go on and of course we can't tell him what we know. He's aware we are helping though,' Rachel reported.

'Did Ben's wife say anything about the funeral arrangements?' Margareta asked.

'It wasn't mentioned, but I saw his address on the case file and I don't think Ben will be joining us here,' Stefan glanced at Rachel for confirmation. She nodded.

'Actually Mum we'll have to go back now. We've left Gavin and Abigail in the pub with Phil and Clare. We're hoping to hitch a lift to the café that Ben told us about. We might get some more clues there. Or rather Phil might. We just need to make sure he picks up some information from the charity shop that's almost next door.'

Anna stalled them. *'Before you go, give me an update on St. Winefride's Hotel.'*

'It's as I guessed. A complete makeover downstairs. One of the walls in the reception area has been knocked down and so it is a very comfortable lounge area just off the lobby entrance. All the furniture has been replaced too. Stylish, modern and comfortable,' I would say.' Stefan supplied the information willingly.

'I don't know why you are so interested Mum,' Rachel raised a curious eyebrow.

'Because I want to keep up to date with what's going on in the town. It might come in handy one day. Look at those old crones over there hanging around in the belfry. They've been here for centuries. They don't mix with us, and scuttle away as soon as they see us, as if they might contract some disease. They don't want to know what's happening in the world. I don't want to end up like them!' She cackled, *'as if that could happen. Besides, you never know if*

we might need the information in the future for our investigations. This is why I encourage Big Steve and the others to mix with the newly deceased.'

They glanced across their niche to see Big Steve's newest acquaintances, Catherine and Kirsten. They hovered a short distance away from the group. Both women had died young within a few weeks of each other from natural causes. Neither spirit had known each other beforehand. They were in their late fifties. Their burials were the most recent in the graveyard.

Margareta chuckled. 'I don't think he needs much encouragement. He's collecting quite a retinue.'

'See you later.' Rachel and Stefan grinned at Margareta's comment as they floated back to "The Raven."

In the pub the friends were getting ready to leave. Clare pulled on her coat and lifted Phil's off the vacant chair next to her where he had flung it. She waited for him to fasten the buttons, then they followed Abigail and Gavin outside. A slight breeze swept around the corner of the pub as the newlyweds led the way through the town towards their house.

'Wow, it's gone quite chilly again,' Clare remarked pulling her coat collar up. The group stopped alongside Abigail's car parked on the street outside their house.

'I'll just dash in to get the keys,' Abi said over her shoulder running up the path to the front door. She emerged a few minutes later and they piled into her spacious hatchback.

'This is a big car,' Phil commented. 'And I don't mean that to sound sexist, though I suppose it is. I'm sorry.'

'I need the space for carrying all my equipment when I visit people at home to do their hair.' Abi gave him a wide smile as she manoeuvred the car down the road. 'I might not look it, but I'm strong. I can handle it very well,' she laughed.

Gavin shared her mirth. 'She's been taking judo lessons. So don't mess with her.'

'Good to know. You never know if she might need to put it in action one day,' Rachel acknowledged. She and Stefan suspended themselves over the vacant rear seats behind Phil and Clare. A portable shop sized hair dryer was stacked on the seat next to Clare and a box of hair styling equipment and beauty products occupied the luggage space; neither inconvenienced the two ghosts.

'Are you learning Judo because of the places you visit?' Clare asked.

Abi nodded, 'Something like that. It was Gavin's idea, and actually I am enjoying it. Now then, which way do we go?'

'Best head for the Chester Road,' Phil advised. He saw Abigail's fingers hover over the GPS screen. 'Sorry I don't know the post code. The place where the dead man worked is on Roman Road Industrial estate, and the café is across the road. It's called "Roman Road Café."'

'Very imaginative,' Clare commented.

Roman Road was on the outskirts of Chester on the West side, approximately seventeen miles away from Holywell.

'So do you do much mobile hairdressing Abi?' Clare asked.

'I've got a few regular customers I see after work. It started when I was training, just with family members, you know, and some of my friends and then their families. I didn't charge because I wasn't qualified, but everybody gave me something. I put the money away towards a car. Dad used to take me to every appointment, and he helped me buy this Vauxhall Zafira. He got fed up of lugging all the equipment in and out of his Toyota.'

'And now you're qualified, do they mind you doing this extra work outside the salon? Your employers, I mean,' Phil asked.

'They know I do it and are OK with it. But they wouldn't like it if I stole their clients, which I won't.'

As they crossed the bridge over the River Dee, a grey cloud burst and pelted the windscreen with rain. The wipers screeched as they were put into use.

'Yuk that's a horrible noise, Gavin grimaced. 'I'll have a look at that when we get back. You might need a new wiper blade.'

Abigail flashed him a loving smile. 'Thanks.' She turned down Roman Road and slowed down as they all kept a lookout for the café.

'I think that's the building that accommodates the engineering company where Ben Sloan worked,' Phil said. He checked his notes then pointed to a three storey concrete building set off the road. 'Look there's the sign for it – *Deesway Engineering Company.*'

Abigail slowed down to read the sign. A large car park fronted the building, with a noticeboard giving the names of the various businesses on the same site. *Deesway Engineering* was the only company of its kind. The other enterprises included a scrap merchant and three warehouses, one of which stored dried animal feed. Another sold art and craft equipment, complemented by the adjoining building that sold sewing machines. The access to the site was a potholed and gritty road. The café where Ben had frequented was nowhere to be seen. Abigail passed the building and drove another hundred metres to a roundabout. She turned all the way round and then drove slowly back down the same road towards a cross roads.

'There it is, almost on the corner. You can't see it very well because of that line of potted stick Cypress trees,' Clare said. 'They've probably been put there to make the pavement and entrance look more inviting. This street is a bit down at heel.' She leaned forward in her seat, 'It's the third unit past that brightly painted mini supermarket.'

Abigail slowed down to look. After the mini supermarket, they passed a chemist and mobile phone shop before spotting the café.

'There isn't a parking space here, I'll go around the corner and try not to park too far from the café.' She turned left into a wide road that was lined on each side with terraced town houses. Vehicles were parked all along each side of the road, though she managed to find a spot to park a few metres away from the junction.

'I think you guys should stay here, and I'll go in,' Phil said.

'No. I'll come with you. I don't think you should go in on your own,' Clare cast him a worried frown as she spoke.

'I'm not in any danger. I'm just hoping to pick up some useful information.'

'She's right to feel uneasy,' Rachel observed. *'Who knows who may be listening when Phil starts questioning the staff? Someone may be in that café with a connection to Dean. Or even the killer himself!' They may not like Phil asking awkward questions.'*

Stefan turned to face Rachel hovering at the side of him. 'You're right. If Phil manages to get someone to give him some information, a nasty eavesdropper might start a rumpus. I hope Gavin goes in with him.'

'A rumpus! I haven't heard that word for a long time,' Rachel laughed.

'I think it's a good word myself.' Stefan cocked his one good eye at his companion. 'I like unusual words, that's why I like languages. I could have used kerfuffle.' He was gratified by another amused stare from Rachel. 'Kerfuffle?'

Stefan inclined his patchy head to one side with a smile then followed Phil out of the car. 'Come on. Let's hope one of the serving

staff, has remembered something significant since the police were here making inquiries.'
Another car door opened and Gavin got out.

'It seems my brother agrees with you,' Rachel said. 'Not with the rumpus though,' she threw a grin at Stefan who held up his bony arms in mock despair. The ghosts glided around the two men as they made their way along the street. They passed the charity shop on the corner and then hovered outside the café as Phil and Gavin considered how they were going to conduct themselves.

'Should we ask for takeaway coffee and then try to get chatting?' Gavin suggested. He tugged at his ear.' You are better at that sort of thing than I am.'

Phil shook his head. 'I was thinking of a more direct approach, like asking to speak to Karen and Danny, the guys the police spoke to.'

Gavin disagreed. 'No I think you should be more subtle, it might put them on their guard.'

'Yes I agree with Gavin,' Rachel said.

'Do you think we ought to make our presence known?' Stefan said.

'Yep. Do you want to do it?'
Stefan gently blew some air to caress the back of Phil's neck. Phil responded by rubbing the area with his hand. Stefan repeated the action with more force. Then gave him a nudge on his shoulder.

'I think we've got company,' Phil said with a grin.

Gavin stared at his friend in disbelief. 'Do you mean Rachel?'

'I'm not sure it's her or her sidekick. Maybe both of them are here.'

'But how did they get here?'

'I wish I could answer that,' Phil shrugged. 'Come on let's play it safe like you said. I'll ask for coffee and somehow try to get into a conversation to say we're colleagues of Ben Sloan.'

'Nice work!' Rachel said approvingly. Just the right kind of pressure.'

'Thanks. I must admit it was a bit of trial and error. I started cautiously first, and it seemed to work.'

'OK, I'll just follow your lead. I hope you know what you're doing,' Gavin said.

Phil opened the door and entered the café. Gavin stayed close behind him. It was larger than it looked from the outside. Tables and chairs covered the floor area from the large window to the central serving bar. Even more seating had been placed beyond the central serving bar reaching the back wall of the café.

A few tables were unoccupied, though Phil didn't choose a place to sit down. He headed to the counter and leaned against one of an untidy huddle of vacant bar stools. Two women dressed in white overalls were busy working. One handed over a tray of drinks and snacks to a customer who walked away to a place at the furthest point of the café away from the central bar. The other worker finished wiping down the work top. When Gavin joined Phil's side, she ignored them then disappeared through a door leading to the back.

'Hello, what can I get you?' The other assistant smiled encouragingly at Phil. She was a large woman, with blonde hair tucked up tightly in a white cap that displayed the name Ellen's Eats which belied the sign on the café outside. Phil noted with satisfaction that she wore on her overall a badge that gave her name Karen.

'Hi, could I have four Americanos to go please?'

'Milk?' 'Yes please.'

After referring to the logo on Karen's uniform Gavin asked why the sign outside said *Roman Road café*.

'Oh that's because the owner hasn't got round to changing it yet. She only took over this place six months ago. She's done a lot of modernising in here. As you can see we've got all the latest equipment.'

Phil and Gavin agreed it looked much nicer inside than out.

An elderly man sitting nearby chipped in.

'Great improvement. I just hope she doesn't put the prices up!' He shuffled out of his chair, tucked a newspaper under his arm, grinned at the small group at the bar and headed for the door. 'See ya.'

'He's one of our regulars. I also hope the manager doesn't increase the prices.'

Encouraged by the assistant's cheerful disposition, Phil asked her if she was new to the job.

'I've been working here several years. Danni and I were lucky that the new owner kept us on when she took over running this café.'

'Actually it's you and Danny we would like to talk to,' Phil said quietly. 'Is he here?'

Karen smirked. 'Danni's just gone for a smoke, *she'll* be back in a few minutes. What do you want to talk to us about?'

Gavin caught Phil's startled expression and stifled a grin at his mistake.

'Just a few questions,' Phil said covering up his misconception over the gender of Danni. 'I think you knew a colleague of ours… Ben Sloan?'

Karen frowned as she reached for the ten pound note Phil held out. 'Ben Sloan. I know that name from somewhere.' She put the money in the cash register and handed him a pound change.

'He's the guy who was murdered on the lake?' Phil prompted her hopefully. 'It was last week end. You may have read about it in the papers?'

Realisation swept her face. 'Yes, that's it. I remember now. A sociable guy. 'He used to come in here now and again. Usually he was on his own, but he seemed to know a lot of our customers. Worked across the road in the big building I think. Such a shame what happened.'

'Did you know him well?' Phil asked.

'Not really. I recognised him whenever he came in here, but I didn't know him well enough to chat properly. If you know what I mean.' Karen eyed him curiously. 'We just mentioned stuff like the weather, you know, that sort of thing. We get busy during lunch times. There's not much time to chat. Mind you, I don't work every day. I work four days a week. Danni though works full time. We have another part timer - Jade she works the days I'm not here – Fridays and Saturdays. Then there's Ellen and Johnny. Ellen, as I've said owns the place and takes it in turns with her partner Johnny to do full days and weekends. Neither of them are here at the moment though.' Karen wiped down the counter as she spoke and adjusted the lid that had slipped over a display of cherry scones.

'Did you notice if he was ever with anyone aggressive?'

'What? Somebody in here, threatening him you mean?' Karen stood still to stare fully at Phil.

'No, I don't think so. I've noticed no-one like that in here. I said the same to the police. He usually came in on his own, but like I said, we get busy at lunch times, so it's possible he was with someone like that and I didn't see him. Are you helping the police with their inquiries?' She laughed. 'Sorry it's not funny, but I always wanted to say that. Here's Danni coming. I'll sort your coffees out in a minute.' She moved away to serve another customer then called over her shoulder,

'Danni, somebody here to see you.'

At that same moment, Phil's mobile rang. Hurriedly he plucked it out of his pocket, then recognising the number he cast an anxious look at Gavin, indicating he needed to take the call. Gavin read the signals in Phil's eyes urging him to talk to Danni. Reluctantly he moved closer to the counter, whilst Phil stepped a discreet distance away to take his call. He watched his friend try to make small talk with Danni. She smiled up at Gavin.

'Hello, did you want to see me?'

Gavin faced the young, slim woman named Danni hesitantly. He hadn't bargained on doing any questioning, he'd just wanted to give moral support to Phil. Gamely he plunged in.

'Yes, hello my name is Gavin, I'm with my friend here because we are helping the police into the investigation of the death of a man who used to come in here.'

'Not bad, Gavin. Go for it.' Rachel urged.

'Do you mean Ben Sloan, the man who was found drowned and stabbed?' Danni asked. She studied Gavin intently as she opened the dishwasher and unloaded a tray of clean crockery. She glanced at Gavin intermittently as she replenished the shelves with clean mugs.

'Yes, that's right. We're wondering if you can think of anything that might give a clue to his murderer. I mean, did you notice anyone who behaved in a threatening manner towards him? Actually, anything you think may give us a clue to his death?'

'I've already told the police all I know. The man was quiet, I didn't know him well, and I only spoke to him to get his meal order. Are you some kind of private detective?' Danni eyed him suspiciously.

Gavin smiled. 'No not really, I'm just…

'Actually yes, I'm a private detective, Gavin is assisting me,' Phil intervened. He put his mobile in his pocket. 'Sorry I had to take that call. That was DI Barker. Do you remember him making inquiries?'

Danni shook her head and switched her suspicious gaze to Phil. 'No, I don't remember no DI Barker.'

Phil racked his brain trying to remember the name of the police officer who had visited the café and written the report. 'Maybe you remember Detective Constable Lucas. I believe he came here to ask you questions.'

Having keenly examined Phil's face, Danni relaxed and unloaded another tray from the dishwasher. He was relieved she had decided to trust him.

'Yeah, I remember him. He seemed to think I knew all the customers that come in here. I told him I hardly spoke to the chap. We get busy, especially at lunch times and sometimes you don't know who is with who. Occasionally, complete strangers share tables so that they can sit down to eat.'

'So you wouldn't know if he regularly met a particular person.'

Danni eyed him suspiciously again. 'You mean like a woman? Do you think he was having an affair?'

'I'm just trying to find someone who knew him well. Someone who could give us a clue to his death.'

'No, I'm sorry. Sometimes he sat down with people I recognised from his building, other times he was joined by others I didn't recognise. Now and again he would call in and order two coffees to take away, but I don't know who they were for.'

'What about your colleague Jade. Did she ever talk about Ben?'

'Not that I can remember. She never said anything to me. But there again she doesn't say much to anybody. She's a good worker though.'

Danni seemed reluctant to talk more and edged to the side as Karen came to the counter with four disposable mugs of coffee. She placed them on a recycled tray with moulded holes that clamped the coffees in place.

Phil sighed and spoke to Danni who was already walking away. 'Alright, thank you for your time.' He nodded to Karen and picked up the tray from the counter. He caught Gavin's eye to indicate they were finished and they strolled out of the café.
Outside they loitered for a couple of minutes. Phil related the conversation he'd just had on his mobile with DI Barker.

'Apparently Ben Sloan's mate Rob Taylor who was on holiday in Scotland is now home and DI Barker is on his way to see him. I told him where I was and he is going to make a diversion to pick me up in fifteen minutes. So I thought we could wait in the car? He'll arrange for me to be taken to the hotel later, if you don't mind taking Clare back?'

'Fine, whatever. So what did you think about that chat with Danni and Karen?'

'Oh no,' Rachel said. 'They need to go in the charity shop and look for Tracey. I hoped that Danni might have mentioned her. She'd have been a familiar face even if she didn't know her name. She's had plenty of time to think since the police asked her the initial questions.'

'Even if she'd recognised Tracey as a customer and knew she worked in the charity shop, there would be no reason to mention her if she hadn't seen her with Ben. She wasn't that interested in the case, I admit,' Stefan agreed. 'I doubt very much neither she nor Karen have given Ben's murder much thought since they heard the news.'

Rachel sighed. 'I suppose not.'

'I got the impression Ben often got takeaways and they drank the coffee in the charity shop.' He focused his one flawless eye on his companion, 'so what do we do now?'

'We've got to stop them walking past. Somehow make them go in to the charity shop. Quick they're moving away, they're almost at the shop door. We need to alert Phil.'

Stefan frowned, 'how are we going to do that?'

'In the only way I know how. It's regrettable but necessary. Use your strength to punch him. I will too.'

Rachel concentrated hard and hit Phil in the stomach, instantly he pitched forward gasping in pain. He tried to straighten himself before Stefan, still learning to handle his own strength, effected a whack across Phil's *chest.* This time Phil staggered then slumped against the charity shop door. The tray of drinks slipped from his hands and toppled on to the pavement, one tumbled on to its side and began to leak.

'Are you alright mate?' Gavin bent anxiously over his friend to pull him up.

Stefan, unused to handling his power gave Phil another punch that made him double up with pain.

'Stefan stop it!' We might have over done it.'

Completely winded, Phil gasped for breath as the door to the charity shop opened and a young woman stood in the portal.

'Hey are you alright? Do you want some water? She spotted the coffee spilling over the pavement and picked up the tray. 'I have a chair here, come and sit down.'

'That was rougher than I intended, I'm sorry,' Stefan said more to Phil rather than to Rachel.

'No you were brilliant. We need to force him into the shop. That should do the trick. A shame to hurt Phil but I think he will realise why we did it.'

'I'm fine, Phil said. Just indigestion.' He turned to Gavin and held his arm out for support.

'You look terrible, why don't you come in here for a minute and sit down until you feel better?' The shop assistant encouraged.

'No, that's fine. Our car is just around the corner,' Gavin said.

'Yes you must go inside,' Rachel urged. She nudged Phil making him sway towards the open doorway. The concerned shop assistant took his arm and guided him to a chair in the shop.

'Brilliant! Stefan enthused. 'He's gone in.'

'Yes, but at a cost, I must say. I'm exhausted now. Rachel observed. 'I hope I don't need to exert any more energy later.'

'Do you think Phil will realise that we pushed him into here?'

'When he gets his breath back he'll work it out.'

Gavin was worried. 'I think you should sit down here for a minute or two, Phil. Your face is white. He looked up at the shop assistant. 'A glass of water if you don't mind please?'

'Of course. But first I must lock the door. That done, she disappeared into the back of the shop.

'Is this really indigestion or is it a message of the other kind?' Gavin whispered. 'The last time I saw you like this was when Rachel was trying to make contact with you.' He looked around him half expecting to see her beside him.

'You're right. It is similar to what I felt before, but I've never experienced such brute force from Rachel. It might be an associate with her. But I can't think why she would want us to come in here. It wasn't in the police report.'

'Perhaps the police didn't come here, or perhaps they might have tried but it was on the day this place was closed. Look on the door, their opening times are somewhat haphazard. In fact according to that notice they should have closed five minutes ago. We're lucky to find someone here to offer you some help.'

The shop assistant returned with a glass of water. She was accompanied by a young teenager.

'This is my son Josh. He volunteers after school. I'm Cynthia by the way.' She handed the drink to Phil who obligingly sipped it. The pain had subsided and he was already feeling better.

'Thanks. I'm sorry to hold you up.'

'That's alright. I'm happy to lend a hand. We can spare another five minutes after all,' Cynthia said.

'Have you been working here long?' Gavin asked, making polite conversation.

Cynthia nodded. 'Though I don't consider it proper work. I'm a volunteer, in fact most of us are volunteers. It's hard to get them you know. So we have to open the shop when we can. We've got a kind of a rota going so it's not too bad. It's mostly sorting donations and sending bags to other shops in the town.'

'*So where's Tracey?' Rachel frowned. Perhaps she works part time too.'*

'That's a nuisance,' Stefan replied.

'Do you always work alone?' Phil asked. He felt fully recovered, and was wondering what questions he should ask. If Rachel had forced him in here, he needed to know why.

'Usually there are two of us each shift, but Andrea left an hour ago to pick up her kids from school. Tomorrow, it will be Tracey and Veronica.'

At the mention of those names a black bin bag which had been stuffed with soft toys by the window began to tilt forward. Cynthia and Josh had their backs to the bin bag and didn't see the movement. Phil and Gavin spotted it and exchanged a meaningful glance.

Concentrating on the bin bag, Phil tested his theory with a bold question.

'So do Tracey and Veronica always work the same shift?' The bag moved again very slightly.

'Usually, but Tracey didn't come in on Monday – one of her days – because she was upset over a friend of hers having died. She came in the day after though. Yesterday, I mean.'

The bin bag shook violently tipping out a woollen hat. Cynthia turned to see where the noise was coming from. She picked it up and replaced the woollen hat inside. She tied the bag with some string. 'I've probably put too much stuff in here,' she said with a laugh.

'You always do that Mum,' Josh chipped in. 'I've emptied all the others and put them on display. Somebody is obviously getting rid of their soft toys.' He pointed to a shelf crammed with teddy bears, elephants, cats and other animals that usually appealed to children. He then disappeared into the back room.

'Did you say a friend of hers had died? So sorry to hear that. Yet she came in the next day that was kind of her.' Phil knew he was on the right track when the bin bag rustled again. He tried to work out how to mention the deceased's name, without raising the woman's suspicions when Cynthia provided it.

'Yes, it was that man who was found in the lake over in Holywell. Apparently she knew him when they were in school together. Tracey was shocked to hear it. So young at fifty three.'

'Oh you mean Ben Sloan. We read about it in the paper didn't we Gavin?'

Gavin nodded. He shot Phil an astonished look behind Cynthia's back. 'Yes it was a nasty business.'

'Did she tell the police, this Tracey…?'

'Roper. Tracey Roper. I don't know. Why should she?'

Phil affected a shrug. 'Just a thought. It might help with their inquiries.' He stood up. Anyway thanks for the water, I appreciate your time. I feel much better now.'

Cynthia was about to speak again but her attention was turned to a knock on the locked door. She called through the shop window. 'Sorry we're closed.'

'Actually those women are our wives. They've probably come looking for us,' Gavin grinned. He stepped towards the window and waved then smiled into their anxious faces, when Cynthia quickly unlocked the door. 'We're on our way.'

'We were getting worried,' Clare started to say. By this time Phil had moved to the door. 'Thank you Cynthia.'

She handed him the tray of beverages. She'd righted the toppled one. 'These coffees might still be hot, it's a wonder they have all kept intact. The grooves in the tray have kept three upright, though I doubt there's much left in one of them.'

'Thank you again,' Phil said. 'You've been very kind.'

Cynthia watched them move out onto the street, and locked the door again, a bemused smile on her face.

'Good teamwork there,' Rachel said.

'Glad you think so. A shame we don't know where Tracey lives. But we're on the right track.' They followed the group to Abi's Vauxhall Zafira and draped themselves over the back seat.

Inside the car, Gavin, with Phil interjecting every now and again brought Clare and Abigail up to date.

'You mean you saw Phil have a paranormal experience?' Abi's blue eyes widened.

'Yes, it's the worst I've ever seen him suffer,' Gavin added. 'My sister, if it was Rachel, can obviously pack a punch when she wants to.' He couldn't help smiling as he examined Phil's face. 'You look OK now.'

'Yes, the pain soon goes.'

'Are you sure you're OK?' Clare asked anxiously. She held on to his arm and squeezed it. Phil nodded. 'Don't worry. I'm fine. Besides, we have more information and a new lead.'

'Sorry but it had to be done. And dear brother that took all my energy, so less of "when she wants to," if you don't mind.' She turned to her companion. *'I shouldn't take all the credit.'*

Stefan eyed her with an amused smile stretching across his patched up face. 'I'm pleased to be of some use.'

Abigail started the engine and then turned it off again when Gavin laid his hand on her arm. 'Sorry, we have to wait for the police.'

'Yes, sorry Abi, I've had a message from Barker. He's picking me up from here to take me to visit that guy who's just got back from Scotland. You know, Ben Sloan's mate.' Phil checked his watch, 'Barker said about half four, it's twenty to five already. You don't mind do you?' This was more for Clare's benefit rather than Abi's, though Phil scanned both their faces for any hint of annoyance. Relieved that there was no opposition to the plan, he suggested they met for a drink at the hotel when he returned. Gavin handed out the coffees.

'We may as well drink these whilst we wait.'

Phil took the carton with the least coffee. Clare poured some of hers in it.

'This will keep me going anyway,' he said.

A few minutes later Phil got out of Abi's Zafira, said goodbye to the occupants and after watching her pull away got in the back of the police vehicle. The DI introduced Phil to Detective Sergeant Malcolm Price from Cheshire Police.

'Though the dead man was murdered on our patch,' he explained, 'some of our lines of enquiry takes us over the border. Though not far over, I have to say. Because we're from North Wales Police we have to liaise with another police authority. It's a courtesy thing really.'

Phil noticed that the DI didn't bother to explain to the DS, the reason for Phil's presence other than to say he was assisting with the inquiry.

On the way to Rob Taylor's house, Phil explained the reason he had been to the café, and then his unexpected findings in the charity shop. He left out his experience with the paranormal.

'Hmm, so you think this Tracey Roper might give us a steer?' the DI asked.

'I have a strong feeling she may be able to tell us a bit more about Ben Sloan's private life. According to Cynthia at the charity shop, she was really upset about his death. That suggests to me a close relationship? Unfortunately I didn't feel I could ask where she lives. I doubt she would have told me anyway.'

'I'll get someone at the station to look her up. There can't be many people with that name in the area, DS Price said, but she might be living on your patch,' he remarked. The DI agreed and pulled out his mobile. 'Yes I'll get my lot to do some checks too.'

A short drive from the Roman Road Trading Park took them to Rob Taylor's mid-terrace house on Saltney Meadows Avenue. The detective sergeant radioed the station and asked them to look up Tracey Roper's address. Then all three went up the steps to the front door.

Rob Taylor conducted them down a long hallway to a small sitting room. An identical pair of suitcases were propped up against a sofa where they had been dumped on their arrival home. Apologising, he picked them up and carried them out in to the hall. He reappeared with his wife who offered them tea. Phil and DS Price looked to the DI for guidance. He shook his head and Mrs. Taylor sat down with her husband.

'Thank you for seeing us so soon after your journey,' DI Barker began, 'it's really appreciated.'

'Anything I can do to help Inspector. Ben was a good friend. I've known him for a long time. I can't believe he's gone. Please sit down.'

'Can you think of anyone who would want to kill Ben?' The detective inspector asked.

Rob shook his head. 'No, I really can't. I've been asking myself that same question ever since I got the bad news. He was a nice guy. Cheerful, kind, that sort of thing.'

'When was the last time you saw him?'

'About ten days ago, just before Linda - my wife here - and I went up to Scotland to see her family. It was her mother's seventieth birthday you see. She's from Glasgow.'

Linda nodded.

'How was Ben when you last saw him? Did he seem worried?'

'No, not that I recall. We were playing pool in the local pub. The only thing that seemed to be worrying him was his next move. He was concentrating on his game. We had a few pints and shared a taxi home. He never said he had any problems.'

'You don't think he had a sexual relationship with someone other than his wife? Another woman or… a man?'

'What?'

'I'm sorry… I have to ask.' Barker tried to soften the question. He could see Rob was disgruntled at such a suggestion.

'No, absolutely not on both counts. Ben would never cheat on his wife. I think I'd know if he did.'

'How long have you known Ben?'

'We were in secondary school together, so I guess nearly forty years.'

'So where did he meet Olive?'

Rob grinned. 'She was in school with us too. Not in the same class though. She was in a year younger than us and hung around with a different group of friends. Obviously we knew her but not really well. They didn't get together until several years after we'd all left. There was a community hall in the village where we lived.' He smiled as he reminisced. 'We youngsters used to hang around the place trying to look cool.' He sighed.

'It's not there anymore, been knocked down. Anyway on Saturday nights they put on discos for us teenagers and that's when it all started. Ben and Olive I mean. They would have been about seventeen maybe older when they started courting. I think they had a bit of a break for a while and then got together again roughly three or four years later. She'd had a baby by then. Not Bens. It's a long time ago'. His chuckle was for his wife's benefit rather than for the detective.

'I hadn't seen either of them for quite some time. We lost touch somehow. Then a few years ago after Linda and I moved here, Ben and I bumped into each other at the Greyhound. I haven't seen Olive for years, though. As I've said, I saw Ben regularly. He didn't really talk about her, to be honest. Is she OK? Daft question I know. She must feel terrible.'

The DI ignored his concern about Olive's welfare. A finger and thumb on his left hand smoothed down his moustache. 'So you can't think of anything at all that would help us? He wasn't involved in any gang, or being threatened or some such thing?'

Rob shook his head. 'The only thing I can think of, and it's a small thing, it might not mean anything, but recently when we were playing pool, he got several calls on his mobile. After each time he seemed agitated. He didn't say anything aggressively to the caller, as far as I can tell because whenever he got a call he turned his back on me and it was only for a few seconds. I didn't think anything of it at the time. I suppose I assumed he didn't want to put me off my game. But it happened about three times one night. I thought he might have had a tiff with Olive and didn't want to say anything. It would've been unusual but I didn't think any more of it.'

'So do you think he might have received a threatening call?' The DI asked.

'I guess it's possible. That's if it wasn't Olive. I've never known her to ring him at the pub. I doubt she would've rang unless there was some kind of emergency and he would have left if there was. She knew where to find him, so there'd be no need to call him just to find out his whereabouts. Not like some women!' He caught the perplexed expression on Phil's face, and laughed. 'You'd be surprised how some women try to keep tabs on their husbands. I have a friend whose wife is forever ringing him wanting to know where he is, what's he doing?'

'...and when is he coming home?' Sergeant Price finished for him. 'Yes we get plenty of that.' He scanned DI Barker's face for confirmation. He nodded.

'Does the name Tracey Roper mean anything to you?' Phil asked.

'Tracey Roper? Tracey Roper?' Rob repeated. He rested his chin on a finger looking at the ceiling as he rolled the name around. 'No I'm afraid not. Wait, I knew a Tracey Hill. She might have married a Roper. Ben mentioned he'd seen the Tracey I know quite recently. Said she was working at a charity shop. Is that the one?'

DI Barker shared a self-satisfied smile with Phil and the DS.

'How do you know this woman?' Phil continued. He sensed that the strange aura surrounding his body urged him to ask the question. Something told him that this unknown woman would be an important link.

The grin on Rob's face widened. 'Tracey Hill's another old school friend. I haven't seen her for years. Neither had Ben. But about six months ago he met her again. I think he told me he'd seen her come out of the café where he sometimes went and they started chatting. He told me about it straight away, said they arranged to have a coffee to catch up on old times.' Rob focused on the ceiling again lapsing back into reminiscence. For a few seconds he seemed to have forgotten his visitors.

DI Barker coughed. 'You were saying? Tracey Roper?'

'I'd forgotten all about Tracey Hill. Oops, sorry I mean Roper. Ben and I always knew her as Tracey Hill not Roper.'

'Do you know where she lives?' DS asked.

'No, I'm afraid not.'

Phil was thinking hard. He realised that there may be a connection with Olive and Tracey. He turned to Rob, 'Do you think Olive knew Tracey?'

'Probably. We all used to hang out at the youth club at one time or another. They would know of each other even if they weren't friends. Ben and I lost touch with Tracey years ago, but he and I often met up for a drink. When he started courting Olive, and I was with my wife Linda here, we used to go out together. We all liked messing around on the river, swimming, taking picnics on the rowing boats and all that.' He turned to his wife for confirmation who nodded enthusiastically. 'Do you remember Love?'

'Yes, I do.'

'So it wasn't unusual for Ben to rent a rowing boat?' DI Barker asked.

'No, not really, but I can't understand why Olive wasn't with him on that lake. She could row quite well herself.'

'She was impressive, I thought,' Linda added. 'It does seem odd that she didn't want to share a boat with Ben, but I suppose she had her reasons.'

'Had he, to your knowledge ever been rowing on that lake in Holywell before?'
Rob shook his head. 'Can't say he'd ever mentioned it to me. I haven't been that way for ages either.'

'Thank you Mr. Taylor you've been very helpful.' DI Barker got up and began to walk to the door, he motioned to his companions to follow him.

'Hey, you're not suggesting Ben was having an affair with Tracey are you?'

'You'll understand that we have to keep an open mind Mr. Taylor. We have to consider every angle. Thank you for your time.'

'I suppose so. I hope you find whoever did that to Ben.'

'We will, Mr. Taylor,' The DI assured him, though he wasn't convinced.

Outside the house DS Malcolm Price answered his phone. As he spoke the DI made a call on his own device. Phil strained his neck trying to listen to both conversations. He needn't have worried. DS Price eyed his superior triumphantly. 'We've got the address of Tracey Roper.'

Barker finished his call. 'Forensics have managed to dry out Ben Sloan's mobile. It seems there were over sixty text messages and about ten verbal calls telling him to stay away from the caller's wife.'

'That's what I call a good start,' the DS said.

'Problem is, there is no mention of a name, and the mobile used to threaten Ben Sloan was a throwaway.'

'So what do we do now Sir?' DS Price asked. Shall we go and see this Tracey woman?'

Barker shook his head. 'I'm tempted to go and see Olive Sloan again. There's a few things she hasn't mentioned to us. What do you think Phil?'

The tickling sensation on Phil's neck caused him to hesitate before answering. He felt sure Rachel wanted him to visit the Ropers. The incident in the charity shop had been for a reason.

'I think it might be useful to see Tracey Roper first,' he said. 'We know she was upset when he died. She may know something that his wife doesn't. Or at least something Olive doesn't want to tell us. We have just learned that she was an able boat rower, yet she told us she didn't like the water. It might be useful to get as much information from Tracey as we can before we talk to Olive again.' He chose not to add that he felt Rachel wanted him to talk to Tracey.

'Good decision Phil. I was hoping not to give him a nudge, it's not necessary now,' Rachel confided.

'Yes, that's saved us some effort.'

'How are you feeling? She asked. Are you tired?'

'A little. It takes a lot of concentration to make an impact doesn't it?'

'Yes. I'm flagging a bit.'

DI Barker checked his watch. 'You sure your wife won't mind? It's almost six o clock. It will be at least seven thirty before I can get you back to Holywell.'

Phil grinned. 'She's used to my coming and going. We don't eat until about eight, and if we get back later she'll eat without me. I'll text her. We're meeting friends for a drink later at the hotel.'

'Ah yes, the newlyweds.' The DI nodded as he recalled Gavin and Phil's involvement in the investigation of Rachel's murder.

They got into the police car. The two ghosts accompanied them.

'We're making progress, but it's slow,' Rachel remarked. *'It seems strange to be working with the same detective who put away my killers.'*

'He seems like a good bloke.'

CHAPTER ELEVEN

Tracey Roper lived at twenty six North Market Street three miles west of Chester and five miles from Rob Taylor's house. As they crossed the bridge over the river, Phil imagined Ben and Rob with their respective wives boating on the Dee. It was a popular place with the locals as well as tourists. He and Clare had enjoyed many river trips when they had days out in Chester before they went to live in Romania. It was a bustling, historic city where they often explored hidden niches and alleys that led off the city wall pathway. The river was within easy walking distance from the shopping centre.

The DS and Phil followed DI Barker up the path to Tracey Roper's doorstep where he knocked sharply on the door of the semi-detached house. As soon as he'd explained their business to a slender woman with long blonde hair who confirmed she was Tracey, sadness swept her face. Repressing looming tears she agreed to talk to them.

'I don't know if I can help but please, come in.' She guided them to a small sitting room.

'My husband Dean is upstairs working on his computer. I say working, I really mean he's playing games.' She managed a sheepish smile. 'Please go in and sit down, I will call him.'

They took advantage of her suggestion then heard her running up the stairs.

'She seems nice and amiable,' Stefan observed. *'She was obviously upset, when the DI mentioned Ben's name.'*

'Yes it'll be interesting to see how her husband reacts when he sees three police officers in his house. Two I mean, but of course they won't know that Phil has no rank.'

'I've noticed our DI doesn't bother to explain Phil's role in this investigation. He lets people assume that he is a detective,' Stefan laughed. *'Good technique.'*

When Dean Roper sauntered into the room, Phil and the detectives rose to their feet again. He acknowledged his visitors with a cursory nod crossing his arms aggressively. His resentment of the intrusion was plain to see. Tightened muscles on his long face partnered a clamped shut mouth set in a wide jaw. He stood silently, waiting for an explanation.

The DI introduced himself and his colleagues. He observed Dean quietly as the man, back rigid sat down next to his wife. Tracey openly wept and in what seemed to Phil a put on show of concern, Dean rested a perfunctory arm across her shoulders. His other arm rested on his leg with his hand clenched in a fist. The performance reminded Phil of a robot. Tracey wiped her face with a handkerchief and leaned into his side, her long flaxen hair spread over his sweatshirt. Phil felt she looked far more upset than

Olive. Fragile too, judging by her small wiry frame. Her blue eyes etched into a pale skin, glistened with tears as she focused on the detective inspector's face.

'I'm sorry to intrude. As I've explained to your wife, we are investigating the death of Mr. Ben Sloan,' Detective Inspector Barker began.

'And what's that got to do with us?' Dean replied harshly. Unlike his wife, he avoided eye contact, preferring to stare through the window, above the police officers' heads. His face hardened, the arm around Tracey's shoulders tightened into a controlling grip.

'Because you are bloody guilty that's why.' Rachel spoke to the air. She nudged Phil gently and was rewarded in seeing his expression change. A faint smile twitched his lips. She knew he was aware of her presence.

'How are we going to get the message across to Phil that Dean's the murderer? He looks like a hard nut to shell,' Stefan murmured.

'I think he's already picking up a bad aura from him. He's also sensed our presence. He knows something's up. Still it's going to be hard to get evidence.'

'We are trying to build up a picture of what we know about our victim, Mr. Roper. We understand that your wife knew Ben Sloan, and so we'd like to ask her a few questions.' The DI studied Dean Roper thoughtfully. 'It's just routine. It shouldn't take long.' Before turning back to Tracey, he deliberately threw a question at her husband.

'Did you know Ben Sloan too, Mr. Roper?'

Dean blinked at the unexpected question. It forced him to take his eyes away from the window and face the DI with a guarded expression.

'Me?' he said quickly. 'No! I'd never heard of him until Tracey told me she'd read about his death in the Chester Chronicle.'

Rachel gave Phil a nudge. Startled, he responded with a frown attempting to interpret the paranormal hint. He focused on Dean who avoided Barker's enquiring expression.

The DI paused, then turned to Tracey.

'How well did you know him Mrs. Roper?'

'I knew him from years ago, when we were in high school. After I left school, I didn't see much of him, then the council built the community centre. It was very popular in the village, because it provided somewhere for youngsters to go. There were discos and sports' groups, table tennis and things like that. I joined the youth club there and so did Ben. We became friends again, then around the time he started seeing Olive, my family and I moved away and I didn't see him for years. She hesitated and took a deep breath. 'Then when I was made redundant six months ago, I started volunteering at a charity shop. It's not far from where Ben worked.'

DI Barker nodded as if this information was new to him. He waited for Tracey to continue.

'Anyway there's a café a few doors down from where I work, and sometimes Ben went there. I saw him pass the shop one day and knocked on the window to say hello. He was surprised to see me and came in to the shop.' Tracey gulped to catch her breath then continued. 'We had a long chat. It was years since we'd seen each other you see, so we agreed to meet up and have a coffee every now and again. Sometimes he would bring me a takeaway coffee.' Tracey sniffed. 'He was kind like that.'

All the time she spoke, Dean remained sitting stiffly at the side of his wife; his arm across her shoulders as inflexible as a board. The two officers regarded him keenly. Phil was perplexed that he demonstrated little effort to comfort his wife.

'So over the last six months you renewed your friendship and saw more of him during that time?' DS Price asked.

Tracey nodded. 'Yes, but like I said, mostly when he popped in at the charity shop on his way home. Sometimes depending on my work rota, we would have a drink in the café. I don't work every day you see. It was all quite innocent.' She turned to her husband then as if to convince him. 'Dean knows I wouldn't do anything underhand.'

Without smiling, Dean nodded his head. 'I know you wouldn't.'

'That sounds like a warning,' Stefan said with disgust.

Rachel agreed. 'I hope Phil is picking up on it.'

'When you last saw him did he seem distressed about anything?' Phil asked. From the corner of his eye he noted the muscles in Dean's wide jaw expand as if he had clenched his teeth.

Tracey shook her head. 'No, he always seemed cheerful.'

'So he didn't confide in you about nuisance mobile calls?' DI Barker asked. He narrowed his eyes as he studied Tracey's face, aware of Dean's intake of breath at the question. The DS noted it too and turned to catch Phil's eye who acknowledged his glance with a nod, frowning as he analysed Dean's body language.

'Did you see that?' Rachel said. She glared at Dean.

'Yes and Phil is studying him with interest. Let's see how this pans out.'

Again Tracey shook her head. Shock seeped into her expression. 'Was someone harassing him?'

'As yet we're unsure,' DI Barker replied, 'but we have to keep an open mind. Did you ever meet his wife?'

'Not recently. I knew Olive by sight a long time ago when we were at school. She was in a different class and I didn't get to know her really well. Ben started seeing her off and on when we were at the youth club.'

'So did you ever have a relationship with Ben when you were younger?'

Tracey looked uncomfortable and looked at her husband for support.

Dean removed his arm from around Tracey's shoulders and clasped his hands together tightly as if trying to keep calm.

'What's that got to do with anything?' He asked sourly.

Tracey laid a calming hand on his arm. 'It's alright Dean, I don't mind telling them, if they think it's relevant.' She turned to face the detectives. 'When we were teenagers, Ben and I had a few dates, nothing serious. Years later Olive came back on the scene, and they fell in love. I haven't seen her since those early days. Like I said we all lost touch.'

'And what about you Mr. Roper, have you ever met Olive Sloan?'

Dean reacted impatiently. 'No, of course not. I haven't met her nor this Ben Sloan you're on about.'

'That's a lie!' Rachel said. You killed him. She stared at Stefan.

'Allow me.'

Phil experienced another change in the air accompanied by a slight nudge to his shoulder. This time he felt it wasn't Rachel but suspected she wasn't far away. He frowned, unsure how to interpret the nudge.

'He definitely knows we are trying to help him.'

'But does he realise it's Dean who is the killer?' Rachel responded with a note of exasperation in her voice.

'Even if he does, Phil can't arrest him. He'll have to confide with the DI. It's up to us to provide him with the evidence. Let's see what more information is forthcoming.'

'Forthcoming? What century is that word from?' Rachel laughed despite herself. Stefan ignored her.

'I take it you didn't attend the same school as your wife?' The Inspector continued with his questions.

'No. I'm not from Chester, I went to school in Wrexham.'

'How did you meet?'

'At a disco in Chester. Me and some mates used to go to a club called "Music time in the Crypt" every Saturday night and so did she.'

Tracey agreed. 'I used to go with some friends. We loved dancing you see and then I met Dean.' She turned to smile at him.

'Have you got children?' The DI asked. He was trying to build up a picture of these two rather than having any interest in their offspring. He studied their body language whilst DS Price asked some supplementary questions. They seemed an oddly matched couple. Both good looking, Tracey's finely chiselled features radiated warmth and a certain openness. He noted a small indentation at the side of her mouth, made, he supposed by chicken pox during her childhood. The scar had no ill effect on her beauty, if anything it enhanced it as it made her look beguiling even now when she was evidently upset.

In contrast, her husband's stiff countenance exhibited a flinty edge. Barker noted his skin was tanned unlike his wife's complexion. Hours spent on a sunbed perhaps, the DI pondered.

'We've got two daughters. They've left home now,' Tracey said. Her face brightened as she talked about her children.

'And where do you work Mr. Roper?' DS Price asked.

'Why do you want to know?' Dean's eyes shot rage at the detective as he momentarily lifted his head to speak.

'It's just a routine question, in case we need to contact you again.'

'I don't think you need to ask me any more questions. I've told you everything I know, which is little.'

'This is a murder inquiry,' the DI intervened. 'Anything that might help us, any little thing could be vital. That goes for you too Mrs. Roper. If you can think of anything, please give us a call.'

The DS took the opportunity to hand Tracey his card with his contact details.

'So, Mr. Roper, can we contact you at work?' DS Price persisted with an intense stare. Phil felt a heavy atmosphere pervade the room. Under such scrutiny Dean rubbed at his neck whilst his jaw hardened. He breathed deeply then scowled at his wife when she took it upon herself to answer for him.

'Oh for goodness sake Dean, it's not as if you were in MI5. Everyone knows you work at the sports centre.' She ignored her husband's glare and turned her attention to the police officer. 'It's that new sports complex just off Saltney Road, Sergeant. A huge place, do you know it?'

The sergeant nodded. 'Yes, I believe I do. It opened about three years ago, am I right? I think it's called "Your Active Time and Leisure."'

'Yes,' Dean's worked there since it opened, haven't you Love? They've got a solarium and a sauna too. That's where you got your suntan. Isn't it?'

'Ah yes, I noted you were bronzed. Perks of the job? I hear the solarium is very popular?'

'Yes, but I don't spend all my time on a sun bed,' Dean replied sullenly. 'I'm there to work!'

'So why don't you tell us what you do there?' DS Price encouraged.

'Maintenance. I just make sure the place ticks over.'

'There's a huge swimming pool there and a café. Dean gets a discount for all the activities, the gym and squash too. He likes swimming most though, don't you, Love?' Tracey said proudly.

'Are you a good swimmer Mr. Roper?' Phil asked. He felt an odd twinge on his shoulder. He was sure he hadn't imagined it.

The question was met with a shrug. 'So so.'

DI Barker studied Dean Roper for a few more seconds. He looked as if he was about to ask more questions then changed his mind. He got up from his chair and took out one of his own cards from his pocket.

'You have DS Price's card, this one is mine. If you think of something that might help, anything, no matter how small, please give me a call.' He indicated to his colleagues that they should go. Tracey got up and smoothed her jeans down with her hands. She still looked upset as she ushered her visitors through the hallway to the front door. Dean remained on the sofa.

'I promise you Inspector, if I can think of anything to help, I will phone you,' Tracey said.

'By the way, where were you and your husband on Friday afternoon?' DI Barker asked.

'I was working!' An indignant clipped voice barked from the living room. Tracey tilted her head; blue eyes looked upwards as she tried to recall the whereabouts of herself and husband the previous week. She faced the inspector again, 'yes that's right. He was in work. I was here.'

'All day?'

'Yes.'

'Alone?'

'Yes.' She bit her lip.

'We had to ask. I'm sorry.' The detective inspector followed his companions down the path. 'When are you due to work at the charity shop again?' he inquired, turning as he reached the garden gate.

'I'll be there tomorrow and Friday, this week. You can visit me there if you need to.'

'Thank you for your cooperation. We appreciate it.' Seeing Dean Roper appear behind her he added, 'both of you. Goodnight.'

Dean Roper wasted no time in closing the door behind them.

*

Outside, leaning against the police car, the three men compared notes.

'Phil, thanks for the lead to Tracey Roper. We're building up quite a picture about our victim now,' the DI said. 'It's interesting that Ben Sloan and Rob Taylor knew Tracey and that Tracey and Taylor knew Olive. So what do you guys make of that?'

DS Price spoke first. 'I have a feeling Dean Roper knows more than he's letting on. He gives me the impression that he's also a control fiend. He certainly didn't like us talking to his wife. She seemed to be telling the truth.'

DI Barker agreed. 'What about you Phil? What's your opinion? Did you get any vibe?' He ignored his colleague's surprised expression.

'I agree with you sergeant.' Phil turned to face the DS. 'Dean Roper seemed very defensive. He got uptight when you asked him if he knew Ben and was adamant that he'd never met him nor Olive. Yet I got the impression he wasn't telling us the truth.' He shrugged. 'Just a feeling I got, that's all.

Phil pursed his lips and continued relaying his thoughts. 'It could be that he's a private man and is annoyed that his wife has got mixed up with the police because of re-acquainting herself with an old school friend.

It was obvious that he didn't like being asked about his work. However I think there's something else troubling him. He openly resented the police in his house and was not disposed to being co-operative.'

Phil's companions sighed at his last remark.

'That's not an unusual reaction, I can tell you,' the DI admitted. 'Anything else?'

'I was thinking,' Phil said slowly, 'and this is just conjecture, that maybe he isn't as easy going as Tracey makes out. Perhaps he's the jealous type, even though Tracey and Ben's fling happened many years ago. I get the impression he didn't like the fact she was seeing him again, even for an occasional cup of coffee. His surly behaviour suggests that he doesn't like change. He likes everything in order.

'There's definitely something amiss there. Tracey seemed open and co-operative whereas her husband seemed the opposite. Something else struck me too. When he insisted he'd never met Ben Sloan, he tensed up. Could it be that he once met Ben or perhaps he's met Olive, but didn't want to admit it because he didn't want to be a suspect for murder?' Phil took a deep breath after sharing these thoughts. Then continued. 'However, it's worth noting that Tracey didn't contradict him when he said he didn't know the Sloans, so maybe he is telling the truth. Again, this is just speculation.'

'It wouldn't be the first time an innocent witness has held back information out of fear of being arrested,' Barker admitted.

Phil didn't mention that he'd received paranormal nudges each time Dean denied knowledge of the Sloans. How to interpret those nudges, he was as yet unsure. Was it affirmation of Dean's denial, or the reverse?

DI Barker lit a cigarette before he spoke again. 'I can accept that he begrudged his wife's connection with our victim that has brought the police to his door. But could there be another reason? He's not giving much away except his antagonism and dislike of detectives in his house. Perhaps he's jealous that his wife was so obviously grief stricken?'

'He tensed up because he is the killer!' Rachel fumed.

Phil shrugged, 'possibly, and now you mention it, I can't help thinking that Tracey seemed more upset over Ben's death than Olive.'

DI Barker dragged on his cigarette and looked upwards to the sky as if trying to get inspiration from the stars. 'I have to agree with you, there was something about Olive's demeanour that seemed odd, this morning. Though I know that people express their grief in various ways. I've seen enough of that in my time!'

Phil turned things over in his mind. He felt sure Rachel had wanted him to go to Tracey Roper's house. Was Tracey guilty or her husband? Although Dean Roper presented himself as a most likely suspect Phil couldn't dismiss Tracey's possible involvement in Ben's death. Whilst he stood analysing his thoughts, the DS cut in with a similar view.

'What if Tracey is a better actress?' DS Price ventured.

Barker frowned. 'What do you mean? She seemed genuine to me.'

'Exactly,' the detective sergeant nodded then continued with his notion.
'Yes her tears did seem genuine and maybe they are. But, is it feasible that her tears are for an unrequited love? I mean did she kill him because he wouldn't leave his wife, yet she still loves and mourns him? A kind of "if she can't have him, no-one else can." I have come across cases like that sadly. Could she be planning to kill Olive next – out of revenge?' DS Price glanced first from his superior and then to Phil. He didn't wait for either of them to comment but continued with his hypothesis.

'For example, look how she told us that Dean is a keen swimmer, but we don't know if Tracey can swim. She deftly suggested that Dean could have swum to Ben's boat and stabbed him.'

'Interesting.' The DI stroked his chin and ran his fingers over his moustache. 'Are you suggesting Tracey killed Ben and is trying to shift the blame on to Dean?"

'Something like that. Furthermore she doesn't have an alibi. She said she was home all day.'
Phil listened to the detectives speculating. He wasn't convinced that Tracey was the murderer but admitted that sometimes first

impressions could be deceiving. Besides Rachel had led him to Tracey.

'What do you think Phil?' The DI asked.

'It's feasible, I suppose. A crime of passion maybe. Ben and Tracey could have been lovers despite what she's been saying. It might also explain Olive's dispassionate reaction this morning. You know, she might be too proud to admit that she knew there was someone else in her husband's life, but didn't know who. She wants people to think her marriage was perfect and has no idea who killed Ben. In any case would she suspect Ben's lover as the killer?'

'No no no! Rachel cried. You've got it wrong.'

'What shall we do? Hit him again?' Stefan suggested cheerfully.

Rachel shook her head. No. if we do anything now, he'll think we agree with this last theory. Let's see what the DI suggests. Besides we need to conserve our energy.'

'I don't think we should worry too much. Phil is just trying to look at all the angles.'

'Maybe. Let's hope so.'

'It's plausible I suppose and you are right, it would explain Olive Sloan's behaviour this morning,' Barker considered. He turned to explain to his colleague the outcome of the interview at Holywell police station earlier that day with Olive Sloan.

'If Olive suspected her husband was having an affair, isn't she the most likely suspect? The DS said. 'We now know she can row a boat. She had a real motive.'

Phil acknowledged this theory yet he felt confused, because that morning he'd got no vibes from Rachel to make him suspect Olive.

The DI took another drag of his cigarette then stubbed it out with his foot. He stared at the stub deep in thought.

'So what now Sir? Do we call to see Olive? She doesn't live too far from here. We could do it in ten minutes. It's only a couple of miles over the river, back on your side of the border.' Price grinned. 'We could take a detour to Juniper Street before heading back to the station.'

Barker checked his watch then shook his head.

'I think we'll leave that until tomorrow. It's quarter to eight. I don't think she's going anywhere. She's got too many things to sort out. I think you and I should visit her again tomorrow morning. Early like, get her unprepared. There are things that we have discovered today, she hasn't disclosed to us. I want to know why. She's hiding something I'm sure of it.'

DS Price nodded. 'Fine.'

'In the meantime we ought to get this fellow back to his wife. We've taken up enough of his time.'

DS Price looked confused. In the end he asked the question that was roaming around his head. 'So where do you fit in to all this Phil? Are you based at Holywell?'

In the dark gateway Phil grinned. He had to hand it to the sergeant he was trying to be tactful. All evening the DS had shot him curious looks. Phil was saved from having to give a reason for his presence by Barker who indicated that they should get back into the car. As they eased themselves in, he imparted a vague explanation to his inquisitive colleague regarding Phil's involvement in the investigation.

'Phil has been doing some undercover work for us. His contribution on a previous case gave us some vital information. But now we need to get him back to his hotel. If you can drop me off at the station DS Price, then we'll call it a night. Just one other thing though. If you have some time tomorrow perhaps you could check out Dean Roper's alibi. See if he was working all day last Friday twenty eighth of February. No sweat about that though. My money is on Olive Sloan!'

'I think we should keep an eye on Dean Roper,' Stefan suggested. 'We could stay here all night and get a lift back tomorrow in some passing vehicles. You said you'd done it before?' He ended his suggestion with a question though he doubted Rachel would disagree. He knew she was as keen as he was to solve the case before Phil returned to Transylvania.

'You're right. One of us ought to watch Dean, but I feel that there's more to Olive Sloan than we thought. Phil and the detective inspector suspect something too. I think it would be better if you stay here, and I go to

Olive's. It might be useful to see what she's doing or where she goes. She might be keeping back information which could be important.'

'Good idea. How are you going to get there?'

Rachel was already drifting into the police car. 'They can take me as far as Saltney, then I'll get out at the most convenient spot before they join the A55. From there I can get a lift in any passing vehicle to Juniper Street.'

'Do you know the number of her house?'

'Not exactly, but I remember reading on the file, that it was forty something. I'll just pop in to every house in the forties until I find her.'

Stefan grinned. 'Are you sure you wouldn't rather stay here, and I'll do it?'

'Very gallant of you, but I can manage. Thanks all the same.' She sat smugly in the back seat next to Phil thinking how nice Stefan was.

Instantly, Phil felt a peculiar presence at the side of him. It was very faint and he was unsure if he was still feeling the effects of the atmosphere from the Roper's house or if there really was a ghost in the car with him.

CHAPTER TWELVE

On the approach to a set of traffic lights outside Saltney, the DS chose the left hand lane that would lead them to the A55 to North Wales.
The lights changed to red and Rachel left her three living companions as she drifted towards a vehicle waiting in the lane heading towards her destination. She grinned at Phil's suspicious expression as he turned to pat the empty space which she had vacated.
Her journey involved travelling in three more vehicles before she reached Juniper Street. After passing through several number forty something houses she found herself inside forty seven. It was a modern, detached house with a long front garden.

Olive sat in the spacious kitchen talking to a neighbour over a glass of wine. *Rachel hovered around the worktop to listen to their conversation. It seemed mundane stuff but she became alert when the neighbour asked Olive if she'd seen a stranger watching their house.*

'A stranger? What do you mean?' Olive asked sharply.

'I'm surprised you haven't seen him. Mind you he doesn't stay for long. About twice a week, a tall, lean man hangs around across the road. He usually props himself against a telegraph pole and he seems to be looking at your house.'

'When was the last time you saw him?' Olive sipped her wine and fixed a worried look on her neighbour. 'Are you sure he was staring at this house?'

'The last time I saw him was the Friday afternoon when you and Ben went away,' the neighbour hesitated. 'Sorry to mention it but it was the day he was killed.' She whispered the last few words guiltily as if she felt it was a crime to mention the dead.

Rachel's eyes swivelled from one woman to the other. She recalled that Ben had said Dean hung around the house sometimes trying to unnerve him. He'd been sure Olive hadn't noticed because she'd never mentioned it. He himself hadn't remarked upon it because he hadn't wanted to alarm her.

Gliding from the kitchen to the front of the house, Rachel examined the distance from the telegraph pole to the front of the house. She felt sure that if Olive had looked out through the window she would have noticed Dean. It didn't make sense, but she accepted that possibly, the woman had been distracted by something, maybe she was sewing or watching television and hadn't noticed him. Perhaps Olive wasn't the sort of person who gazed out of the window very often. She glided back to the kitchen.

'When the police knocked on your door to make their inquiries, did you tell them you'd seen somebody loitering outside?' Olive asked. Nervously, her fingers gripped her wine glass. Her neighbour topped it up and poured herself another generous amount.

'No, actually I didn't. They never asked me that and I didn't think of saying. It was such a shock to hear Ben was dead. They just asked me how long I'd known him and if I knew of anyone who might want to kill him. It didn't occur to me to tell them about that man. Do you think it's important? Should I tell the police?'

Olive breathed deeply. 'Did you just say you haven't seen that man since Ben was killed?'

'No. I don't think so. Oh, wait a minute, yes, now I come to think of it. The Monday evening, after Ben died, he was there again. He wasn't where I usually saw him. He was sitting in a car opposite my house. I recognised him because of his dark glasses. It seemed odd to me to wear them when the light was fading outside. I wouldn't normally have looked twice, but I was walking home from choir practise and I passed the car and when I saw him wearing those glasses, I remembered him.'

'If you saw him again, so soon after Ben's death then he couldn't have anything to do with Ben's murder. Just a coincidence. I don't think the police would be interested,' Olive said carefully. 'Did you notice what type of car it was?'

'Not really. Blue I think. I didn't take much notice of the vehicle.'

Olive hid a smile as she got up and lifted a cloth from a cheeseboard resting on the kitchen work surface.

'This cheese should be at room temperature now.' After the cheese was placed on the table she seized a baguette and savagely tore it into pieces. 'Please help yourself Doris and get some bread. I've got plenty.'

Olive's mobile vibrated on the work surface and she picked it up quickly when she saw the name on the screen. She stepped into the hall towards the lounge, turning her back on her neighbour who could see into the lounge from the open door of the kitchen.

'Hi Barbara,' she said.

Curious, Rachel glided towards the mobile to listen. The deep-toned voice on the other end didn't sound female to her, but she supposed the low pitch could be a woman.

'Just thought you might want to come for a sauna tonight. I missed you yesterday.'

Olive frowned and met the eyes of her neighbour who had walked into the lounge with her wine and a plate of cheese. Olive modulated her voice as she spoke into her phone.

'I didn't think it was appropriate to go for a sauna yesterday Barbara. The police wanted to interview me again. There was also a tiresome journalist here yesterday afternoon. I was thinking it would be better to go tomorrow night or maybe next Tuesday.'

'Are you sure?'

Olive was about to say no again, when her nosey neighbour interrupted. She made no effort to conceal she was listening to the conversation.

'Yes, you should go for a sauna. I know you like to go on Tuesday and Thursday afternoons. It will take your mind off things. You deserve it.' She picked up a wedge of cheese from her plate.

It seemed to Rachel that Olive observed her neighbour with suppressed dislike. She also appeared desperate to think of something flippant to say to her caller. Rachel frowned trying to puzzle it out.

'Is there someone with you?' The caller questioned warily. Olive moved away to the window and looked out on to the garden.

'Yes, my neighbour is here. She's come to offer her condolences. We're just having a snack. She brought a bottle of wine to cheer me up and insisted upon opening it now. She's having a drink with me.' Olive turned with a forced smile to look at her neighbour. Doris reciprocated holding up her glass of wine in salute. She took a long drink.

'The one from next door?' The voice groaned.

'Yes.'

'Can't you get rid of her? I would like to see you tonight. We could meet at our usual place?'

'Alright…Yes should be alright in an hour. I won't have any more to drink.' Olive turned to see the neighbour's disappointed expression.

'Great. I'll see you later then. I'll hang around outside and wait,' the caller said.

Olive finished the call and hiding her pleasure in an act worthy of an Oscar, Rachel noted, she spoke to her neighbour.

'Sorry Doris, I'm going to go out to see some friends. They can't come to the funeral and they haven't been able to visit me since...it happened, so I'm going there for an hour. I'll have to go soon. Thanks for coming round. But please do take your drink with you. I can collect the glass tomorrow.'

'Oh that's a shame. Can't they come here to join us?'

'No...no they have small children in bed so it's easier if I go there. Ben was very fond of them.' Olive managed a sad smile and made a pretence of wiping her eyes with a tissue.

Rachel frowned as she recognised the performance as a put-on similar to her behaviour in the police station earlier that day. Something about the phone conversation seemed odd to Rachel. The caller had put pressure on Olive to go out which seemed heartless considering Olive was grieving. Yet she didn't take much persuasion.

As Olive ushered her neighbour out of the lounge towards the front door, their conversation concentrated on the coming wake.

Rachel realised that she wouldn't get much more information about the circumstances leading to Ben's death. She turned over in her mind what she'd learned. It seemed odd that Dean had continued to observe Olive and Ben's house. Though she accepted it was a known fact that some murderers returned to the scene of the crime, it seemed bizarre that a killer would want to return to the house where his victim had lived. Was Olive in danger? Was Dean a psychopath and wanted both of them dead? And who was the mystery caller putting pressure on Olive to go out?

She speculated upon what might be happening in the Roper's house. She hoped Stefan was able to find out something concrete to prove that Dean killed Ben. She worried about how they could tell Phil what they knew. Somehow they had to get evidence. He had only one more day before leaving the country again. That meant she and Stefan had one more day to get a result.

Since getting the freedom to roam as a ghost and develop her psychic energy as she saw fit, she had noticed her ability to communicate had improved. It had been difficult to do the last time she'd had the status of ghost. She hoped she could develop it even more. The downside of this enhancement meant that each exertion sapped her strength.

CHAPTER THIRTEEN

Clare was in the hotel lounge studying a menu when Phil got back. She'd reserved a table and had explained to the manager that her husband may be late joining her.

'Just in time for dinner,' she greeted him as he lumbered in. He kissed her quickly, then rubbed his hands, shivering as he took off his coat.

'It's getting cold out there! I thought you would have eaten. It's twenty past eight.'

'I thought I'd hang on a bit longer for you. I told the manager that if you didn't arrive by eight-thirty I would eat alone, and you'd get something later. I've texted Gavin and Abi to say we're running late. They'll be in "The Raven" from nine o clock onwards.'

'Right. Let's get some food, I'm starving.'

They waited until they'd placed their order and had been served with a bottle of red wine before they discussed the case.

'Do you think Olive knew that her husband was having the occasional coffee with Tracey?' Clare asked. She watched as Phil poured her a generous glass of wine. 'I mean, if he hadn't told her, it's possible he was acting suspiciously so she spied on him and saw them together?' She twirled her wine glass around in her hand as if it helped her to analyse Olive's actions. Phil watched her, thinking hard himself.

'If he didn't tell her, it might be because he thought it wasn't worth the hassle of arousing possible jealousy,' Clare continued…'especially as he wasn't having extra marital sex…'

'Or so Tracey says,' Phil reminded her. Clare nodded. She continued to speculate.

'On the other hand, he might have told Olive, because he felt his marriage was rock solid and his relationship with Tracey was years ago and it hadn't been a long meaningful one? But he under-estimated her outrage and she killed him?'

'Hmm. Maybe you have a point. Olive denied her husband was having an affair. Tracey also denied having an affair with him. They both could be lying.'

'What about Tracey's husband? Jealousy is a strong emotion. It makes people do terrible things. I'm assuming the police have thought of that?'

Phil nodded. 'The detectives and I noted Dean's surly demeanour, but that doesn't mean he is a killer. He says he didn't know Ben and Tracey didn't contradict him. Yet something bothers me. When Dean denied knowing him, I got a curious twinge of the paranormal kind. It was like as if Rachel was trying to tell me something. I'm not sure she was warning me he was lying or that he was telling the truth. It's hard to interpret her nudges. She was definitely in the house with us, and later in the car when we left the

Ropers. Then I sensed her wafting away just before we got on to the North Wales Expressway.'

'I wonder why. Maybe she went to do some sleuthing on her own. But where would she go?' Clare wrinkled her brow.

'I would hazard a guess she went to Juniper Street.'

'Juniper Street? Why there?'

'It's where our grieving widow lives.'

'Oh I see. Perhaps Rachel hopes to pick up some more clues.'

'Hmm. But why go to Olive's? Why did she want me to go to Tracey Roper's house? Does she suspect Tracey the spurned lover, or Dean the jealous husband or Olive the deceived wife?'

'Tricky questions. Could it be that Rachel suspects them all and as yet unsure which one is guilty?'

'And what's the motive?' He asked this more of himself, staring into his wine glass as if looking for answers.

Clare exhaled an exasperated sigh and sipped her drink. 'Jealousy fits all three. It's all conjecture. I'm just trying to look at it from different angles. I give up. Perhaps Rachel will find something in Juniper Street. At least she's given you two extra suspects.'

Phil nodded absently and picked up the bottle of South African Merlot. 'This is a very good wine don't you think?'

'Yes, not a bad price either, considering we're in a hotel. I'll make a note of it for next time.'

'It's our last night tomorrow. Have you heard the news from Transylvania about this virus thing?

'It was on the radio in the police car. There'll be restrictions on travel as from Friday evening. It's a good job our flight is for Friday morning.'

'I'm not looking forward to fourteen days quarantine, but I suppose we'll manage.' Glancing at her husband's face, Clare frowned when she saw he was deep in thought.

He lifted his head to meet her eyes.
'I feel certain that Rachel has gone to spy on Olive. I'm not sure if she's working alone or whether there is another spirit of some kind with her. If she is working with another force it would be nice to know who it is.' His sigh accompanied a rueful grin. 'At least she can't get into trouble either way.'

*

In Dean Roper's house, Stefan shadowed their suspect with great interest. After the police officers left, Dean returned to his computer games in a room upstairs leaving Tracey to prepare their evening meal. Their conversation seemed stilted to Stefan. An oppressive unease veiled the dinner table and neither mentioned the police visit. Stefan wondered whether it was a waste of time spying on them.

As soon as Dean finished eating he told Tracey he was going for a walk to clear his head.

'I'll come with you if you like.'

'No, no, if you don't mind I'd rather be alone. I don't want to talk. I've got a headache. Some fresh air and quiet will help. I'll see you later.'

'You're not annoyed with me for telling the police where you work?'

He shrugged. 'I'd rather you hadn't.'

'Why not?'

'I don't think it's any of their business coming here asking questions about someone you knew years ago.'

'They're only doing their job.'

'If you say so.'

Stefan read unhappiness in Tracey's face as she sighed and cleared the table. He watched her stack the dish washer with a grim expression. Their relationship appeared to be unhealthy.

They heard him come down the stairs then scrabbling for his coat off a hook in the hall. Finally a clinking of keys as he closed the front door behind him. Tracey pressed her lips together and sighed sorrowfully. She seemed to Stefan, fed up.

Stefan followed her upstairs to a small bedroom that had been set up as a study. He supposed she intended to use the computer to send some emails.

She stepped to the small window to draw the curtains then swore as she heard Dean start his Toyota Corolla hatchback parked on the drive, then reverse out.

'Now where are you going? Have you got another woman somewhere?' she muttered.

She watched Dean position the vehicle outside the house. On the passenger seat beside him the blue light of his mobile flickered and he turned off the engine to answer a call.

At that point Stefan felt it would be better to follow Dean to wherever he intended to go. Knowing Tracey to be innocent he would be better off tailing Dean. Yet he lingered hoping she might turn up some kind of evidence to prove Dean's guilt.

From the desk Tracey picked up a mobile and frowned. She appeared to Stefan to be perplexed. Absently, she took her own purple phone out of her pocket and switched it on. A picture of her husband on the screen saver stared at her. Sighing she walked again to the window. She peered through a gap in the curtain at Dean who was still talking on his own device. Tracey turned the alien mobile over in her hand frowning all the time.

Stefan wondered if it was the phone Dean had used to threaten Ben.

Driven by curiosity or maybe suspicion, she checked the recent text messages and contact list.

Stefan hovered around her to read them.

The last ten messages were short. They seemed to be from women making bookings for saunas. The contact list was also very short. Just half a dozen names, the same people in the messages, presumably making regular bookings.

He concluded that it was a work phone and that Tracey thought the same.

Sighing heavily, she put the mobile down again and logged on to her email account.

Stefan observed Tracey's agitated face. He wondered if she knew something about Dean that she didn't want to tell the police. When he heard Dean start his engine again, he decided to leave Tracey to her thoughts.

Dean pulled away from his parking space just as Stefan floated into the car and settled around the back of the driver's seat. Within ten minutes they were out of Chester and were heading towards Saltney.

When the vehicle passed through a set of traffic lights at a roundabout, Stefan realised they were going to Juniper Street.

Dean parked a little way down the road from Olive's place, then reached in to his jeans pocket for a mobile phone. For a few seconds he cradled it in his hand glaring at it. Then swore.

Stefan guessed that Dean had realised he'd forgotten to pick up the other mobile when he'd left the house.

His face contorted angrily. Then evidently deciding to take the risk, he made a call on the device he had with him.

After he had punched in a number, he hunched down in his seat and focused his attention on number forty seven. A minute later Olive appeared at the door of her house. She stood on the doorstep a few seconds, as if checking for something. Satisfied, she got in to her silver Volkswagen

Polo and drove off with *Rachel suspended over the seats at the back.*

Dean allowed five minutes to pass, then started up his engine and manoeuvred his blue Toyota Corolla hatchback in the same direction. After driving six miles, Olive left the A483 then turned on to a B road. It was a narrow country lane that twisted and turned towards a small village called Nant Bach. From there she followed an even narrower lane that gave on to a rough track. After a hundred yards, Olive was forced to drive slowly as the hedgerows brushed against the windows; overhanging conifer branches skimmed the windscreen impeding her vision. The muddy track suggested little traffic used that area. Olive stopped in a small clearing shaded by a sycamore tree. Seconds later, Dean parked behind her. Before getting out of his vehicle he pulled on a baseball cap forcing it down hard to press above his eye brows. Then he strode to Olive's Volkswagen. He slunk inside on to the back seat. Olive slipped out of the driver's seat and got in the back beside him.
Rachel drifted out over Olive's head. Revolted, she watched them passionately embrace.

As soon as she saw Dean opening the car door, Rachel realised that Barbara was their code name. Seeing the lovers embrace, explained why she'd been confused in Olive's kitchen listening to the phone conversation. Stefan glided towards her and together they hovered over the bonnet of Dean's hatchback.

'I didn't expect to see you so soon,' he said.

Rachel giggled, 'Neither did I. But what do you make of this? I'm staggered!'

'Obviously they were in it together. Olive lured Ben to Holywell knowing Dean was following. He saw Ben hire a boat and decided to get one too, follow him, lure him to the edge of the lake where they couldn't be seen and stabbed him,' Stefan said.

'Yep. I think you're right. I also reckon that if Ben had decided not to go on the lake she would have lured him to a quiet spot for Dean to do his ugly deed. But come on let's get out of here, I'm not into voyeurism. We can go and hang over there near those trees, it looks like this murderous pair are taking full possession of the back seat. Their passion is soaring.'

'Nicely put,' Stefan smiled. 'So what do we do now? We can't tell anybody and we're a long way from Holywell even if we could.'

'When I was in the car with the police and Phil, that Detective Inspector Barker said he intended to visit Olive in the morning – early – to give her a shock, get her off her guard. That kind of thing. I reckon we should stay tonight at her place to wait for them, so we can see how she reacts. Then we can get a lift back in the morning to Holywell.'

Stefan stared into space as he contemplated Rachel's suggestion. 'The thing is, if Phil isn't coming with the detectives in the morning, we won't be able to prod him into action.'

Both ghosts looked at each other in despair. 'What's the alternative?' Rachel asked.

'We need to get back to Holywell tonight and somehow make Phil think he should go with the police to interrogate Olive in the morning. We have to make him see that Olive and Dean conspired to murder Ben,' Stefan said.

'Yes, but how?' Rachel threw him an exasperated look. 'Any ideas?'

'I know that's easier said than done. But time is running out. We'll have to think of something,' Stefan said.' Tomorrow is our last chance.'

'That reminds me. 'I've discovered that Olive is going to the sauna tomorrow afternoon. She pretended to her next door neighbour that she is going with a friend of hers. The sauna must be in that sports complex where Dean works. I think that's where she meets lover boy.'

'Wow. Do you suppose that's where they met, fell in love and concocted this plan to kill Ben?'

Rachel nodded. 'I wonder how long it's been going on.'

'Long enough for them to realise they wanted Ben out of the way. It's possible they may have first met each other at the sports centre not realising that their respective spouses had a connection. When Tracey told Dean she'd bumped into Ben, I think that's when they put into action their evil plan. At

first, I think they tried to frighten him off with anonymous phone calls and texts hoping that he might stop seeing Tracey.' Latching his one eye on Rachel's face, he continued with his theory.

'Obviously that didn't work. But then their relationship got serious and they wanted more. Perhaps they tried to unhinge him hoping he would commit suicide, so they intensified the threats. That didn't succeed either. Ben was stronger than that. He didn't even tell Tracey. She's completely in the dark.'

'Hmm, I suppose it's feasible. So when the phone calls didn't work, and Ben threatened to tell the police, they decided to kill him?' Rachel suggested. *'But why? If they'd fallen in love why didn't they just get a divorce?'*

Stefan frowned, his one eye in his patchwork face and his good arm resting against his hip gave him a swashbuckler appearance.

'Good question,' he said. *'Also, does Tracey suspect anything? Is she as innocent as she seems? If he's been carrying on with Olive for a while, don't you think she might be a little suspicious? People's behaviour changes no matter how slightly; surely she'd have noticed something?'*

Rachel shrugged. 'I don't know. Maybe Dean's behaviour has changed but Tracey didn't notice, or if she did, she's totally trusting and didn't suspect something was going on. Even if she thought he was having an affair, would she suspect him of murder?'

'Hmm. Or she didn't want to admit it to herself!' Stefan focused on Rachel as he spoke, covertly studying her as she pondered over what he'd said. She'd died during her late teens, with scarce opportunity to have romantic liaisons of her own. Apparently she'd had one boyfriend, who she discovered later had been cheating on her. Stefan, ten years older had had several romantic liaisons during his life time. However when he was killed at the age of twenty seven there had been no-one special in his life other than his family.

'Actually, I think Tracey is beginning to get suspicious about his behaviour. That is not a very happy household.' Stefan related to Rachel what he'd recently witnessed.

'Look their session of passion seems to be over, he's getting out of Olive's Volkswagen. What shall we do?' Rachel turned to her fellow ghost. 'Think, think! What shall we do?'

'I know. Let's get a lift as far as we can, with one of these horrible people and make our way back to the graveyard. We can talk it through with your mother and the rest of the gang. Maybe they'll have some ideas.'

Reluctantly Rachel agreed. 'Alright, we can travel as far as the A483 roundabout, then look for some passing cars going our way. We might have to make a few transfers to get us back to St. Winefride's.' They glided back to the parked vehicles.

Olive, her face flushed, pushed stray hairs from her face as she stood in the open driver's door of her Volkswagen. Dean leaned on the other side of the car. His baseball cap lay crumpled in his hand. He put a fist through it to widen the opening then pulled it tightly over his head.

'I'll see you tomorrow afternoon, five o clock at the sports centre. Book into the sauna as usual with the name 'Barbara' wait for about ten minutes and I'll find us a nice warm room where we won't be disturbed. Remember, don't call me on this mobile.'

'OK. Goodnight, Darling.'

'Yuk,' Rachel grimaced.

They watched Dean drive off in his Toyota, then slipped into Olive's Volkswagen. As planned, the ghosts got out of Olive's car at the roundabout and coasted across to the other side of the road to wait for vehicles going in the direction they needed. A few minutes later they were travelling along the A55 towards Holywell. Another change after that and in thirty minutes, they arrived at St.Winefride's cemetery. They glided inside the cathedral as the clock struck eleven o clock.

Anna saw them as they approached her favourite niche. 'Any news?' she asked eagerly. Margareta, Desmond and Tom hovered nearby.

'Yes and no,' Rachel said.

'We are at an impasse,' Stefan said. 'We thought you might have some ideas.'

Anna looked pleased to be asked. 'Tell me what you've got so far.'

She was shocked to discover that Ben's wife was not only having an affair, but had conspired to murder him.

'Think how Ben worried that his dear wife would be heartbroken, waiting for him at the café, when all along she knew he would be dead. What a bitch!'

The other spirits agreed.

'We have to make sure she doesn't get away with it. Neither of them!'

The spirits nodded their approval. Big Steve floated in towards the end of the conversation, with a few acquaintances from his growing retinue. They hung back discreetly. He looked shamefaced. 'I agree they shouldn't get away with it, but I have to confess I wasn't completely faithful to my wife. We had an unusual relationship, it was kind of an open one if you know what I mean. But I would never have killed her.'

'Would she have plotted to kill you?' Margareta asked. She noted Janice and Olga hovering closer as she spoke. A wry smile spread over her bony features. 'By the way, I see you haven't wasted much time acquiring new female acquaintances.'

'My wife spent too much time plotting how to juggle her lovers to contemplate murdering me. Besides, now I'm dead what difference does it make if I spend time with Janice and Olga or the others?'

Margareta shrugged. 'Whatever.'

'Never mind Big Steve's love tangles. This is more important,' Anna remarked. 'We need a plan. Come on, think.'

'Didn't you have a séance last time?' Margareta asked.

Rachel nodded. 'Yes and that was effective to some extent, though it wasn't perfect. It worked because we were trying to find evidence that concerned my death. Also my dad and brother were involved, so it was all connected. It made things easier to communicate.'

Anna agreed. 'I can't see Olive consenting to a séance. She'd be worried in case she got found out. Besides, not everyone believes in that sort of thing. My husband only took part because my son persuaded him and I think even he was fairly sceptical. Come to think of it that Detective Inspector would take some convincing too.'

'He is impressed with Phil so far. He might be slightly more amenable, than you think,' Stefan observed. 'Though in any case I think Rachel is right. A séance in this particular case isn't going to work. We don't have a connection. It might be possible if we could get Ben involved. What do you think Rachel?'

'I don't know, and we haven't time to find out. We only have twenty four hours, and in any case Phil would have to suggest it. I think he would have done if he felt it would be useful.'

'What worries me,' said Anna, 'is there is no apparent motive. It's not as if he was a millionaire or at best very rich. And if they are prepared to kill Ben, will they kill Tracey?'

'That's what's worrying me too,' Stefan confessed.

'Me too,' added Rachel.

'People have killed for all sorts of reasons,' Big Steve cut in. *'For them, it might be the convenience. Have you considered that Olive wouldn't want to share the proceeds of the sale of the house, if there was a divorce?'*

'Good point,' Anna conceded.

'She has a nice house,' Stefan reported. *'Double garages, long driveway, large gardens, sought after location. It might not be a mansion, but worth hanging on to. Ben's death will ensure she keeps it.'*

'Not if we have anything to do with it,' Anna remarked resolutely. *'We must make sure that she and that evil man don't get away with it. They might plot to kill his wife.'*

'Somehow we have to get evidence to Phil. So far we haven't got any,' Rachel said. *She looked down at her "Save the Orangutan" Tee shirt for inspiration.*

'The evidence is in Ben's mobile phone,' Stefan commented. *'The police found it and heard the messages. They know he was threatened, and they know the threats came from one of those devices that you can't trace. I'm wondering if the detective inspector has listened to the messages himself rather than read the transcript that the IT team at the police have put together for him. If so, he should listen to the messages because he might recognise Dean's voice, now that he has interviewed him. Not that he was particularly talkative.'* *He sighed. Stefan floated away to the ceiling of the cathedral and hovered horizontally.*

'Now what's he doing?' Margareta asked.

'He's cogitating. He does that sometimes when he wants to think something through.' Anna surveyed Stefan's irregular outline. His jagged leg lop-sided asymmetrically alongside the rest of his patched up frame. 'It's what he did when we were fixing up Rachel's mobile.' Her eyes gleamed. Before she said anything, Rachel shook her head vehemently.

'No, Mum we can't do that again. It was such a shock for Dad last time.'

'He got over it. Besides he's got used to Phil being psychic and communicating with the afterlife. But in any case, I don't think Saint Winefride will co-operate with us a second time. She was freaked out for days afterwards.'

Tom's eyes twinkled as he recalled the occasion. 'It was very entertaining though.'

'Have you managed to regain the skills you learned last time?' Anna asked Rachel suddenly. 'I recollect that you had trouble controlling your energy when you first got permission to roam out of the zone. Then as time went on you were able to do things like lift things like sheets of paper and then heavier things. Do you remember? You told me how you managed to lift pizza boxes and even that letter box at Nicky's neighbour's flat?'

Rachel nodded. 'Yes I remember very well and yes I have managed to regain those skills and put them to good use. In fact I *packed quite a punch in our faithful Phil's stomach today, more heavily than I intended. Stefan is learning fast too.'*

Anna gazed at her daughter thoughtfully, just as Stefan returned to their circle. 'I think you and Stefan ought to concentrate on improving your skills to see if you can give Phil more clues,' she said.

Stefan agreed. 'I was thinking something similar.' He turned to Rachel. 'As we don't have much time, we should go to the hotel to see if we can catch Phil and Clare before they go to bed. We must make him phone the inspector to ask if he can go with him in the morning to interrogate Olive.'

Rachel groaned. 'I don't know how we're going to do it.'

'We'll think of something. Even if we have to wake him up with a few prods. He'll guess we're trying to tell him something and will work it out. Come on.'
Rachel wasn't convinced.
Outside St. Winefride's hotel, Phil and Clare chatted to Gavin and Abigail, making arrangements for their last evening.

'I'll need to say goodbye to Emily at some stage tomorrow, and my parents said they'd come over too.'

'Do your mum and dad know you've got mixed up with this murder inquiry?' Gavin asked with a tug at his ear.

'Yes I sent my dad a text yesterday. He's not keen that I'm involved. He told me to take care.'

'He's right to warn you to be cautious. There seems to be a lot of loose ends. Who knows what you could be getting into?'

'You can say that again,' Phil agreed.

'Maybe the police will get some more information from Olive tomorrow morning. Didn't you say they were going to make an early unannounced visit?' Clare asked. 'Perhaps the DI wants to get her off her guard and ask again what happened the day they were in Holywell. It's what I would do.'

Phil ran a hand through his hair. 'It's strange that she didn't get in the boat with her husband on the day he was killed. That mate of Ben Sloan's, what's his name, err... Rob Taylor said Olive was an accomplished rower. So it seems odd that they came out together for a drive and then didn't hire a boat - together.'

'Unless they had a tiff. She went for a coffee and he got in a boat,' Clare suggested.

'Fine. I would accept that, but why did she say she didn't like the water?' Phil frowned.

'Because she was afraid that if she'd told the police they'd had a row, they would suspect her of murder?' Abigail suggested. 'So she invented another excuse.'

'She's automatically a suspect. Immediate members of the family are always suspects. I should know. I was one myself,' Gavin said grimly. Abigail squeezed his hand sympathetically.

'Too bad you can't sit in on Olive's impromptu interview tomorrow,' Clare said. 'It would be nice to get this sorted before we leave.'

Phil made a face. 'I suppose DI Barker thinks he's got a lead and doesn't need me anymore. I gave him Tracey and Dean Roper. Now he's spoken to Rob Taylor he's suspicious of Olive. There seems to be some kind of link. He probably thinks he can work it all out without me. It would be nice to see it through to the end.'

'He needs evidence though. You know how difficult it was getting proof of Rachel's killer!' Gavin met his friend's eye. 'Why don't you give him a call in the morning, and suggest you sit in with him? It's not as if she hasn't met you. Besides if you are in her home you might be able to sense something. Like Barker said, if you get the suspect unawares, they let their guard down.'

'That's what he is hoping will happen yes.' Phil acknowledged. He scratched the back of his neck, he felt sure he could feel Rachel's presence.

'Gavin has a point. I think you should go in the morning as he suggests. It would be nice to get a satisfactory conclusion before we leave, or at least see how far he has got,' Clare said. She caught hold of Phil's arm. 'You know it will be on your mind tomorrow anyway.'

Again Phil sensed an aura around him, he wondered if Rachel and her partner were agreeing with Gavin's suggestion. So as not to unsettle his companions, he tested his theory on Clare.

He loosened his wife's grip on his arm and cradled her face with his hands. 'So you think I should go?'

She smiled. 'Look at you. Your eyes are gleaming; you won't be able to stop thinking about it.'

'You're right. Thanks. I'll give the inspector a call.' He received a light nudge on his shoulder that convinced him he had made the right decision.

'But, take care mate. Let me know if I can help in any way.' Gavin squeezed his friend's shoulder and then took hold of Abi's hand. She leaned over and kissed Phil's cheek. 'Yes take care. See you tomorrow. Get a good night's rest.'

On their way upstairs Phil got hold of his wife's hand. 'It's good of you to put up with all this, but we may be mistaken, Olive might be totally innocent.'

'That's where you're wrong Phil,' Rachel said excitedly as she turned to Stefan. His collage face crinkled into a smile. 'Great. He's going to call the DI. That conversation saved us a task. I didn't know how we were going to get Phil to contact the DI without some strong blows whilst he was sleeping.'

'I must admit that was worrying me too. It doesn't seem fair to keep hurting Phil all the time, but I think we would have had to do it if Gavin hadn't encouraged him. A few tickles on Phil's neck was all we needed. But I think he was secretly up for it anyway. We're in business. Now let's practise our

extra-sensory powers, like your mother suggested.'

CHAPTER FOURTEEN

It was almost midnight before the last of the guests left the hotel lounge. Whilst Rachel and Stefan had been hovering around waiting to start testing their strength on various objects in the room, they listened to random conversations.

'It's amazing what information you pick up when you're eavesdropping,' Stefan said laughing. 'I reckon that chap over there is cheating on his wife. I read over his shoulder a text from his lover. He told the woman at the side of him it was his mother! He's deleted it too. Very wise!'

'Perhaps he's not interested. In the caller I mean.'

Oh he's interested. You should see the message he sent back!'

Rachel made a face. 'Never mind them. Come on we've got work to do. Let's try lifting those beer coasters. I ought to be able to do that. I'm not sure about you Stefan. It's one thing to be able to effect a jolt in Phil's back, it's different trying to lift objects. You haven't really had the chance to develop your skill and tomorrow we will need all our combined strength. It's a shame that tomorrow night we have to return to the graveyard. I hope we can solve this case, or at least make some good progress before we return.'

'Right. Let's get started. Show me what you've got.' Stefan's eye patch wrinkled, making him look mischievous. 'You go first oh Maestra.'

Rachel rolled her eyes at her companion then focused on the table nearest to her which had been cleaned and set up ready for the next day. A small tower of six beer coasters had been placed in the centre. To her delight she managed to lift the top one within seconds. It floated high above the pile then tumbled down again, sending the rest of them careering off the table.

'Well done, now try to lift one and place it somewhere down again.'

'Right.' Rachel tried again on a different table. Unfortunately, the next attempt ended in a similar fashion as the previous one.

Stefan looked on eagerly waiting to have a go himself. 'That's all very well if you want to attract Phil's attention to let him know you are with him, but he already senses your presence. You need to be able to bring something to his attention - to convey a message. It has to be better than turning a page on a file.'

Rachel frowned. 'I know that! I am trying!'

'Perhaps you are trying too hard.'

Annoyed, more with herself than with her companion, Rachel allowed herself to be distracted from her efforts and said more sharply than she intended, 'Why don't you *have a go?' Unexpectedly, a whole stack of coasters flew in the air then crumpled into a muddled heap onto the floor. They stared at them in amazement.*

'Did I do that?'

Stefan laughed. 'I think that's a good indication of what I was trying to tell you. I think you were over concentrating. I could tell by your face. You let yourself get distracted to talk to me and as soon as you diverted your energy the tower rose and collapsed. Don't glare at me, I know you've got the experience. I think your annoyance with me created a different type of energy, but it was misdirected. You just need to adjust your focus. Don't be too intense. Try again on another table. We've got plenty to choose from.'

He drifted away, not waiting for Rachel's indignant response. He chuckled to himself. Her reaction reminded him that she was a lot younger than he and she suffered her youthful pride. He also acknowledged, that he had had the benefit of having known about her struggles with her energy force, the first time she roamed out of the zone. She'd related everything to the spirits. That information had helped him to prepare himself. He was fond of her and didn't want to hurt her feelings.

Aware that Rachel was watching, Stefan focused on the next pile of coasters. His first try lifted one from the top of the tower and he watched it topple down pretty much the same as Rachel's first attempt. That encouraged him to try again and he succeeded in lifting and placing down flat another coaster. His next effort lifted what was left of the entire tower. Keeping them together he replaced the pack intact. Delighted with his progress he moved to another table to practise again. This time he managed to lever the second pile into the air allowing it to hover before levering it back into position. He turned around to see if Rachel had witnessed it. She acknowledged his achievement with a nod then focused on her next target. This time she managed to do the same as Stefan.

Satisfied with their progress, she turned to smile at Stefan. 'Let's see if we can both do it at the same time and see how high we can get them to hover.'

The ghosts did this several times and after a few more practises were able to lift and replace each tower of coasters, as they trailed each other from table to table.

'That's great,' Rachel exclaimed. But Stefan wasn't done. 'Come on let's go into the restaurant and see what we can achieve in there,' he said.

Eventually, following several failed attempts, they managed to unfurl and move several napkins out of place. Some fell to the floor and though they could lift them back to their correct position their skills did not stretch to being able to fold them properly. Pleased with their exertions they turned their attention to the long brocade curtains at the wide windows of the hotel restaurant. To their delight their combined focus enabled them to draw and close them.

'That's great work,' Rachel said delightedly. *'They're quite heavy, I think we've earned a break.'*

'Totally agree.' Stefan checked the clock in the hotel foyer, *'it's half past one. We've got time for some rest before we return here in the morning. At least we know that Phil is going to contact the DI in the morning. What time do you think the inspector plans to knock on Olive's door?'*

'I suppose he'd want to be there before eight o clock? I don't know really. They'd have to leave here about seven thirty ish or a bit before. So we'd better get here at seven I suppose. Come on I'm dead beat,' Rachel said.

'Really? Dead beat?'

*

Phil had wondered what time he should contact the DI. Before going to bed he'd sent Barker a text offering to accompany him to see Olive Sloan, but hadn't received a response. He decided to get up at six-thirty to call the detective inspector.

'You know when he said he wanted to do an early morning call, I didn't think he meant before eight o'clock, but now I'm not sure,' Phil confided in Clare the following morning. She rolled over in bed to face him, blinking as he turned on the bedside lamp.

'I shouldn't think so, though it has been known for police to do dawn raids,' she yawned.

'You can hardly call this a raid,' Phil smirked.

Clare yawned again and turned over in bed. 'I s'pose not,' she agreed sleepily. She closed her eyes again and made herself comfortable whilst Phil leapt out of bed and into the shower. He dressed as noiselessly as he could, taking extra care with his choice of clothes which he thought suitable for a formal visit, then searched in his pocket for his mobile. After scrolling down his contacts for the DI's number he pressed the relevant icons. He was relieved to hear it being answered within two rings and was impressed that his own number had been saved into the detective's contacts list.

'Phil, good morning. What can I do for you? I got your message by the way. Sorry I didn't get back to you sooner, things didn't go according to plan. I had intended to text you this very minute.'

'Good morning. So what do you think? Would you like me to accompany you to Olive Sloan's house this morning?'

'Absolutely. I was reluctant to ask last night. You'd been so helpful yesterday. I was conscious I'd taken up a lot of your time. Your wife won't mind?'

Phil turned towards Clare who was half awake listening to the conversation. Phil leaned over her and put a hand on her shoulder. 'No she doesn't mind, as long as she doesn't have to get out of bed, she's happy for me to go along with you.' He saw Clare's mouth curve into a smile.

'Great. I can pick you up at seven fifteen. Will that be enough time for you to get some breakfast?'

'Yes, that's perfect. The hotel serves breakfast from seven onwards. That's enough time for me to have a continental.'
After the phone call he took the small kettle from the hospitality tray and filled it to make himself a cup of tea, taking advantage of having twenty minutes to spare. At the sound of the water boiling, Clare stirred again. 'If you're making tea, I'll have one please.'

Propped up against pillows, sipping her tea a few minutes later, she asked Phil if he'd come up with some possible questions to ask Olive.

'Yep. Though it all depends on what Barker has in mind. My questions will have to be supplementary ones. But it seems he has my trust, so we can plan how we handle it on the way there. I suppose he'll have another detective with him from Holywell station, since Olive Sloan lives just inside the Welsh border and not in Cheshire.'

'He might have arranged to meet DS Price though, mightn't he?'

Phil shrugged. 'I don't know, possibly.' He stood up again and adjusted his trousers, then checked his tie in the mirror. Clare watched him run a comb through his damp, wavy brown hair as she enjoyed her brew. One of the many things she admired about him, was that he always made sure he looked clean and tidy. He turned towards her, 'I'm going down to get my croissants. I won't come back up, there won't be time. I'll text you later. Have a nice morning.' He kissed her forehead and left the room in pursuit of his breakfast.

In the restaurant Phil was bemused that he couldn't find a table that was properly set. Or rather the cutlery was set but the napkins which were usually folded so neatly were askew. At first he thought that other guests had unfolded the napkins to make it look as if they'd reserved a place, but there were only four other early risers and they were already seated. Choosing a spot near the buffet, he placed his mobile on it as his marker, then got himself some food.

As Phil finished eating, Rachel and Stefan sashayed into the hotel and hovered around Phil's table. They stayed as close together as they could, hoping he could feel their presence. It seemed to work; Phil sensed a slight change of air. He hoped he wasn't imagining things.

'Rachel?' he whispered.

In response, his napkin floated to the floor.

'Did you do that?' Phil asked in surprise.

Another napkin found its way to the floor. Phil picked them up, putting his soiled one over his plate.

'Are you alone?' Phil asked.

Rachel looked at Stefan for inspiration. He shrugged. 'If you drop another napkin he'll take it as a yes. We need to do something for a negative.'

'I think if we do nothing, he'll take it as a no.'

They waited, as Phil tried to think how he could make it easier to communicate. 'So you have someone with you?'

A napkin moved from the table on to the floor. Phil retrieved it again then got out of his chair, brushed crumbs from his trousers and picked up his phone, a grin spreading across his face.

'I get it. I'm going with the police to see Olive Sloan. Are you both coming with me?' He watched as another napkin fell to the floor. Phil's grin broadened as a waiter came to his table and took it away with the used crockery to the kitchen. Phil waited for another waiter to clean up the table and set it up for the next guests, before trying to communicate again.

'By the way, thanks for the lead to Tracey and Dean Roper. But I'm less grateful for those thumps to my chest. I'm guessing if you hadn't hit me so hard I probably wouldn't have landed in that charity shop; so I forgive you.'

Rachel and Stefan exchanged smug looks.

'He's getting it.' Stefan enthused.
Outside the hotel, DI Barker waited near the entrance blowing on his hands to keep warm.

'Good morning. A change in the weather I'm afraid. It's gone chilly again. Come on get inside the car, it's warmer in there. Detective Sergeant Watson has the heater on full blast.'

Enroute to Olive Sloan's house the DI laid out his plan. He would begin the interview and Phil and DS Watson should ask supplementary questions as they felt fit, even if they'd already asked the same ones before.

'That way, if she's hiding something she might trip up, hopefully.'

'Do you suspect her of having something to do with her husband's death?' Phil asked.

'I'm not ruling anything out. I've been in this game for too long. I suspect everyone. There is definitely something shifty about her.'

At five past eight, DS Watson knocked hard several times before Olive drew the curtains of her bedroom window to look down on to her doorstep. Furrows of indignation wreathed her face which deepened when she recognised the three individuals standing on her garden path. DI Barker waved to her, whereupon she closed the curtains with a resentful scowl.

'I'm assuming she's going to answer the door,' the inspector smirked. 'She doesn't look happy. Brace yourselves.'

'What time do you call this for making calls Inspector? It's indecent! I was in bed.' She pulled her fleecy dressing gown tightly around her and shivered as the cold morning air drifted into the hallway.

The two ghosts entered the house coasting along the gentle whorls of the breeze.

'Come in quickly before I freeze.' She led the way through the wide hallway to the spacious kitchen and motioned them to sit down at the pine table in the centre of the room.

'This is a murder inquiry Mrs. Sloan, we don't have time to waste.' DI Barker had no intention of apologising. 'No don't bother with the kettle, this won't take long.'

Disgruntled Olive put the kettle down. She raked her hand through her tangled hair.

'That'll rattle her. Roused out of her bed and denied her morning cuppa. Nice one,' Stefan observed.

'More questions Inspector? I've told you everything I know.' She sat down at the kitchen table scowling at her uninvited guests.

'First of all let's start with Rob Taylor.'

'Rob Taylor...?' The name startled Olive. She sat upright in her chair. 'What about him?'

Phil thought she seemed afraid.

'Why didn't you tell me about your husband's lifelong friend? He played snooker with him regularly enough.'

'Pool, actually,' Olive amended then looked guilty. She bit her lip as if regretting her correction.

'Ah so you did know him.'

'No. Yes.' The suspect shrugged trying to regain her composure. 'A long time ago. I haven't seen him for years.'

'You must have known that they met up almost every week. Contacting him has been very useful.' The detective held her eyes. She looked away miserably fumbling with her dressing gown belt.

'Ben used to say he was going to the pub to play pool, he rarely mentioned names. I didn't know that Rob went to the Greyhound.'

'She's been caught out! She hasn't covered her tracks properly,' Stefan said triumphantly.

Phil got the sense that Olive was actually telling the truth. Her excuse seemed reasonable yet her initial reaction upon hearing Rob Taylor's name displayed fear. He studied her body language and facial expressions guessing that she worried that Rob Taylor may have given the police some background information about her that she'd kept secret. But what else was she hiding? Her next words astonished him.

'Has he got something to do with Ben's murder?'

Her fearful expression altered as she calculated that Rob could be a convenient scapegoat. Deceit crawled over Olive's face.

'Wow, look at the evil in her coming out now.' Rachel turned to catch Stefan's incredulous visage. *'She's realised that her lack of interest in her husband's activities at the Greyhound may be her undoing. She knows that Rob Taylor has probably informed the police about her rowing and swimming ability. Now she's trying to turn it to her advantage.'*

'She's panicking. Anyway DI Barker knows that Rob was in Scotland when Ben was killed,' Stefan said.

'Why do you say that Mrs. Sloan?'

She shrugged. 'I thought that's why you mentioned his name.'

Barker frowned at Olive's remark. He noted his suspect's uneasiness and took advantage with another attack.

'What about Tracey Roper? You probably know her, if you know Rob Taylor.'

Olive's shoulders slumped. She fidgeted in her chair then pushed back a lock of dark hair from her pallid complexion.

'Tracey Hill?' She snorted. 'What of her?'

The DI paused, digesting what she'd said. 'Tracey Hill was her maiden name. So you know she is married and her name is Roper?'

The colour in Olive's face rushed back. She nodded, biting her lip. DI Barker pressed on. 'Didn't she and your husband have a fling a long time ago?'

'Something like that. A long time ago, yes. What of it?'

'So why didn't you tell us?'

'Like I said it was years ago. I didn't think it mattered. I hadn't even thought of it.'
Olive shifted in her chair, her eyes downcast. She cupped her hands around her flushed cheeks.

Phil leaned against a work surface studying Olive's ever changing demeanour. He exchanged a glance with DS Watson who raised her eyebrows before returning to focus on the DI's next words.

'We asked you for all your husband's contacts, past and present, anything that could help us find his killer.'

'I'm grieving. You can't expect me to remember everything.' Olive cast a longing glance at the kettle.
Whilst Phil conceded that it may have been a genuine mistake to not reveal Rob Taylor's

identity, he felt she used her husband's death flippantly as an excuse. Her attitude gave him the impression she didn't care about finding the murderer. Later when he discussed this with the inspector he admitted he'd felt the same and that something didn't sit right with him. Underlying her obvious distress with the unexpected intrusion he noted a hint of deviousness. He also noticed she didn't exhibit any trace of grief.

The inspector chose again to take advantage of her discomfiture.

'Mrs. Sloan we know you are bereaved, but it appears to us that you've been telling us a string of lies. For example you are an expert boat rower according to Rob Taylor. Yet you told us that on the day of your husband's death you didn't like the water. Why did you say that?'

'I…I…don't know why I said that. I was confused.'

'So what really happened that day in Holywell? Why don't we start at the beginning? Whose idea was it to go out for the day? Was it yours?'

'Yes…No…I mean it was his.'

DI Barker's eyes glinted as he focused on his suspect.

'Did your husband suggest going boating on St. Winefride's Lake in Holywell?' DS Watson cut in. She flashed a questioning look at her superior who inclined his head slightly for her to go on.

'No…I mean yes.'

'Make your mind up. It's a simple question.'

Olive breathed deeply obviously trying to think what she'd previously stated. 'Ben suggested a ride to the North Wales Coast, but when we got to Holywell I thought we could have a detour to see St. Winefride's well. It's a tourist attraction and I'd never been…'

'Yes, I'm aware of that. So why didn't he go with you to the well? Did you have a tiff? I think you actually hired a boat together then you stabbed him and swam back to the boathouse? You could do that. Rob says you're a strong swimmer.' The DS bombarded Olive with questions hoping to trip her up. Her reaction disappointed the detective.

'No, no, no, it wasn't like that.'

'Well we know that bit isn't true,' Stefan said. Rachel nodded. *'But the DS is on the right track. Yet despite her method of interviewing I don't think she believes Olive did it.'*

'Suppose you tell us what it was like.' The DS softened her approach. 'Did you have an argument?

Olive nodded. 'He'd been edgy for a few weeks. I thought he was stressed about something at work but he wouldn't tell me what it was about. He'd taken the day off. I told him he should calm down and that we should have a coffee somewhere to discuss it. He refused. Then I suggested we go for a ride in the car.'

'Oh, so it was you who suggested going out?' DI Barker interrupted.

'Yes.'

'You just said he suggested it.'

'Inspector I've told you this before. Why don't you look at my previous statement? I can't remember what I said now.'

'When we asked you if your husband was stressed, you said no. Now you are telling us he was. How can we believe anything you said in your statement?

'That's because it's all a pack of lies! Stefan said. Rachel nodded.

'Mrs. Sloan you keep changing your mind. Tell me the truth. Did you suggest the North Wales Coast?'

Olive nodded.

But you didn't get there did you?'

Olive shook her head again. Tears formed in her eyes.

'They look like real tears this time,' Rachel commented gleefully.

'Probably because she knows she's been found out. She's desperately trying to think of a way to wriggle out of it. I wonder what she and Dean had agreed to say. She's good at telling lies, but she can't remember what she said.'

'So why did you end up in Holywell?' DI Barker asked again.

'I told you. I wanted to see the famous well.'

'Then after you'd both seen the well, you suggested going for a row on St. Winefride's lake?' DS Watson asked.

'Yes. He liked that idea. I said hiring a boat on the lake would help to calm him down.'

'He liked that idea?' DS Watson repeated slowly.

Olive nodded.

'So you went to the lakeside together and when you got there you changed your mind?'

'Yes.'

DI Barker inclined his head towards the sergeant then picked up the thread.

'No! That's a lie. The footage on the cameras at the boathouse only show your husband in the reception area hiring a boat. You are nowhere to be seen!'

It seemed to Phil that for a few seconds Olive's lips twitched, almost as if she were suppressing a smile. He observed her intently.

The DI folded his arms and glared at Olive. 'Or did you hire another boat and like my sergeant here suggests, you murdered your husband?'

'No, I said. No, I didn't!'

It was obvious to the detectives and Phil that Olive was getting flustered. She looked disconsolately down at the table. Phil felt her distress did not exhibit grief but fear. He also suspected that the DI's last remark about the footage brought her some relief. He wondered why. Did she feel she needed to prove her innocence?

Olive lifted her head, breathing heavily. 'Half way to the lake, I told him I'd changed my mind. I had a headache. I said I would meet him later. By that time he'd made his mind up to go on alone.'

'Are you sure you didn't force him to go on his own? After all you were out together on a day trip. Wouldn't he have wanted to stay with you, especially as you had a headache coming on? Did you follow him, hire a boat and kill him?'

Olive said nothing. She looked down and nervously pleated the belt on her dressing gown.

'Mrs. Sloan. Answer the question please?'

Olive looked up with new resolution in her expression. 'He was stressed. I encouraged him to go on his own, and said I would go and get a coffee.'

'So why did you lie to us? Why didn't you tell us he was stressed? Barker relentlessly held her defiant eyes. 'You told us in your previous statement that he wasn't.'

'I didn't want to be a suspect, I suppose.' Olive's face brightened, almost as if she'd just thought of an excuse.

Phil who had been quietly observing the proceedings followed up on the line of enquiry the DS had taken previously.

'So Rob Taylor tells us you are a good swimmer as well as a rower Mrs. Sloan?'

Startled at the returning question, Olive answered quickly without thinking, 'Yes of course I can swim and row.' She hesitated then added, 'but I'm not strong enough to swim in the lake to stab my husband and swim back, if that's what you are implying.' She ignored Phil and glared defiantly at DS Watson.

Surprised at her response, Phil quizzed her again. 'Is that what you think happened? Someone swam out to him and stabbed him?' He was aware of the detectives observing Olive intently as she answered. She shook her head vehemently finding the strength to fight back.

'No, no, I don't know what happened.' Rattled she got out of her chair. 'Look I'm fed up of this, I didn't kill my husband. I think you should go now.'

DI Barker nodded and stood up. 'Thank you for your time Mrs. Sloan, you can have your breakfast now.'

Phil turned to go then taking advantage of her distress asked another question. 'Was your husband having an affair with Tracey Roper?'

Olive laughed. 'No, he wasn't. I've told you he wasn't having an affair!' She faltered… 'Why? What's she been saying?' A wary expression masked her face. Phil wasn't sure how to read it, but he recognised panic in her reaction. Another thought came to him.

'Do you know Tracey Roper's husband? Dean Roper.'

DI Barker stopped and listened at the front door to hear Olive's response.

'No, I don't! Now please go.'

Taken aback at her vehemence, Phil followed the detectives out of the house simultaneously aware of a strange sensation on his neck.

Rachel was trying to tell him something. He tried to figure out if it meant

Olive lied about an affair between Ben and Tracey or about not knowing Dean.

'She might not have killed her husband, but she's a conspirator to the fact,' Stefan observed.

'I can't understand why she would conspire to have him killed. After all those years of marriage,' commented Rachel as they floated out of the house behind the police officers. 'And they have known each other since high school.'

'Sad I know. Maybe she was forced into it, by our hard hearted ruthless Dean Roper.'

'Nothing forced her last night, the way they were going at it!'

'Going at it! What a way to describe passion.' Stefan frowned and rolled his one eye in his patchwork face.

Rachel grinned. 'Funny that she mentioned the murderer might have been a swimmer, when we know Dean fits that description.'

Stefan nodded. 'Whichever way he did it he obviously wasn't picked up by the cameras.'

'Yeah. There are places around the lake out of range of the cameras.' Rachel grimaced, remembering the scene of her own murder. 'Unless he hired a boat to do it and then swam away from the scene? But that would entail leaving two empty boats on the lake and the investigation report only mentioned one. The one with Ben's rucksack.'

'Yes. Good point. If Dean hired a boat to kill Ben, he could have rowed back after killing him? It would make more sense.'

Rachel tilted her head. 'I think so. Let's see what our detectives are thinking.'

Phil's thoughts were on the same lines as Rachel. He checked the information with the DI who leaned against the garden gate outside Olive's house inhaling on his cigarette. The smoke swirled into the air captured by the mid-morning mist.

'That bit you mentioned about the security cameras, is it correct?'

Barker nodded. He inhaled more nicotine before adding, 'yes we've checked the footage. Olive isn't visible in the reception area until the time she was seen at the desk making inquiries about her missing husband. That was about five thirty - after dark. Her clothes were distinctive. She was wearing a pink jacket I believe.'

DS Watson nodded her agreement. 'The cameras concentrate mostly on the lake to alert the staff of any difficulties on the water. Nevertheless, some edges of the lake are not exposed,' she added. 'Images of Olive weren't picked up anywhere else.'

The inspector sighed. 'Unfortunately, even the cameras miss things occasionally. They're not hundred percent fool proof. Sometimes luck plays to the murderer.' He took another drag of his cigarette and jerked his head towards Olive Sloan's house. 'What do you think Phil? Do you think she's still hiding something?'

'Yes. I don't buy this ad hoc decision to visit Holywell. The fact that she keeps changing her story, then forgetting what she'd said, which ought to be a simple explanation, implies, she knew what was going to happen.'

Phil hesitated before continuing. 'It's as if she laid a trap for her husband's murder! She was flustered when I mentioned swimming and then came up with a theory of her own to try to convince us that she didn't do it. Almost like a guilty conscience playing tricks on her, forcing her to say the very thing she was hiding?'

Barker stubbed out his cigarette on the ground with his foot.

'It happens that way sometimes.'
Phil raised curious eyebrows though said nothing as he digested the detective inspector's comment.

'Do you think she had planned for someone to knife him?' DS Watson inhaled deeply on her e-cigarette as she asked the question on Phil's lips.

'It's certainly possible,' Barker asserted.

'I suppose you've looked at the CCTV cameras for other lone rowers that afternoon?' Phil asked. 'I can't help thinking that the two boats I saw late on the afternoon that Ben Sloan went missing may be a clue.'

'Yes. We have been able to identify the majority. Most are regulars. However there were a few individuals we don't know. The boathouse has got a record of their names but not addresses. Of course one of the names could be fake. We've narrowed the list down to five separate characters, each one wearing jeans, dark sweatshirts, dark jackets and similar baseball caps.' He grunted, 'typical clothing, and not very helpful to us. They all paid cash for the boat hire, so we don't have a paper trail.'

DI Barker watched his DS turning off her e-cigarette. 'We need to keep an eye on her. 'I think she is capable of this deed, but why would she go to such lengths to do it? And how did she manage to do it? It doesn't make sense.' Barker sighed raising his eyes to the sky as if looking for inspiration. 'Or she could be innocent and just acting oddly. Maybe we'll pick up another lead at the funeral tomorrow.'

'You know I fly back to Bucharest tomorrow, so I can't be of much more use,' Phil reminded him. He tightened his stomach muscles half expecting a supernatural nudge.

'Do you want to visit the Ropers again Sir?' DS Watson asked.

The DI shrugged. 'Not yet. I've nothing new to go on, though I suppose Tracey might be able to give us a bit more about Olive's character. That would be a shot in the dark really, since they haven't been friends.'

'Olive has admitted that she knew Tracey as Tracey Hill. Is it possible she knew Dean Roper?' The DS asked.

'She's just denied knowing him,' Phil reminded her. 'Though I think she's lying. But why would she? Mind you she's told us a lot of lies over the last few days.' He scratched at the tickle on his neck interpreting it as confirmation from Rachel. But how did Olive know Dean?

The DI pondered over this. 'Dean Roper insisted he didn't know her. It was obvious that the connection with the Sloans was Tracey so I think he's telling the truth. When we spoke to the Ropers, Tracey didn't mention that Ben and Dean knew each other and she was completely open about her relationship with Sloan. Neither did she contradict Dean when he said he didn't know either of the Sloans. He's a surly character I know but we have nothing on him. Still it's odd that Olive knew Tracey was married to Roper.'

'Possibly a mutual acquaintance told her, Sir?'

The detective inspector mulled over his sergeant's theory. 'Yes, or Ben actually told her that he'd re-acquainted himself with Tracey and that she was married to Roper.'
Phil admitted that either theory seemed possible. He recalled something Clare had suggested the night before.

'Could it be that Dean Roper was jealous of his wife's relationship with Ben – no matter how slight it was, then followed Ben and Olive to the lake and killed him?'
Phil scratched his neck, the irritation seemed stronger making him convinced that the tickling sensation was Rachel trying to tell him he was on the right track.

'It's possible, I admit, but we have very little to go on. DS Price is going to check his alibi. But I don't think he's our man.

However I won't rule it out,' DI Barker said. 'Come on let's get back to the station. We'll drop you off at the hotel Phil.'

'How much you bet Olive rings Dean to warn him that they have linked her with Tracey and that Rob Taylor?' Rachel said.

'She might. Though Dean told her not to contact him. Besides neither the detectives nor Phil have linked him with Olive so if they do go to the Ropers again, they will probably concentrate on asking Tracey more questions. Mind you, I think Phil suspects that Olive and Dean know each other, he's just not sure how or what bearing it has on the murder.'

'Olive is unnerved, and she might want moral support. She's not very good at keeping track of what she said,' Rachel argued. 'It's a lot for her to cope with even though she didn't physically kill him, or at least that's what Ben told us.' She frowned, focusing on Stefan's good eye.

'What do you mean?' He screwed his face up causing the lines of his complexion to run into each other creating a spider's web effect.

Rachel pursed the bony framework of her lips, 'I'm thinking that Olive could have been in the boat with Dean. It would have made the murder much easier. She would have kept out of sight, keeping the boat steady so that Dean could slip into the water. Ben wasn't expecting any trouble, and by the time Dean had toppled him and stabbed him, he would have been trying to save himself.

He wouldn't have seen Olive,' Rachel sighed, *'that's if she was there of course.'*

'Wow, you could be right. It would explain her reaction to Phil's question about her swimming.'

Rachel nodded. *'We must make Phil ask Barker about her mobile and to find out whether the police have checked it and we also need to know if Barker has listened to, rather than read the transcript from Ben's mobile.'*

'Right, I see what you mean. 'How do you propose we do that? Mobile phones are heavier than napkins.'

'I know. But somehow, we have to get him to ask DI Barker about the audio transcripts.' She stared at Stefan trying to find inspiration.

'Although I'm tempted to stay here and shadow Olive, we ought to get back into the car, wait for Phil to text Clare as he promised, and combine our energy to force the mobile out of his hand. Perhaps draw his attention to it in some way which will make him think about messages. Instead of a jolt in the stomach we could try his arm or his hand?'

Stefan stared at Rachel thoughtfully. *'OK, let's do it and wait our chance, our combined strength just might be enough.'*
They watched Phil get into the police car and as anticipated, he reached in his pocket for his mobile to text Clare. As soon as it was in his hand, he felt a pain surge across his wrist. He dropped the phone on to the floor of the car and bent down to pick it up.

Before he could press the contact number, he experienced another pain, this time in his fingers. For good measure Rachel tapped him on his shoulder, not too much pressure but enough to alert him. He bent his head down and whispered 'Rachel?' Another light clout on his hand confirmed his suspicions. Catching her passenger's discomfort, in the driver's mirror, DS Watson threw him a perplexed look. 'Are you alright Phil?'

This caused DI Barker to turn his head. When he saw Phil juggling with his mobile he blinked his surprise.

'That phone causing you some problems?'

'No, no it's fine. I dropped it and now it seems to have a mind of its own. I just need the screen to clear.' He stared at his device trying to figure out why Rachel didn't want him to use his phone.

The DI turned to face the road again and Phil attempted to scroll down the list of contacts on his mobile. This time the pain on his shoulder was harder, and Phil winced audibly.

'Are you sure you're OK?' DI Barker asked. He saw Phil's arm crossed over his chest towards his shoulder, his mobile gripped in his other hand.

'Rachel,' Phil whispered what are you trying to tell me?'

Barker frowned. He thought Phil's wife's name was Clare. Why was the man repeating the name Rachel? He thought he'd heard him whisper it earlier but wondered if he'd made a mistake. He racked his brain trying to think where he'd heard that name before.

'What are you trying to tell me?' Phil whispered. A harder blow on his hand coincided with the DI turning around again to see Phil's anguished face. He spoke abruptly to his sergeant.

'Stop the car, Watson. I think Phil needs to get out for some air.' He followed Phil on to the pavement and studied him as he rubbed his hand and wrist.

'Are you sure you are alright? You looked pretty bad just now. Do you suffer from travel sickness?'

'No. It's nothing like that. I need to tell you something which you may not believe, or not want to believe, but it's the truth, and with a bit of luck I might get some backing to convince you.' Phil looked around him even though he knew he wouldn't be able to see Rachel.

Perplexed, DI Barker followed Phil's stare into the vacant space. His expression contrasted with his companion's expectant visage.

'You're beginning to worry me now. Whatever it is, you'd better spit it out.'

'As you know I'm a psychic. That's the reason you asked for my input in the first place.'

'Yes, of course. What of it?'

'The fact is I'm getting assistance of the paranormal kind.'

'Isn't that normal? I mean you getting communication from the other side?'

Phil couldn't prevent a hint of a smile to twitch his face. 'So how do you think I get it?'

The DI frowned. 'I don't know. I suppose you get vibes or visions?'

'I certainly don't get visions. It would be simpler if I did.'

'Well vibes then. Strong smells?'

'Smells no, vibes yes and something extra.'

'Something extra? Like what exactly?'

'Is this guy a comedian or what?' Stefan said.' We don't smell!'

Rachel shrugged. 'At least he's willing to listen. We might be able to help him, if Phil can convince him we know something.'

'The thing is, apart from the vibes, Rachel sometimes physically punches me to communicate. I don't know how she does it, but it can hurt!'

'Rachel? Who's Rachel?' For a few seconds they held each other's eyes. Phil waited for him to work it out.

'You mean Rachel Bellis? The girl who was murdered?' Barker's jaw dropped. 'Never!' Yet even as he denied it, part of him wanted to believe Phil. It would explain a few mysterious events during Rachel's murder investigation.

As he saw the light dawn on the DI's face, Phil pressed on. 'Just now she deliberately hurt my wrist and then hit me on the shoulder to knock my phone out of my hand. I think she is trying to tell us something important about Olive.'

'But how do you know it's her?' Barker asked.

Phil looked around him helplessly. He needed to convince the DI of how he communicated with ghosts.

'Rachel can you give me some kind of proof that I'm not going mad?' He pulled out an unused handkerchief from his jacket pocket and placed it on the garden wall behind him. 'Perhaps you can demonstrate with this handkerchief? I saw the mess you made of the napkins in the hotel! Please?'

'The napkins in the hotel?' DI Barker whispered. He raised his eyebrows, at the same time pressing down his moustache with his finger and thumb trying to make sense of what Phil was saying.

'Anything to oblige.' Rachel grinned and lifted the handkerchief off the wall and dropped it on a rose bush. She was gratified to see the DI's incredulous expression.

'Bloody hell. I can't believe it. Are you trying to tell me that you can actually talk to the dead?'

Phil nodded. 'Not usually as well as I can with Rachel. I think it's because I knew her and her family.'

'So that's how you managed to find out the names of her murderers, because you had a special bond?'

'I suppose so. I've had no contact with her since then until now. And, I've never been able to connect so directly with ghosts in other circumstances. I get vibes when I'm in Transylvania, some stronger than others. I've even been able to pass on messages to the living. Some ghosts want to communicate and others don't.'

'Why do you think she wants to solve the Ben Sloan case?' The DI scrutinised Phil intently, scarcely believing what he was hearing.'

'I'm afraid I don't know. Maybe she knew him, or maybe because I asked her to help, after you had approached me.'

The DI took a deep breath. 'Alright, let's assume I'm convinced, though I must say this is unbelievable; why is she preventing you from using your phone?'

'I don't know. Maybe she is trying to avoid punching me in the stomach, like she sometimes does. The only thing I can think of is that she is trying to tell us something about Olive. She was in the house with us.'

The inspector stared at Phil incredulously.

'I'll have to give it some thought. In the meantime I need to let Clare know I'm on the way back.'

'Use mine. Do you know her number?'

Phil grinned. 'Fortunately hers and mine are the only ones I've memorised.'

When Phil eventually managed to ring Clare, he was relieved there was no interference from the ghosts. She was finishing her breakfast and answered the call as she was chewing a piece of toast. Not recognising the number her voice was cautious until Phil explained.

'How's it going?' She asked.

'We're making progress. I'm on the way back to the hotel. I'll be ready for a cup of coffee when I get there. Do you want to meet me at the café near the post office?'

Clare checked her watch. 'About forty minutes? I've just finished a pot of tea, so yes, I'll see you there.'

Before they returned to the car the DI asked Phil not to mention anything about the supernatural to DS Watson.

'I don't think it's something I want to share with my colleagues just yet.'

'At least Phil will think about it,' Stefan said.

'I'm sure he'll work it out,' Rachel agreed. 'Give him time. He won't let it go. But our work isn't over. We need him to get the police to the sports centre later today.'

DS Watson dropped Phil off just outside Holywell town square. Before the officers moved on, DI Barker called to him, 'if you think of anything, let me know. Thanks for all your work.'

Clare was waiting under the clock tower of the town hall. She watched him step out of the police car and waved as Phil walked across the cobbled square to join her.

'I'm glad you got back in one piece. I take it your suspect didn't cause a fuss?' She kissed him, taking his hand to leave the square and lead him towards the café.

'It's fair to say she was not amused and I can't blame her. Two detectives and me, people she scarcely knew knocking on her door at eight in the morning.'

They found a table by the window to enjoy a view of St. Winefride's tower, visible through the branches of the tall Acacia trees at the side of the town hall.

'They're supposed to represent immortality of the soul, you know.'

'What?' Clare threw a confused stare at her husband as she took off her coat and flung it over the back of a chair.

'Those trees. Acacia. Often found in graveyards.'

Clare followed his gaze, 'I like them, though they're not at their best this time of year.' She stood at the side of her husband whilst he placed his order at the counter.

When they sat down, he gave Clare more details about the interview with Olive then explained what happened to him in the police car.

Clare frowned. 'I was worried you might get hurt by your suspect, and instead you get attacked by Rachel! Was it as bad as the other day?'

'No, but bad enough. I'm convinced that she, or I should say, they, because she is working with someone, were trying to tell me something. I can't think what it is other than I suspect there's a stronger connection between the Ropers and the Sloans than I initially supposed. In the car I was prevented from using my phone and then they let me use the inspector's and the nudges stopped.'

Clare frowned trying to make sense of the puzzle Phil presented. She pushed a stray strand of hair behind her ear. 'So could the clue be mobiles and not about Olive?'

Phil shrugged. 'It might be, but what?' He removed his scarf and coat then turned his attention to his Americano and pastry.

Finally Clare's creased brow slackened and she put her hand on her husband's. 'I think I've got it. Did you say that the dead man's mobile had threatening messages on it, but they couldn't trace the caller?'

Phil nodded, his mouth full of egg custard.

'How much do you bet there's a clue in the messages? Maybe Rachel wants you to listen to them.'

'Yes!' The ghosts spoke in unison.

Phil was sceptical. 'I'm assuming the detectives would have listened to it, over and over already. They've probably got a typed transcript of it. They have experts to do that sort of thing.' He got up to order another coffee, then turned to his wife. 'Are you ready for one now? I needed the first one to warm up. It scarcely touched the spot. It's pretty cold out there.'

'Yes, I'll have a cappuccino please.' A waiter standing nearby cleared their table, smiled and offered to bring fresh drinks to save going to order at the counter.

Turning back to her husband Clare caught hold of Phil's hands. 'Perhaps you should listen to it – the audio version I mean. A fresh pair of ears as it were.' She smiled wryly. 'It's worth a try. Perhaps Rachel is trying to get you to read the transcript as well as listen to the message. Maybe she thinks you'll pick up something that the police didn't.

They'll probably have a typed version of all the messages.'

Phil felt a familiar irritation on his neck and released one of his hands from his wife's to scratch it. He looked lovingly into his wife's face. Her enthusiasm and his itchy neck persuaded him that she might have a point.

'Right, I'll give Barker a ring later. Perhaps he can arrange for me to go to the station and do what you suggest.'

He felt a confirming tickle on his neck and smiled at Clare. She was right. He didn't want to alarm her, so said nothing about the ghostly caress.

'Good. It's possible that an odd phrase or sentence had been missed out. I believe it can happen sometimes when transcribing tapes. But how Rachel would know beats me.

'She and her partner were in Olive's house listening to the conversation. I wonder if they want me to listen to Olive's device as well. I'm not sure the police checked hers. I'll ask Barker. Anyway I'm glad you figured it out. Thank you Darling.'

Rachel shrugged. 'I suppose that won't be a bad thing to do, to listen to Olive's messages?' She turned to Stefan for his thoughts.

'It depends if the police have checked and copied her text messages and calls. Did you say she was using her phone yesterday when you were in her house?'

Rachel nodded.'

Clare sipped her coffee then unwrapped the cellophane from the gratis biscuit and dipped it into her drink. She pulled it out quickly then put the whole thing into her mouth. Phil observed her performance as he had done numerous times before. He grinned. 'One of these days you'll get the timing wrong.'

She laughed. 'Tell me. How can a ghost know anything that's going on in the current world anyway?'

'That's something I can't answer. I wish I knew how ghosts find out things. It's a mystery to me as it is to you. All I know is I get weird sensations and an awareness that is without doubt paranormal. It's hard to explain.'

'It's proved useful on many occasions. But I don't envy you, especially when you get doubled up in pain when someone from the other side wants to get in touch. It worries me.'

'Fortunately, that doesn't happen too often. So far only with Rachel and her sidekick, whoever that is. But going back to the mobile transcript I suppose everyone makes errors, even the experts. I'll give Barker a ring now.' After several engaged beeps on the DI's phone, Phil left a message and put his mobile away.

'Right, not much else I can do. That aside, how do you want to spend the rest of the morning? Sightseeing in Holywell?'

Clare smirked. 'I think we've exhausted that possibility.' They both laughed.

'It would be nice to see the coast. How about getting a bus to Flint Castle, have a quick mooch around there, then a walk along the coastal footpath? We could grab a sandwich for lunch in that little café that overlooks the estuary.'

'Alright. I wouldn't mind seeing that crumbling old ruin of King Edward the first's again. At least we know it's still there. The café might not be. Thirteenth century building against a twenty first century shack. What are the odds?'

Clare gazed out through the window. 'A lot of businesses especially cafés don't always do well, hopefully that one has survived. The weather is improving now. There's a smidgeon of blue in the sky. Perfect for a walk and to get a sea breeze.'

'Great.' Phil used his paper serviette to wipe the mist from the window. 'The sea air will help me think. If it warms up later we can eat our food outside.'

Rachel sighed. 'If that's how they are going to spend the morning, we might as well report back to the graveyard.'

'Don't worry, I think Phil will follow up this morning's revelations. He just wants a break and to spend some quality time with his wife. Can't blame him.'

'I suppose so,' Rachel said grudgingly.

Come on, let's chat with your mum. She'll be dying to hear what's happened,' Stefan said kindly.

'Dying?' Rachel laughed.

CHAPTER FIFTEEN

Phil and Clare had finished their lunch at the seaside café and were strolling along the coastal path towards Flint castle when DI Barker rang Phil.

'Sorry to disturb you, I've been mulling over your message about your paranormal experience this morning. Thanks for your thoughts on that. I did start to wonder myself if it could be something to do with the phone we retrieved from the dead body, though I just can't fathom why a ghost would know about such things! However, if you think it might be a clue from your er...ghost contact it's worth a shot. I seem to be going round in circles with this case. I feel as if I have all the pieces yet not sure how they fit together.

'Anyway I have the file here in front of me – very flimsy it is, I have to admit and I picked up the transcript from the dead guys' mobile to read again. Then a thought occurred to me that just maybe the clue from the incident you experienced was about hearing rather than reading messages? So I decided to actually get the damned device out of the evidence store and listen to it again. I thought there might be something we may have missed. It happens sometimes, but usually the transcribers are spot on. The team who do this kind of thing are pretty good. But still. Anyway, I've played back the messages a few times and I have to say the voice is familiar. I can't figure out where I've heard it before. I've interviewed several people over the last week – not all of them connected to this case. It's hard to recall the voices of each one. It might not even be a man, though based on what is being said, something tells me it is. Speech gets distorted sometimes over the phone, it can be deceiving. I just thought you might like to come over and listen to it?' He broke into a whisper. 'Maybe your paranormal assistant might be able to help?'

Phil groaned. 'Inspector, I would be pleased to come over, I was thinking of that same possibility myself. The thing is, I'm in Flint with my wife. We're just outside the castle and will need to get to the town square to wait for a bus. It's due in twenty minutes or so. We can be at the police station about three fifteen?'

OK. 'I'll see you then. Thanks for your cooperation.'

Clare looked at her watch. 'You go on ahead. If you hurry you'll catch the bus. You can run faster than I can and besides I want to have a proper look at the castle. I can catch a later bus.'

'Are you sure? I don't have to go.'

'We both know that's what you want to do. Besides I'm as interested as you in this case. I'm also interested in those ruins.' She raised her hand to gesticulate towards the historic building. 'It's pretty unique in history. It was one of many that King Edward the first built in his campaign against the

Welsh, not that there's much left of it. As I'm here I may as well have a closer look at the remains. You go and catch your killer. I will go back to the thirteenth century.'

Phil bent down to kiss her. 'I'm so lucky to have a wife like you.'

'Yes you are. When I get back to the hotel I think I'll have a soak in the bath whilst I'm waiting for you to come back from the hub. Text me if you think you'll be delayed. I'll fix a time with Gavin and Abigail for the farewell dinner later. I've forgotten the name of the restaurant they suggested.'

'The Dee View,' I think they said.'

'That's it. I'll ring to make a reservation.'

'Great. Can you let Emily and Jack know the details?'

'OK.'

'Can you ask Gavin if he wants to book a taxi? We might need to book more than one if there's seven of us, possibly nine if my parents decide to come.'

'Will do. Now go!'

In the graveyard Anna and her spiritual companions were impressed with Rachel's and Stefan's adventure and even more so with their increased communicating skills.

'You see, I knew you could do it if you tried!' Anna said triumphantly. 'A shame you only have until midnight tonight to try to develop even more expertise. It's also a pity you can't lift objects heavier than a tower of beermats.'

'That took some time to accomplish! For both of us! It requires a certain amount of

concentration,' Stefan said, slightly offended. Much though he liked Anna, she was never satisfied. Always pushing for more.

'The hotel curtains were heavy, and we managed to make Phil drop his mobile, even if we did have to hurt him,' Rachel added.

'Yes, I wondered about that,' Tom offered. 'Strange that you can deliver a punch or hurt him physically yet you can't lift things. Heavy ones I mean,' he added, as he caught the exasperated expressions on his young friends' faces.

'Maybe our bony remains have more in common with the living flesh and bones of humans than inanimate objects, because we are organic,' Tom mused. 'It's similar to how I can use my titanium knees to tickle the bell ringers when I float in the bell tower.'

'You're not still doing that! Are you?' Anna admonished him. 'You might frighten them off thinking the place is haunted!'

'Too late for that. It is haunted!' Desmond chipped in. He'd been hanging around listening to the conversation and laughed. The others joined in. Tom's mischievous ways kept them amused.

'Don't you see that if you stop the public coming we will lose contact with what is going on in the outside world?' Anna persisted with her castigation. She tried not to laugh because Tom's antics amused her too.

'The bell ringers would still come. There's a group of them. It's not as if they come alone.' Tom's defiant eyes twinkled as *he addressed Anna. 'As for scaring other people away, I doubt that. I reckon even more would come. Haunted places always encourage visitors.'*

'What are you two going to do now?' Margareta asked in an attempt to change the subject. 'Presumably Phil and Clare aren't going to stay in Flint all day.'

'They were going to have lunch and then make their way back to the hotel. I'm assuming they'll be back before four o clock. They will have things to organise for their departure tomorrow. They will want to say goodbye to family and friends and whatever. Phil definitely left a message for the DI though. He won't forget about the mobile transcript.' Rachel stared at her companion for inspiration to plan their next move.

'Perhaps we should hang around the bus station for an hour or so and wait for them to come back. Hopefully the DI has made arrangements with Phil to contact him,' Stefan suggested.

'If I know Phil, he won't let it go. Come on let's go and see if we can find them. We need to get them to catch Olive and Dean together at the sports centre,' Rachel added.

*

Sitting at his desk in the police station Detective Inspector Barker read through his scant notes again as he waited for Phil to arrive. He had reserved a small room where the audio equipment had been set up along with a duplicate copy of the transcript.

At the bus station in Holywell, Rachel and Stefan saw Phil hurry up the street. He seemed relaxed, so they weren't worried that he was alone.

'Perhaps Clare is sight-seeing and Phil decided to meet the DI?' Rachel suggested.

'Hopefully he's going to the police station,' Stefan said.

They followed Phil to the council hub that housed the police station and the tourist information office as well as the library.

Phil was expected at the reception desk and after signing in, was conducted to the room where the inspector sat experimenting with the volume of the audio equipment. On the desk in front of him beside copies of the transcript, sat the case file.

DI Barker shook hands with Phil. 'Good of you to come at such short notice. I don't want to waste your time, but your input is very much appreciated. It's evident that Ben Sloan was being threatened. But we knew that, even though his wife claims to be unaware of it. He may have been having an affair with Tracey. That still isn't clear. Here sit down and make yourself comfortable.

'I've just listened to the messages again, including our recorded version of all the verbal messages as well as the originals on the mobile. It seems our victim kept all of them. There were ten in total.' He breathed heavily handing a set of earphones to Phil.

'I've been thinking over what we discussed this morning and I keep returning to my original thought that Olive Sloan knows more than she is letting on. Her story doesn't ring true about what happened on the day of Ben's death. She could have followed him, got her own boat and stabbed him. Her motive? Simply that she wanted him dead. But maybe I'm biased. I dislike the woman. There's something crafty about her under those attractive features. She's lied to us several times. Her performance of the grieving widow doesn't wash with me. But hey, I must keep to the facts.'

He threw up his hands and shrugged then eyed Phil with a trace of a smile on his tired face.

'Here's a bizarre theory: She set the whole murder up; she discovered he was seeing Tracey Roper and was enraged. So she hired a man to threaten Ben with anonymous phone calls.' Here the DI sighed. 'Unfortunately, the caller doesn't mention names, though Olive's plan is that Ben is supposed to think he's being threatened by Tracey's husband. The caller says "keep away from my wife?" When these calls didn't work, Olive got him killed. She either paid the man to kill him, or, like I mentioned earlier, she followed him to the lake and killed him herself. We know she is a good swimmer. We also know she can row a boat. But of course we have no evidence.'

'That's a bit far-fetched, isn't it?' Phil wrinkled his brow. 'Hiring someone to make telephone threats then a contract killing I mean? The other bit of your theory about her doing it herself sounds plausible though. But how did she manage to avoid the security cameras?'

'That bit about CCTV I agree is puzzling. But that apart, believe me, people will do anything for revenge especially jealous wives and husbands. Sadly there are also unscrupulous people who will kill for money. But they make mistakes. I'm looking for the mistake that gives us the essential clue.'

'If Ben really was having an affair with Tracey, even though she denies it, Dean Roper could have made the phone calls – you know the jealous husband?'

A caress on his neck convinced Phil he was on the right track

Barker agreed. 'It would certainly fit. I'm not ruling Dean Roper out – the jealous and controlling husband. He sends a few threatening messages to no avail and then takes the matter in to his own hands.'

Phil folded his arms and leaned against the wall. 'Yes, I admit it crossed my mind on more than one occasion. Yet he insisted that he didn't know Ben, and Tracey didn't contradict him when he said it. But Rachel took us there for a reason. This theory makes sense, but how do we prove it? Is it possible Tracey suspects her husband and is covering for him?'

'She wouldn't be the first wife to cover for the misdeeds of a husband. Didn't she say Dean was a good swimmer? Was that a hint? She knows but is too afraid to tell us. It's possible.'

'Has Dean Roper's alibi been checked yet?' Phil asked.

'Yes. DS Price has checked with the manager at the sports complex. Apparently Dean Roper checked into work on Friday at 8.00a.m. The thing is, the nature of his work – that being maintenance - meant that after checking in he could be anywhere on the complex during the day. None of his colleagues can confirm nor deny that he was there all day or whether he knocked off early. They can't remember much other than they know they saw him earlier in the staff canteen. His whereabouts that day are a bit sketchy.'

'Don't they have time sheets?'

'Yes, he signs them himself and they're checked randomly every week by the manager. They depend on their employees' honesty.'

The DI smoothed his moustache. His eyes locked with Phil's.

'So he could have left work early and followed Ben Sloan to the lake?' Phil suggested.

'Yes.'

'How the killer got into Ben's boat and out of the water again without being caught under the CCTV is a mystery,' Phil said slowly. 'If he'd been in another boat close by, it would've made it easier for him to swim back to it unseen after stabbing Ben, especially as the light was fading.'

'Barker agreed. 'You yourself said that you saw two boats well away from the boathouse on the opposite side of the lake, separate from the rest of the rowers.'

'Yes, it worried me at the time and now it makes sense,' Phil acknowledged.

'But the fact is, whoever did it, got away unseen, a fluke. Luck was on his side, the cameras didn't pick him up.' The detective inspector sighed.'

Phil sat down at the desk, took the earphones from the DI and waited for the machine to play back the messages.

The DI watched him as he fiddled with the buttons. 'Of course, we could be barking up the wrong tree.'

Phil started the recording. 'Here we go.'

Rachel and Stefan hovered around Phil to listen.

'Do you really think Olive was in the other boat?' Stefan questioned. 'We considered this yesterday. She could have disguised herself with a hat or scarf or something and hung around the reception area when Dean was paying for the hire, then she caught up with him. That way, if she'd been picked up by the cameras, the police wouldn't have suspected them, because they would appear to be a couple?'

'Hmm. Not a bad notion,' Rachel mused. 'Olive could keep the boat steady whilst Dean did the dirty deed!' She gazed at Stefan with new admiration.

'But Phil didn't see a boat that far out with two people inside. He told the police that he saw just one person struggling with the

oars and no-one in the other,' she reminded him.

'Olive would have crouched down because she didn't want Ben to see her. We don't know at what moment Phil saw the boats and for how long he watched them.'

'Wait, I think Phil is getting it,' Rachel interrupted him excitedly.

'That voice is familiar. He's made an amateurish attempt to disguise it but not very well, Phil said.'

Rachel and Stefan hovered around Phil to listen.

'There's a recurring timbre that despite his efforts to conceal it, it's still coming through. In addition to that he has a deep bass tone. Also there's a pattern where he seems to clip the end of each sentence. That combination of inflection and pitch I have heard very recently. I have an inkling I know it. I need to play it again.' Phil stroked his chin, thinking deeply as he waited for the recording to restart.

After three more play backs, Phil smiled exultantly. 'I have it. I think it's Dean Roper. In fact I don't think it, I'm convinced.'

'Dean Roper? Sure?' The detective inspector's eyes brightened.

'I've studied languages for years. In my line of work I get to meet people from many countries and I've developed an ear for dialects. I recognise that resonance. I've heard it as recently as yesterday.'

'Fantastic Phil. We knew you could do it.' Rachel shared a triumphant grin with Stefan.

'OK let's hear it again.' Hope wreathed the detectives face. 'This could be the break we're looking for.'

After listening to the messages once more, the DI nodded. 'Yes, I believe you're right.'

Phil frowned. 'I had a feeling he wasn't telling the truth.'

The DI eyed Phil with a shrewd smile. 'Tracey under-estimated Dean and thought he wasn't interested in her old school friend. He probably checked her mobile to read her messages. Then without her realising, got her to give him more information to track him down. The phone calls didn't work so he followed him to the lake. Like I said, there's no accounting for what a jealous husband might do? The thing is; how much of this does Tracey know?

'After Ben's untimely death, did she start to suspect Dean and is covering for him? He may have threatened her and she's scared. She was visibly upset about Ben's murder. Far more than Olive, I might add!' The inspector beamed triumphantly.

Phil breathed deeply, relief and shock ran through him. In addition he felt the familiar tickling sensation on his neck confirming his suspicion of Dean Roper.

'Do you think Olive suspects Dean Roper and he's threatened her too?'

'Bloody hell, you could be right. Your ghost contact was right to lead us to the Ropers. Otherwise, I doubt we'd ever have discovered that link.'

Barker leaned back in his chair speculatively. 'We need more evidence. This isn't enough. We need to track him down and bring him in for interrogation. We also need his mobile. Let's hope he still has it.' The DI got up and paced the room excitedly.

'So Olive Sloan and Tracey Roper have been telling us lies out of fear?' Phil looked up. Then let out a groan.

'Are you ok?'

'Yes, I think I'm getting a message from Rachel.'

'What is she saying?' The DI looked half amused half expectant to see Rachel in the room. He looked around him to see nothing but empty space.

'I don't know. She doesn't talk to me as such, I get a series of light punches to let me know she's there or sometimes, if she wants to tell me something urgently, I get especially hard thumps.'

'Like what happened this morning in the car?'

'Yes. Sometimes she moves things. I'm guessing she can only lift light objects.'

'I think he's getting us,' Stefan said enthusiastically.

'Good, but he's not getting the full picture. How can we tell him that Olive is involved?'

'Did you get the pain when you were listening to the messages?'

'No.'

'But you know she's here listening?'

'I'm sure of it.'

'Can you ask her something?'

'Yes, kind of. So far I get yes answers but not negatives. I think it's easier for her to nudge me for a yes but not a no.'

'So when you first got this pain, what were we saying?'

'We agreed Dean Roper murdered Ben.'

'Can you ask her if we are correct that he is our killer?'

'Rachel are we correct that Phil is our killer?'

'Instead of lifting up a piece of paper let's try something more convincing. There's a pencil on the desk, do you think between us we could manage to write a 'Y', Stefan suggested.

'Let's try it, Phil's suffering with my blows. I'm getting too excited and over doing it.'

Lifting the pencil was relatively easy with their combined effort, but balancing it to write a letter was more difficult. However a long straight line that went over the edge of the page and another smaller one angled at the top created a lop-sided 'Y'.

'Bloody hell!' The DI expostulated.

Phil grinned. 'Cheers Rachel. We just need some proof.'

An attempt at an 'O' on another piece of paper made both men look at the pencil in shock.

'Olive?'

This time the piece of paper with the 'Y' on it was lifted into the air.

'I don't get it. How can Olive Sloan be linked to Dean Roper?' Phil asked.

'Easy,' the DI said. 'He killed her husband!'

Several pieces of paper floated in the air. The DI turned white and sank back in his chair dazed.

'Something's wrong,' Phil said. 'I think it is to do with Olive.'

'Now what?' Rachel said frantically. 'We haven't the ability to write enough letters to make sense.' She stared helplessly at the paper strewn across the floor.'

'Quick, get that piece of paper with the 'O' and bring it to Phil,' Stefan yelled.

The two men stared incredulously as the paper floated in the air. Phil grabbed it and turned to his companion.

'I'm guessing Rachel and her sidekick believe Olive's connection is more than being the widow of Dean's murder victim. We know she has told us many lies. She knew Tracey, but denied that she knew Tracey's husband. I think she knows that Dean killed Ben. He has been threatening her just like he threatened her husband and she is afraid he might kill her too. He could be a psychopath.'

It was Stefan's turn to say, 'bloody hell. No' NO. You've got that bit wrong.' He threw up his arms in frustration and turned to see his exasperation mirrored on Rachel's face. The combined frustration of the ghosts unexpectedly lifted the case file from the desk and scattered on the floor. They stared at it fascinated by their own exertions.

Phil stared at the mess too and bent to pick up the papers. 'We're on the right track but I think we might be missing something else,' he said.

'I think we have enough evidence here to pull Dean Roper in for questioning.' The DI checked his watch. 'In all probability he's still at work. Get your coat. First we're going to Olive Sloan's. Then we'll go to the sports centre and catch him before he goes home. If he's left, we'll go to his house.' The DI stepped out of the room shouting instructions to DS Watson to get the car and meet him and Phil at the hub door.

It amused Phil that the DI had commanded him to accompany him to Olive's. He acknowledged to himself that he would have been disappointed if he hadn't been included. He followed the DI to the open plan office catching the DS's glance at the clock on the wall as she muttered calculations on mileage and time. As they waited for their transport, Phil sent a hurried text to Clare.

'What time did Olive say she was having her so called sauna with Dean?' Stefan asked as he too noted the time was ten past four.

'I think they arranged to get it together for five,' Rachel replied. 'We'd better hurry, or we won't catch her before she goes to the sports centre. I've no idea how we can get Phil and the DI to go straight there instead of Olive's.'

'Don't worry. If she's left already, they'll make their way to find Dean.' He grinned. 'Actually it might be better.'

In the car, the DI explained to his colleague that they suspected Olive Sloan might know her husband's killer and she could be in danger. He informed her that the anonymous caller they previously couldn't identify from Ben's phone, they now believed to be Dean Roper.

'Do you think Tracey Roper suspects her husband of murder Sir?' DS Watson asked.

'Probably. We need to question her again later.'

Outside Olive's house, the DI rapped on her front door impatiently. On getting no answer he peered through the living room window trying to see if she was in. He shrugged, turning back down the garden path with a disappointed detective sergeant and Phil trailing behind him. As they approached the gate, they heard a shout from the window of the next door neighbour.

'Hello, are you looking for Olive Sloan?'

DI Barker hurried to the window fumbling for his ID badge. 'Yes, do you know where she is?'

'Of course I do. She's gone to the sauna like she always does on a Thursday. She goes on Tuesdays too. But she didn't go last Tuesday, you know, what with her husband and …'

'The sauna? Where?'

The neighbour enjoyed showing off her knowledge and was put out by the interruption.

'At the sports centre in Saltney. It's that new place…,' she began to explain. But the DI was already flying down the garden path to the waiting car.

'She's gone to the new sports centre in Saltney. Isn't that where Dean Roper works?'

'Bloody hell, is that how she knows him?' Phil asked.

'The sports centre, Saltney,' DI Barker instructed his bewildered colleague behind the steering wheel.

'What do we do now?' Rachel asked.

'Let's see what develops. At least they're on to Dean, though I don't think they realise that Olive is in it too. The important thing is they get Dean.'

'Something about all this is wrong,' the detective inspector said. 'Things don't add up. Why is Olive having a sauna there of all places?' He took a deep breath. 'When we get there we can talk to Dean and arrest him on suspicion of murder. See how he reacts to that.' He sent a message to DS Price to tell him what they were doing.

From the "Your Active Time and Leisure" Sports Centre car park, the detectives ran up the steps to the reception desk with Phil following closely behind. DI Barker flashed his ID at the three receptionists sitting at their computer screens. They shot him bemused glances from the other side of the glass partition. One of them motioned to a tall man with a receding hairline, who had stepped into view from a side door. He slid open the enquiries window and scrutinised the DI.

'I'm looking for a Mr. Dean Roper, I believe he works here.'

'Yes he does. But he finishes work at five o clock.' He checked his watch. About five minutes ago, actually. Can I help? I'm the Sports Centre Manager.'

The DI let out an exasperated sigh, but looked hopeful again when one of the receptionists interrupted.

'He won't have gone home yet. He's booked a meeting room. He usually does on a Thursday. Says he's studying. He likes to study in peace. He does it on a Tuesday too as a matter of fact. Locks himself in for an hour.'

DI Barker exchanged a worried expression with Phil. 'Is there a Mrs. Olive Sloan booked in here for a sauna at five o clock?' he ventured.

The manager checked his computer screen. No, sorry. We don't have anyone booked in of that name. Just the usual six names. One of them books in on Tuesdays too. Barbara Mason.'

'Tell me which room is Dean Roper in?'

'That's two one six. It's on the second floor, same as the sauna as it happens. Take the lift it will take you up to room two ten on the top of the stair well. Turn right after that. The rooms are in consecutive numbers. Two sixteen is opposite the ladies' changing room.'

Reading the manager's name tag on his jacket, he said, 'Thanks Steve. Do you have a master key to this room?'

'Yeees but I'm not allowed to give it to anyone...'

'Come with us and bring it with you. We might need it. This is urgent. Now!'

Steve, responding to the tone of the DI's voice, opened a metal key safe and took out a bunch of keys. He motioned to his staff that he was going out of the office. The receptionist, who had been listening to the conversation intently, cast an astonished expression towards the four individuals as they strode to the lift.

Scarcely had the sliding door of the lift opened fully on the second floor, than the DI pushed through it; DS Watson, Phil and the confused sports centre manager hurried after him down the corridor. Outside room two hundred and sixteen, the DI knocked hard, then tried the handle. As he suspected, it was locked. He motioned to Steve to open it. After a fumbled attempt with the keys, the sports centre manager unlocked the door.

All four characters entered the room in a huddle. Their expletives matched those of the guilty occupants inside.

'Fucking hell, what's going on?' Totally naked, Dean leapt away from Olive who, equally devoid of clothing, stared in fright to see who'd barged in.

'I might ask you the same question,' DI Barker snarled. His mouth twitched as he took in the scene, quickly assessing the situation.

'Dean Roper, I am arresting you for the murder of Ben Sloan.' The DI completed the caution and turned to his sergeant. 'Got that DS Watson?'

'Yes sir.' The DS smirked. She held a pair of handcuffs in her hands and eyed Dean's naked body. She waited for instructions as the DI turned his attention to Olive.

'Olive Sloan I am arresting you for conspiracy to murder.' He continued with the caution, whilst Olive tried unsuccessfully to cover her modesty. Her eyes cast around the room, frantically looking for clothes carelessly tossed aside in the heat of passion. Nothing was in near grabbing distance.

Rachel couldn't hold back her mirth. She enjoyed the luxury of being able to laugh and stare without being observed. Stefan shared her amusement and did nothing to avert his one good eye. He had the civility to say that they ought not to stare, nevertheless he enjoyed the naked couple's discomfiture.

'I wonder if this is the first time the DI has arrested someone in the nude?' Rachel murmured.

Having issued the formal warnings, Barker motioned to his companions to leave the room to allow the suspects to find their clothes. 'I'll give you two minutes to make yourselves look respectable.' He closed the door.

'Respectable is probably not the right word,' he muttered to the detective sergeant as she cradled the handcuffs. After the allotted time he reopened the door, dismayed to find that Dean Roper had vanished. Olive, half-dressed was making her way through a door in the panelled wall clutching the rest of her belongings.

'Fucking hell! DS Watson quick get her.'

'It's a partitioned wall sir, we use it for conferences. Dean has the key,' Steve said unnecessarily.

Barker and Phil ran down the corridor. They swore when they saw the lift had left the floor, but then caught sight of Dean scaling the stairs two at a time dressed in just his trousers and his unlaced trainers. Over his arm he carried his shirt and jacket.

Stefan and Rachel waited until Dean got to the near bottom of the staircase, then combined their efforts to jerk the lace of one of Dean's shoes. He tripped, tried to steady himself then slumped down the remaining three steps on to the floor. His clothes fell from his arm to lie strewn across the bottom step of the stair, whilst one of his trainers slipped from his foot to land at the glass door. Giddily he got back to his feet again. The ghosts, determined not to be beaten, repeated their joint action on his lost trainer. It flew in the air, knocking Dean on the side of his head. Unbalanced he fell to the floor again just when the detective inspector and Phil caught up with him.

Phil recognised Rachel's intervention and smirked. 'Nice work. Thanks Rachel.'

'Yeah, that was phenomenal!' Stefan said. His good eye sparkled.

'You can say that again. We make a great team.' Rachel grinned.

Meanwhile, the DI glanced at Phil with disbelief. Triumph seeped through his incredulity as he recognised what had happened. They shared a conspiratorial grin. Together they hauled Dean to his feet and forced him back up the stairs to room two one six. Olive fully clothed sat handcuffed to a chair whilst DS Watson radioed for another police car. Steve stared at Olive then Dean, unable to take in what he'd just seen.

'I never thought this was going on, honestly,' he said to the detective inspector. He gawped at his workmate in astonishment. Dean growled at him malevolently. DS Watson produced another set of handcuffs and secured him to a chair just when DS Price arrived at the scene.

'You've missed all the fun,' she said gleefully.

Dean snarled as she brought her colleague up to date.

Meanwhile, Phil spotted two abandoned mobiles on the floor. Aware he might corrupt forensic evidence, he touched the DI's arm to get his attention. Barker's eyes gleamed as he took a couple of plastic evidence bags out of his pocket, then with disposable gloves carefully placed a device inside each one.

Olive was crying. This time her distress was genuine. The inspector ignored her tears as he gave instructions to the sports centre manager.

'Steve, will you do me a favour? Go downstairs ahead of us to wait for the police to come. Then send them up here please?'

The manager got up from his chair to obey the instructions, evidently reluctant to leave the drama behind him.

'As soon as they get here, we'll take you back to the hotel,' Barker promised as he turned to his ally. 'We need to get these two to the station in separate vehicles,' he explained.'

Phil grinned and checked his watch. He was surprised to see that the time was only five minutes to six. 'Not bad for a day's work,' he whispered contentedly. 'I'm in no hurry. I'll be back in time to change for dinner and to say goodbye to my friends.'

'I appreciate your efforts in this, and of course Rachel's.'

'I have a feeling she had some help of her own in this,' Phil returned quietly.

'It would be good to let Phil know you were involved,' Rachel turned to Stefan.

'Maybe later. I have a feeling we'll see him tonight, at the graveyard. He won't be able to resist.'

'Yep. I think you're right.'

*

Just over an hour later, the DI walked the few metres to the hotel entrance with Phil where they shook hands.

'Thanks for everything Phil. Too bad you're leaving the country. You would be a valuable asset on the crime team. How I am going to explain all this in my report is going to be challenging. Not everyone in the 'force' will believe me if I tell them how we got the information so quickly.'

'You will have to be creative with the truth. In the meantime, though, if it's alright with you, I wouldn't mind knowing how all this pans out. I'm still getting my head around the knowledge that these charlatans were having an affair, and that their spouses were having an affair too.'

Rachel sighed. 'You've got that bit wrong, Phil. Tracey and Ben were innocent in all this.'

'Don't worry, it will all be revealed after the police have finished their investigation,' Stefan assured her.

'I'll get to the bottom of it pretty soon. Don't worry. I think Olive will crack easily. I'm going to let them stew for an hour or so. Meanwhile I'm going to see Tracey Roper. If I strike lucky I'll have some news for you before the night is through. What time is your flight in the morning?'

'Eleven ten. Gavin is taking us to the airport.'

Phil watched Barker walk across the square to join DS Watson where he turned. They both called, 'Have a good flight.'

CHAPTER SIXTEEN

Clare looked up from her book when Phil walked through the entrance doors of the hotel's lounge. Her legs were tucked under her on a leather arm chair, a position she favoured when reading. At her side was a gin and tonic. He eyed it enviously. 'I could murder a pint.'

'Is murder an appropriate word?' She put down her book to look at him as he slumped into the armchair beside her.

'Probably.' He signalled to the waiter who promptly took his order. 'It's been quite a day. The killer or killers have been apprehended, but I'm at a loss as to how the murder took place. And why? None of it makes sense. It's over to the police now. I've done my bit - with the aid of the paranormal of course. Rachel if you can hear me. Cheers. Absently he looked around him even though he knew it was futile. 'I don't think they're here.'

The waiter returned with Phil's drink, just as his mobile rang.

'It's my mum.'

When he'd finished the conversation with his mother he told Clare that his parents weren't coming for dinner. 'They're worried about this virus that seems to be affecting the elderly. She's reminded me that Dad is seventy and she's sixty-nine, so they've decided they won't take the risk. They are avoiding pubs and crowds. Apparently an acquaintance of mum's has sadly died of it - Jenny. I didn't know her. She lived in London. Anyway, it's not as if we haven't seen them during our trip, and we can Skype every week as usual.'

'It's understandable they don't want to come out, I suppose. Are you disappointed?'

Phil shook his head. 'No, not really. I want what's best for them. They would only be uneasy if they came. Besides it's cold out. They are better off staying at home in the warm.' He finished his pint and got up. 'I'll go and get a shower and change. Did you have a nice walk around the castle and a soak in the bath?'

'Yep. It was good to revisit that old ruin and yes, I had a relaxing time in my bubble bath. So I'm good to go. You've got about half an hour to get ready. We're meeting here. I'd better ring the restaurant and tell them it's a table for six and not nine.'

'Six?' don't you mean seven?'

'No. Emily is coming alone, because they can't get a babysitter. Jack's staying at home with the kids. I hope Dan doesn't cancel. I think he must be getting on for seventy. He seems to be fit though.'

At that moment Dan was sitting in Gavin's Suzuki Ignis, having been collected from his house, to save him driving to the restaurant. Leo snoozed on the back seat. The news on the car radio was dominated by the latest statistics of Coronavirus and advice on how to avoid it. Gavin glanced at his father 'You OK Dad? If you want to change your mind, they'll understand.'

Dan shook his head. 'Don't worry I'm fine. I've been following the advice, there's not much more I can do. After tonight, I will avoid going to crowded places. Anyway the restaurant we're going to is spacious, so let's not worry and enjoy ourselves. It will be a while before we see Phil and Clare again. Phil has done so much for us, it seems right that we say goodbye tonight.'

'As long as you are sure.'

Dan nodded.

*

In the graveyard Rachel was relating to her mother and their spirit friends the events of the afternoon.

'So they were starkers?' Big Steve said with a gleam in his eye.

'Not a stitch between them,' Stefan confirmed. He couldn't hide a twitch of his bony face as he recalled the drama of the early evening.

Rachel rolled her eyes at their hilarity though she allowed herself to smile. 'It was funny to see the shock on their faces,' she said, joining in their glee.

Anna shared their amusement and congratulated them on their efforts to apprehend Dean Roper.

'The thing that troubles me is how they all got mixed up in this and why poor Ben Sloan had to die. He was adamant that he'd only met Tracey a few months ago and that it was just platonic. In fact they didn't see each other that often. Neither did they always formally arrange to meet. Most of the times they got together were ad hoc. Just a

question of them running into each other every now and again.'

'I think it was slightly more than that Mum. I'm not saying they were having an affair, but Tracey was very upset over Ben's death. A lot more than Olive seemed to be. According to Tracey they all knew each other from their school days, except for Dean. He got involved with Olive long after he'd married Tracey.'

'I've been thinking about that too,' Stefan offered. 'Is it possible that by some freak coincidence, Olive met Dean at the sports centre, neither of them realising until much later down the line of their affair, that both Olive and Ben knew Tracey? That knowledge probably would have been manageable, until the day Tracey confided in Dean that she'd bumped into an old friend in Ben Sloan.' Stefan paused letting his words sink in. Before he could finish, Anna seized upon the likely ending.

'Yes, and that would make Dean feel threatened of discovery and even jealous. You know, double standards. Alright for him to have an affair but not his wife.' She paused thinking hurriedly. 'Then he hit on the idea of threatening Ben to keep away from Tracey…' She trailed off.

'You might be right Anna, but I think Tracey genuinely wanted a normal friendship and despite everything else she loves her husband. She seemed warm and affable to me. Her distress over Ben's death was that of an old friend grieving,' Stefan interrupted.

'I bet she won't love her husband any

more when she finds out what he's done!' Margareta put in.

'I daresay not,' Stefan agreed. I reckon Dean played on Ben's nerves to try to keep him away from Tracey knowing that he wouldn't tell Olive in case she thought he really was having an affair. Ben couldn't risk telling Olive what was happening and for whatever reason couldn't confide in Tracey. So he kept the anonymous text messages to himself. It must have been stressful having no-one to talk to.' Stefan's one good eye swivelled across each of the gaunt faces of his companions as they thought up theories of their own.

'Then when Dean got more and more involved with Olive, they hatched a plan to get rid of Ben,' suggested Margareta who had been listening intently to the various hypotheses the spirits had put forward.

'Hence the increased threatening messages and hanging around the house. Dean's not very bright is he?'

'No he isn't. I agree with that,' Stefan nodded smiling at Margareta. 'I think it would only have been a matter of time before Ben found the courage to confide in Olive. He might even have gone to the police. If he'd told Tracey, she might have challenged Dean and things could have turned out differently. Worse, probably. Meanwhile, Dean decided that Ben had to be disposed of. Olive had to entice him away from the house so that they could kill him.'

'It's hard to believe that Olive would agree to it,' Rachel said. 'After all those years together.'

'Perhaps Dean gave her an ultimatum,' suggested Margareta. Tom who had wafted behind Margareta agreed. 'Yes, it was Ben's death or the end of their affair and neither wanted to end it because…'

'The sex was too good,' Big Steve added. Anna cast him a withering glance. Rachel turned her face away to hide a smirk. Her mother's looks were enough to kill.

'I agree with Big Steve. Olive and Dean were obsessed with each other. They were enjoying steamy sex sessions and they wanted more than clandestine meetings. It was obvious,' Stefan said, recalling to mind the scenes he and Rachel had witnessed. 'I think they were in love. Bizarre though it may seem.'

'I wonder if Olive's old loyalties to Ben would demand a trade off. You know, eye for an eye, tooth for tooth?' Anna aimed her question at no-one in particular. 'They'd known each other such a long time. So sad to think of a marriage ending like that.'

'You mean Tracey would be next?' Rachel suggested.

Anna nodded.

'I doubt Tracey will still love Dean when she finds out what he did,' Margareta repeated.

*

Speculation over Ben's death was being discussed amongst the friends gathered around a table at "The Dee View" restaurant.

'I'm finding it hard to believe that Tracey might have been involved romantically with Ben Sloan,' Phil was saying. 'She seemed genuinely sincere. I realise now that Rachel led me to Dean through Tracey. How she knew about the charity shop beats me. There was no mention of it in the investigation report.'

'I'm astonished that my daughter has been helping you Phil. Those paranormal events took some getting used to when you were here last. Now it's happening again. Everything returned to normal after you left. At least as normal as you can expect after losing my wife so soon after my daughter.'
Abigail put a reassuring hand on his and squeezed it tightly. Dan appreciated the gesture and smiled at his daughter-in-law.

Phil shrugged. 'I've had no contact with her since I left here actually. It's uncanny that we're working together again. But just as before, I knew Rachel wasn't working alone and that she had some help. I was sensing another spiritual presence. This might sound peculiar but I felt it was male.'

How can you be sure?' Gavin cut into his sirloin steak and threw a perplexed expression at Phil before putting the meat into his mouth.

'When I first made contact with Rachel this time round, I think it was in the hotel actually…I managed to ascertain that she wasn't alone, and that neither Anna nor her old colleague Laticia were with her. Also, the power of the nudges I got were stronger. It's the type I get normally, when a male spirit is trying to make contact during a séance. Through all my dealings with Rachel in the past there has been a distinct edge. Something recognisable, so I knew it was her. Other nudges were different. They were rougher, sharper. Sorry I can't explain it better than that.'

'You didn't see either of them throughout their involvement in this case?' Emily asked.

'No. I've rarely seen any of the spirits that contact me, though there have been occasions when I could see the outline of something intangible.'

'So you communicate almost the same as you did when we had séances?' Dan asked. 'Pieces of paper flying around and you getting punches.'

Phil sighed. 'Yes, though the questions I ask Rachel and her comrade are based on what I know, and their answers have to be easy for them to respond in the negative or the positive. They can try to influence me in my actions but without extra knowledge it's difficult to get to the root of the matter. It's a bit easier working with the police because they have theories of their own and a lot more experience in dealing with criminals. We were able to share information. That nosey neighbour of Olive's also gave us a push in the right direction! We got to the sports centre just at the right time.' He smiled as he recalled the scene. 'I know I shouldn't laugh, but...' He took a sip of his wine.

Gavin laughed with him. 'Not the best circumstances to be arrested, with your trousers down. So to speak.'

*

At the police station, DI Barker allowed himself a cup of tea. He read through his notes and waited for DS Watson to return with the suspects and confiscated mobile phones. Two were taken from Dean Roper and one belonging to Olive Sloan's. When the detective sergeant arrived at the station she'd followed the procedure of getting the devices recorded in the appropriate files and arranged to join the DI in the interview room. Meanwhile Barker got himself a snack from the petrol station shop across the road from the hub.

When the two detectives were ready, they played back the messages on the three devices and were shocked to learn that the pair had planned to dispose of Tracey Roper.

'This evil duo are not the innocents they would have us believe, DI Barker remarked as he finished off the last of his sandwich.

DS Watson agreed. She munched on a cheese and onion pasty allowing flakes of pastry to fall on to a serviette which she'd carefully laid out in front of her. After she'd finished eating, she scooped up the mess, folded the paper serviette provided by the service station and threw it into the wastepaper bin.

'I think we'll go for the throat with this one,' DI Barker confided. 'She's a mess as it is. I wouldn't be surprised that with some careful prodding we'll get a confession pretty quickly. Let's get that new Detective Constable Shahida Massey in on it to listen. Give her some experience dealing with this kind of case. Nobody can say that we didn't give Olive Sloan plenty of female company. We have a Geraldine Draper acting as her solicitor. I haven't met her before, have you?'

'No sir.'

When the three police officers entered the interview room, they found Olive Sloan slouched in a chair, her head resting on the table. She looked up, red and bleary eyed as they walked in. She nervously watched them take their places.

DC Shahida Massey positioned her chair near the door, away from the table. DS Watson carried Olive's mobile in a transparent evidence bag. She put it on the table in front of her and observed their suspect's eyes warily resting on it.

'We're waiting for the duty solicitor to arrive, Mrs. Sloan, she said.'

Olive nodded dispassionately. She barely lifted her head when Geraldine Draper arrived.

After the preliminary introductions, recorded on tape, DI Barker plunged straight into the interview.

'So, Mrs. Sloan, not only were you a conspirator in the murder of your husband, but you conspired with Dean Sloper to murder his wife Tracey Sloper.'

'I didn't kill my husband,' Olive bleated. Tears ran down her cheeks and she glanced at the detective constable looking for sympathy. DC Shahida Massey's expression remained impassive. She'd been warned that the suspect might try to appeal to her feminine side.

'I agree, you didn't kill him,' the DI said slowly, and congratulated himself how Olive looked pathetically hopeful that she might get away with non-imprisonment.

'No, no,' the DI repeated softly, then his tone hardened. 'You didn't put the knife in, but you helped Dean Roper to do it, didn't you? All along you told us you knew nothing about your husband's murder, but you facilitated his death. Didn't you? You deliberately led him to Holywell, encouraged him to hire a boat, and accompanied your lover on to the water to stab him. Didn't you?'

Olive's breath was taken away and she began to sob. 'It wasn't my idea. It was Dean's.'

'You collaborated with him though. Why Mrs. Sloan? Why didn't you divorce him? Was your marriage so bad? Was he a wife beater?'

Olive shook her head, still sobbing. She took the box of tissues from DS Watson whose expression was as poker faced as DC Shahida Massey's.

'No, none of those things. He was boring,' she choked. 'Boring, boring. I was bored with him!' She sniffed and managed to control her tears. 'Dean wanted him out of the way. He said it would be better for both of us, not having him around.'

'And part of the deal was that his wife had to be out of the picture too. You didn't want Tracey around either.' This time DS Watson spoke. 'If Ben had to go, then so did Tracey?'

She nodded, her head kept bent low.

The police officers scrutinised the weeping woman capable of conspiring to kill two innocent people.

DI Barker seized the evidence bag and switched on Olive's mobile. He pressed the saved sent messages button and scrolled back until he found the right place.

'Here we are, listen to this message sent just yesterday; a conversation between you and your lover,'

"I told you not to ring me on this mobile!"
"Dean I had to warn you, the police have been here again, they're on to us.'
"What do you mean? Did they mention my name?'
They asked about Tracey. They think I was jealous of her and Ben."
"Don't worry about Tracey, they've been to see her. Don't panic Olive, they don't know anything. I'll see you tonight."

'So how did you do it Olive? Did you watch your husband go to the boathouse then creep behind him in a disguise? Did you get in a boat with Dean Roper? I'm sure we'll be able to pick it up on the CCTV cameras now we know what we're looking for. No doubt the clothes you wore will be in your house. I'm sure a search warrant will find them. So why don't you save all of us some time.'

Olive took a deep breath. The police officers could tell from her hunched body language she'd given up. They listened intently as she explained how she had taken an extra set of clothing with her to Holywell and had put them in the boot of the car without Ben knowing. This included a black bobble hat and a navy blue full length quilted coat.

After Ben left her at the well to go to the lake, she'd rushed to the car park, removed her pink bomber jacket, put on the fresh guise then met Dean outside the boathouse booking office. Over her arm she held a holdall containing her pink jacket and a towel. Her accomplice wore a dark jacket over a tracksuit. Underneath he wore his skin tight swim wear leggings and vest. A baseball cap covered his head. Olive waited outside whilst he went into the office to pay for the boat hire.

In the vessel, he'd removed his tracksuit and jacket and had slipped into the water. The leather sheathed hunting knife fitted safely inside an inner pocket of his vest.

Meanwhile, Olive slipped her coat off so that she could expertly keep the craft moving a safe distance away from Ben's. They waited for the roving ranger to carry out his checks on the opposite side of the lake. After Dean had stabbed Ben, he meticulously returned the knife to its sheath and put it back in his inner vest pocket. Then making sure no-one was looking, he lowered Ben into the water. He easily swam back to his accomplice and deftly pulled himself out of the water to re-board. He lay on the bottom of the craft, using the towel Olive had provided to dry himself. He wrapped the towel around the weapon still in its cover and put it in Olive's bag. He removed his damp clothing which he put on top of the towel and then pulled on his tracksuit. Meanwhile, Olive manoeuvred the oars as quickly as she could to get away from the murder scene.

'This is where you utilised your skill as a rower,' the DI acknowledged.

'Yes. I thought you'd begun to suspect me when you told me you'd been to see Rob Taylor and you asked me about my rowing abilities. I wondered if you mentioned Tracey to unnerve me and if you suspected Dean.' She stopped sniffing, appearing relieved to confess her guilt.

The DI had no intention of enlightening Olive that it was only a few hours ago when they discovered Dean Roper's involvement.

'Tell me, what happened next.'

Olive explained that after Dean stabbed Ben, they left the boathouse together hand in hand, all the time looking down to avoid any cameras. Olive carried the holdall with their clothes and the knife.

They thought if they looked like a couple they wouldn't be suspected of murder if picked up on the cameras.

The three police officers listened with disgust as Olive related her story without a trace of remorse.

'Finally, Mrs. Sloan I know you are telling the truth,' Barker announced.

After hanging around to wait for Olive's explanation, the ghosts circled the room triumphantly. 'Our suspicions were correct. She was in the boat with Dean,' Rachel said.

'Yes, they planned it together. She actually knew what was happening to her husband when she hid from view. Evil,' Stefan added with disgust.

'She won't get off lightly and she's incriminated Dean, so I think we can go, Rachel said.'

'I agree, I've had enough of this vile pair.'

On his return to the station after the arrests the DI had asked his staff to have another look at the CCTV footage of the boat house. A sharp eyed detective constable had examined it more closely and noticed an image of Olive waiting outside the reception area for Dean. The footage showed the two suspects walking away from the boathouse together to get into a boat and again half an hour later on their return. The information had been passed to Barker prior to his interview with Olive.

DI Barker breathed deeply, declining to admit to Olive that the police had seen the image of a woman and man on the video tape previously, but had originally dismissed it, as they were looking for a single person.

After Olive and Dean left the boathouse, they separated. Dean sprinted to the outskirts of the town to his parked Toyota Corolla hatchback. Olive went to the public toilets in the town centre where she changed back into her original clothes. She then took the holdall containing her dark coat, hat, the towel wrapped knife and Dean's damp leggings and vest to the town car park. There she put them in the boot of her Volkswagen. She returned to the boathouse ostensibly to wait for her husband.

'And that's when you started the charade of your husband going missing.' DI Barker said.

She nodded her head, avoiding the DI's eyes.

'And the bag with the clothes and the knife? Do you still have it?"

She nodded.

Barker didn't bother to hide his contempt. He signalled that Olive Sloan could be taken to another room to talk to her solicitor. He noticed that the solicitor hadn't attempted to stop Olive talking, all through her confession. He wondered what her tactics were. Perhaps she would get Olive to plead that she'd been manipulated by Dean and so get a shorter sentence. The DI grunted then put measures in place to search Olive's house for the bag of clothes. He was hoping that there would be residue from the boat, and possibly some blood from the weapon rubbed on to each suspect's clothing. Though her confession was enough to charge her; at that point he only had circumstantial evidence to prove Dean was guilty. He anticipated that there would be fingerprints on the knife and its cover. A thought struck him that she may have washed the contents of the holdall. He followed her to the adjoining room to ask her.

'No, I haven't had time. There's been too many prying journalists and visitors to my house. They're still in the boot of my car. I intended to burn them.' She hung her head but the DI turned away in disgust, impervious to what he perceived as a charade for grief and remorse. He sent a message to his offices to check Olive's car then returned to his office with DS Watson.

'They made several mistakes Sir,' the detective sergeant said.

'Big ones,' Barker agreed. 'Roper kept the knife and Olive left the holdall with all their belongings in her car. Another stupid thing to do.'

DS Watson shrugged. 'I suppose she was waiting for the opportunity to dispose of them without anyone watching her. 'It's less than a week since her husband's death. Perhaps she was sorry for what happened and couldn't face it.'

'I doubt it,' the DI grunted.

Armed with extra knowledge the police officers began their interrogation of Dean Roper. He proved to be a harder nut to crack. He continually denied any involvement in Ben Sloan's death. He insisted that although he was having an affair with Ben's wife, that he had nothing to do with his killing.

'Mr. Roper we have plenty of evidence. We have your messages on your two mobiles and on Olive Sloan's. Furthermore we have managed to identify your voice on the messages to Ben Sloan on his own device which we retrieved from the back pocket of his jeans.'

'You can't prove that was me,' he said.

'How about this then?' DI Barker asked patiently. He smoothed down his moustache between his finger and thumb and looked Dean in the eye. 'Olive called you and we have that conversation on her device that mentions you by name. Furthermore, she has confessed and told us everything. We have checked the CCTV at the boathouse again and we have no doubt that the camera has picked you up. She has given us a good description of the image you tried to effect. You may have had your heads down after you killed Ben Sloan, but we have a good picture of you standing at the reception desk where you hired a vessel. We have another image of Olive standing nearby. Furthermore she kept your clothes and the knife.'

'The stupid bitch. I told her to get rid of them.' Dean flew into a rage and screamed out more uncomplimentary expletives about Olive. The police officers left him alone to cool down.

Outside the hub, the two detectives enjoyed their cigarettes. Dean's last few words rolled around in DS Watson's head and presently she voiced her thoughts. She exhaled a whirl of apple scented smoke.

'Roper is annoyed with Olive for keeping the clothes and knife. I'm amazed he didn't put the knife in the lake?'

The DI dragged on his fag. 'His own meticulous controlling methods played against him. It was his possession and automatically he replaced it in the holder instead of having the sense to get rid of it. Good for us, but bad for him.' He grinned.

'They made too many mistakes Sir.'

Back in his office, DI Barker found a message from Tracey Roper. As her husband hadn't come home from work she'd rung the sports centre and been told that Dean had been arrested. She wanted to know why and when she could see him. Sighing he asked DC Shahida Massey to accompany him to see Roper's wife. An hour later they were greeted by a tearful Tracey who led them into her sitting room.

After she'd got over the initial shock, the DI asked her if she had any family living close by who could keep her company.

Tracey shook her head despondently. 'My daughters will be devastated. I will leave it until tomorrow before I tell them.' She choked on her words, speaking incoherently. 'Neither of them live locally. I can scarcely believe it myself.' Her body shook as the horror took hold of her.

'What about your friends, Mrs. Roper. Can we call them for you?' DC Massey suggested. She eyed the DI for approval as she spoke. He nodded and got up suggesting he made some tea.

'No, I don't want tea thank you Inspector. My friend Tilly lives a few streets away, I'm sure she'll come round if I ask her. I need something stronger than tea. I've got a bottle of wine in the fridge. We can share it.'

'Do you want to call her now, whilst we are here?' We could ask the family liaison officer to come and sit with you if she isn't available.'

Still shaking, Tracey pressed Tilly's contact number on her mobile. Without going into detail, she asked her to come round.

'She said she'd be half an hour, Inspector.' She turned her tear stained face to him. 'I feel so ashamed.'

'You shouldn't feel any shame at all Mrs. Roper.' He didn't tell her that her life had been in danger. He guessed she would work that out herself in time.

'He's been acting strangely for about a year now. It got worse in fact ever since I ran into Ben Sloan again. But when I asked him if he minded me seeing Ben every now and again he seemed fine with it. I never tried to hide anything from him because there wasn't any need. Then I started to wonder if he had another woman because I found another mobile and he kept slipping out of the house. At first I thought it was a work phone because the only contacts were a list of six women. I didn't think anything unusual about that because I know women like to go to saunas.

But he started working later than usual or he would come home and then go out again never telling me where he was going. I convinced myself I was being ridiculous and it couldn't be happening and that the phone was for work. I was obviously right about the other women, I never dreamt he would kill though.'

'I'm afraid there was only one woman, Mrs Roper. The other names were fictitious to not only make you think they were sauna bookings should you or anyone else find his phone but to conceal her identity.'

'Oh. You mean they were all Olive?'

'Sorry, but in a manner of speaking yes.'

Tracey fell into a fresh torrent of sobs. The DI waited for her weeping to subside before speaking again. He felt sorry for the woman but he still had a task to do.

'Talking of mobile phones, Mrs. Roper, would you mind if we borrowed yours for inspection?'

'Mine. Why? Surely you don't think I'm involved in Ben's death?'

'It's just to eliminate you from our enquiries. We will return it to you tomorrow. I promise. I need to make sure I have tied up all loose ends.'

Reluctantly Tracey handed over her phone and watched DC Massey put it in a plastic evidence bag.

'Thank you. Much appreciated.'

When they heard a knock on the door, Shahida Massey got up to answer it. In the sitting room, DI Barker and Tracey heard the shock in Tilly's voice when the DC introduced herself.

'Police! Oh no! What's happened?' She pushed her way through the hallway carrying a bottle of wine, then stopped and blinked as she took in the scene before her. Tracey got up and collapsed in Tilly's arms. Cradling the alcohol in one arm and her friend in the other, the two women sank down on the sofa. The police officers left Tracey to make the necessary explanations.

CHAPTER SEVENTEEN

In the *"Dee View"* restaurant the group of friends were getting ready to leave. Clare and Abigail went to the cloakroom, whilst Gavin made arrangements for a taxi. Waiting in the restaurant foyer, Phil received a call from DI Barker.

'I thought you might like to hear the details, since you played a big part in the investigation.'

'Yes, please go ahead.' He mouthed silently to his companions to tell them the name of the caller. He grinned as they all clustered around him trying to listen.

The call finished just as the taxi arrived. They sat silently, bursting to talk, but waited until they were dropped off in the centre of town. Dan was going to spend the night in the spare room at Gavin's and Abi's.

'So, did I hear right? Dean Roper has confessed to killing Ben Sloan?' Gavin asked. He put his arm around Abi shivering in the cold night air, despite wearing a thick coat.

Phil nodded. 'It seems Olive capitulated almost straight away. She admitted that she had planned with her lover to kill her husband.' He quickly related to the astonished group gathered around him, everything the DI had informed him.

'In broad daylight – well almost,' Clare amended 'and under the noses of the boathouse staff,' she commented shaking her head incredulously. She turned to Phil.

'Your instincts last Friday were correct. Almost as soon as we'd looked out of that hotel window, you felt something was wrong.'

'Yes, it's true but I couldn't figure out what I was sensing.'

'It was a cold and calculated murder. Olive knew what she was conspiring to do.' Clare shuddered as her thoughts drifted back to the evening before the wedding.

'Did you say that Ben Sloan's funeral is tomorrow?' Abigail asked, she leaned heavily against Gavin's arm. 'Will Olive be allowed to attend?'

'Yes, it is. I should imagine the police will permit her to attend - under guard of course. She might be handcuffed, I don't know,' Phil shrugged. 'It might be her last chance of freedom as it were, before she's locked up for a very long time.'

'Do you think a woman who plotted to kill her husband with her lover is going to want to attend his funeral?' Gavin asked. 'Not content with that, she shamelessly conspired with her lover to kill his wife too. She's really evil under all that façade of grief.'

'It sounds like not only have you helped find the murderer but you have saved Tracey's life,' Dan said quietly. 'Well done.'

'I bet that unhappy woman feels terrible to know that she is married to a murderer,' Abigail said.

'And worse to think that her husband was plotting to kill her,' Emily chipped in. 'She might not have figured that out. Let's hope she never does.'

Phil sighed. 'Barker hasn't told her, but I should imagine Tracey will eventually suspect that she may have been Dean's next victim.'

Dan grunted. 'Shall we discuss something more cheerful now?'

Gavin immediately assumed a serious expression. 'Yes, you're right Dad. This is macabre conversation especially on Phil and Clare's last night. Anyway I think it's too cold to stand around talking much longer. Abi here is almost shaking! Let's go Dad. I think it might start to rain soon.' He turned to face Phil and Clare. 'I will pick you up at seven thirty tomorrow morning to take you to the airport.'

'Thanks Gav for doing that. I would have managed somehow, but it's pandemonium in the morning getting the children ready for school,' Emily said. 'Jack is on an early shift so he won't be able to do it.'

'No worries. Goodnight everybody.'

Dan turned to shake hands with Phil and hug Clare. 'Have a good flight both of you. I won't come to the airport. I'll walk back home in the morning with Leo. He'll enjoy the exercise. He's probably wondering where I am. He isn't used to being left on his own in a strange house. It's a good job he's not a puppy, he'd have chewed up all your lovely cushions by now.'

Abigail's eyebrows shot up. 'What?'

Dan reassured her quickly. 'Don't worry. He's past that stage. I've left him some toys to play with and some of his favourite treats to eat. He'll be fine. I'll just walk him around the garden for a few minutes before we go to bed tonight. We had a good walk this afternoon in the woods. I threw a stick for him lots of times. He likes to run and fetch. So he'll probably want to sleep off all that exercise.'

'Perhaps he should sleep in the spare bedroom with you tonight in case he gets distressed,' Gavin offered.

'Thanks. That's good of you.'

'I'll walk you home Em,' Phil offered. 'What about you Clare? Do you fancy a short stroll to Bell lane?'

'Sounds good. The exercise will work off some of that rich food.'

On their way to her house, Emily asked her brother about his new career prospects. He explained his plans in more detail.

'So if it all goes well, I will be seeing more of you even though you won't be coming home permanently?' Emily's eyes danced.

'With a bit of luck, yes. It will mean travelling back here a few times each year. They said they'd contact me sometime tomorrow, so I'll know more then. I don't know when. I'm sorry I won't be able to tell you the outcome face to face, but we can Skype as usual.'

'Right. Let's do it tomorrow night. Say about nine o clock. It will give you time to sort yourselves out and I will have put the children to bed. Even if you haven't heard anything I want to know if you are home safely.'

'We'd better make it later. We have a long drive from the airport. If we are delayed I will text you, and of course I will let you know as soon as I can when I hear about the job.'

After they'd said their goodbyes, it came as no surprise to Clare when Phil suggested a last visit to St. Winefride's graveyard.

'I just want to thank Rachel and let her know that the case is solved. I'm not sure I will be able to make contact. For some reason making a connection with her here in the cemetery has always been very faint except that time in the church at the wedding.'

'You said that it was because it was the twenty ninth of February. A leap year when anything can happen!' Clare's eyes twinkled as she teased her husband.

'True.'

'She may already know the outcome,' Clare suggested, pulling her coat collar up. A gust of wind blew through the dark cemetery.

'It's more than likely. She might have gone to the police station after the arrests to listen to the interrogations. I didn't sense her presence in the car when they dropped me off at the hotel.'

In the darkness, Clare, her face full of admiration for her husband, listened to him explain his reasons for visiting the grave yard one last time. His explanation was no surprise to her, she'd half expected him to suggest it. 'I get this feeling that she is waiting for me to visit her here tonight. Almost as if we have unfinished business.'

'Tying up loose ends,' Clare acknowledged.

He took her hand and guided her along the concrete path towards Rachel's grave.

Hovering nearby, Rachel, Stefan and Anna observed them. Just a few metres away Margareta, Tom, Big Steve and Desmond hung around waiting to hear the outcome of this late night visit. Very soon other curious spirits hovered in the background. Even more drifted around the old abbey roof top unaccustomed to seeing visitors in the graveyard at such a late hour.

'*As I guessed, he's here. He's brought Clare with him too,' Rachel commented.*

'*Didn't you say they were going out with your father and Gavin and Abigail for a farewell meal? They probably decided to call here for the last time before going back to Romania,' Anna said.*

'*It will be good to use up the last of our powers to say goodbye,' Stefan said. 'I'm hoping he'll realise that I've been helping Rachel. We knew each other well when I was on the other side. It was only two years ago. If we just give him a little nudge so that everyone here will be able to witness it before our extra powers vanish, it will be a good farewell. It's a shame really just when I was getting used to it - the energy force I mean,' he finished his last sentence wistfully.*

'*We must try not to hurt him too much,' Rachel said. 'I don't want our goodbye to be a painful experience for him. Perhaps we can take it in turns with gentle nudges and shoves until we get him to stand at your graveside. Then we will just have to hope he will figure it out that it was you working with me.'*

'It's a shame that Abigail's lovely bouquet has withered,' Clare observed sadly. 'Perhaps she'll come and tidy up the grave.' She looked down at the loosened stems of the white and pink ranunculus. The wind had blown them about. Stray petals tangled with a cluster of late snowdrops that grew in the grass verges.

Stefan gazed at Rachel thoughtfully. 'I think I've got a better idea. A painless one.'

Phil let go of Clare's hand as she stooped to collect the wilting flowers. He took the opportunity to stand closer to Rachel's headstone.

'Hi Rachel, I feel you can hear me. Unusually your presence is very strong here tonight. It's all around me. I thought I'd let you know that the police have got a confession from both those detestable people. I could think of worse words to call them but I respect the spirits in this cemetery. Suffice to say Dean Roper and Olive Sloan will be spending a lot of time at Her Majesty's pleasure.'

At this point Phil looked around, half expecting, half hoping to see Rachel. Annoyed he'd allowed himself to get carried away with such fancies, he continued speaking.

'Thanks for all your help in getting justice for Ben Sloan. It would have been impossible for me without your help, even though some of your punches were a bit painful. I know you didn't mean to hurt me and it was your best way to communicate with me. Another good outcome from all this is, that the detective inspector is a convert. He didn't take a lot of convincing actually. He told me when we first met that he wouldn't rule anything out, even the paranormal. You communicated earlier in the week that you weren't alone. I wish I could find out who was with you. I know it wasn't your mother. But still, maybe you can pass on my gratitude.'

Rachel positioned herself as close as she could get to Stefan. 'Right are you ready?'

He nodded, then together they concentrated on lifting the loosened white petals that had drifted away from Abigail's bridal bouquet. Several were raised to Phil's eye level. He blinked as they trailed in front of him.

Assured they had his attention, the ghosts propelled the petals away from Rachel's graveside and along the concrete path towards Stefan's grave. Half way towards their destination, the trail of petals hovered in a cluster waiting for Phil to follow.

Fascinated, Phil grabbed Clare's hand as she straightened up bewildered at the appearance of a cloud of dismembered flower heads. Together they tracked the fluttering white line.

'What's happening?' Clare gasped. She held her husband's hand tightly, half afraid, half excited.

'It's a sign. I think she or they, are trying to show us something.'

The trail of petals circled in the air, waiting for them to keep up. Satisfied they had Phil and Clare's full attention, the ghosts propelled the petals further along the path. Finally, they scattered the flora over Stefan's grave.

Phil knelt down to peer at the name engraved on the headstone. 'I can't read the epitaph.' He pulled his mobile out of his pocket, hoping to use the torch. 'Damn the battery is flat. Have you got yours?'

Clare shook her head. 'I left it in the hotel.'

'I don't suppose you've got a match?'

'As it happens I have.'

Phil looked at his wife in amazement. Neither of them smoked. He knew his wife carried an assortment of tiny useful things in her bag, but he'd never known her to have matches. She handed him a small flap of safety matches with the name St. Winefride's Hotel emblazoned on the front. He caught her eyes in amusement.

'Thought they'd come in handy,' she grinned. 'Though I hadn't expected this.'

Phil struck a match and knelt down to hold it against the headstone. 'Bloody hell, it's Stefan Kadinsky! Rachel is this who has been helping you?'

The petals rose up in the air then fluttered to the ground again.

'Is that the Stefan you told me about?' Clare bent down to read the epitaph. 'The one who was on that computer course with you and Gavin?'

'The very one. He got killed in a terrible explosion, unlucky chap.' He blew out the match which was near its end, then struck another so that Clare could read the full inscription.

'Well, Stefan, I can only say thanks again old mate for your help along with Rachel's. So sorry that we are meeting again like this.' He blew out the second match then reached for Clare's hand again. 'Come on, our work is done.'

The spirits followed them as far as they could to the cemetery gates. As they hovered, watching the pair walk back to the hotel, they heard the cathedral clock strike eleven o clock.

'That went very well!' Anna exulted, doubly pleased at having witnessed the two ghosts demonstrate their power in the cemetery as well as having helped solve the crime. 'It's good that you were able to convey to Phil that Stefan was involved too!'

Rachel nodded, pleased with their joint work.

'It's a shame you've only got an hour left to use your special ghostly skills. After midnight you'll just be like the rest of we spirits,' Margareta commented. 'Bloody powerless!' she lamented.

'In the meantime we could have a bit of fun with those sixty minutes?' Tom said with a twinkle in his eye. How about going

up to the belfry and see if you can get a bell to ring?'

'Impossible!' Stefan said. It's hard enough with paper and cardboard!'

'You managed to lift Dean's shoe at the sports centre. They are quite heavy,' Tom replied stubbornly.

'Trainer actually, they are lighter than a shoe…' Stefan corrected.

'There must be something you could do together with your combined strength. It seems such a waste.'

'Now Tom, you know full well that these powers are to be used for good, not for frivolity!' Anna rebuked him, though she couldn't stop a hint of a smile to trace her lips.

'The clanger might not be too heavy,' Tom persisted wilfully. 'Perhaps the leather loop that the clanger hangs on could be moved. I could use the energy in my titanium legs. Combined with your powers we could shift it?'

'How about trying to open one of those hymn books?' Big Steve suggested. 'If some fall off the pews it won't damage them too much,' he winked.' You could say it was in the line of your duty. You know, practising to see how far you can increase your energy?'

'I'm having nothing to do with it,' Anna said. 'Remember I am an Assessor. A respectable one at that!' She left the rest of the spirits and glided back to her grave, slid into her coffin and made herself comfortable for the night. Anna was well aware that *without her presence, they would get up to mischief. Tom was always looking for a diversion to amuse them all, and the others would encourage him. She closed her eyes whispering the words she'd heard uttered several times in and around the graveyard. 'You're a long time dead.'*

Stefan caught the mood of their pals and grinned at Rachel. 'What do you think? We ought to celebrate somehow.' She returned his smile. 'What have you got in mind?'

He gesticulated with his hand that she should follow him. 'Come on!'

In their hotel room, Phil and Clare were getting ready for bed. They'd turned the television on just loud enough for them to check the latest news and weather. Their immediate concern was air travel. Once they'd put their minds at rest that their flight hadn't been cancelled their anxiety shifted upon hearing how Coronavirus was affecting Transylvanian life and the rest of the world. They learned that tougher measures would take place the following evening which may lead to a lock down in Romania.

'We knew we'd probably have to go into quarantine when we got back,' Clare remarked, but I wasn't expecting this bug to impact the way it has.' She got into bed and turned off the bedside lamp.

Phil got into bed beside her and yawned. 'Perhaps it will blow over in a few weeks and we'll be back to normal by Easter. Let's get some rest, another early start in the morning.' He turned off his bedside lamp and closed his eyes. Just as he nodded off he thought he'd heard the sound of a church bell ringing.

CHAPTER EIGHTEEN

Walking through the reception area on their way to the hotel restaurant for breakfast, they were surprised to see Sergeant Ward in the lobby. As soon as he saw Phil and Clare he moved towards them excitedly.

'Good morning. I'm so pleased to have found you before you leave for Bucharest.'

'What's up officer?' Phil said cheerfully. 'Don't tell me they've escaped from custody.'

The sergeant laughed. 'No, no, nothing like that. I just wanted to come and say thank you for all your work and to say goodbye. The DI has told me how much your invaluable input has helped us to solve that terrible murder case.' He held himself straight with pride. 'He thanked me too, would you believe, for getting you involved.'

Phil shook hands with him. 'I was glad to have been of some use. It was a nasty affair.'

'Yes, indeed it was. Well, I mustn't keep you from your breakfast. Goodbye to you both. Safe flight. Give my regards to your sister too.'

'That was nice of him,' Clare commented as she laid their room card on a table.

'Yes, it was. I wonder if he's lining me up for another case in the future,' Phil grinned broadly. He helped himself to scrambled eggs and toast.

'Well if they ever do need your services again, let's hope it won't be another murder. Clare raised her eyebrows and breathed contentedly as she reached for a croissant. Do you want tea or coffee with that?'

'Tea please. It's not as if we're going to be around that much. Even if I manage to get this project off the ground, the time I spend here will be limited. I wouldn't be able to go swanning off at the whim of the police.'

Clare unfolded a napkin and put it over her knee before spreading butter on her croissants. 'Let's hope they keep their word and let you know today about the funding. It'll be marvellous if you can go ahead with it.'

Phil poured tea into two cups. 'I have a good feeling about it and I'm sure they'll let me know as soon as they can.'

At twenty five past eight Gavin parked his Suzuki Ignis outside the hotel and helped them put their suitcases into the back of the car. Abigail sat in the front passenger seat, her blonde hair pinned up at the back with a silver slide that looked like a buckle. Clare admired it and asked her if it was antique. Three red garnets were set where the clip rested.

'It's quite old actually. My grandmother gave it me for the wedding. You know, something old, something new and all that. I've taken a fancy to it. I don't think the stones are valuable, but hey I don't mind.'

At Manchester airport, Gavin dropped them off at the entrance. 'You'll have to be quick getting your luggage out, we're not supposed to stop, but it'll save you a long walk from the car park. You may as well go straight through passport control and get ready to board, so it's pointless us coming in with you. It will take ages getting everything checked. Thanks for everything, hope to see you soon.'

Waiting for the gate to be announced for their flight, Phil got the text message he was waiting for. He caught Clare's anxious expression as he started to read it. Her face relaxed as she saw a relieved smile curve his lips. 'The funding is through, we can start working on it next month.'

'Congratulations darling.' Clare kissed him just as their flight was called for boarding.

THE END

Dear reader, if you enjoyed this book perhaps you would consider leaving a review on Amazon or Goodreads. Your comments would be gratefully received.

Meanwhile you might enjoy reading how Phil worked with Rachel to investigate her murder in
Text me from your Grave

Other cosy paranormal novels

Waltzing with Ghosts
Restless yew tree cottage

Family saga novels

Bluebells and tin hats
Rhubarb without sugar

All these novels are available on
www.amazonbooks.co.uk

Author's note

This is my fourth cosy paranormal crime novel. When I started writing a few years ago I hadn't intended to write in this genre. Maybe having lost a sister who was a psychic plus losing a few other close family members all within a short space of time has influenced me.

Restless Yew Tree Cottage was a tribute to my sister. Text me from your Grave came next. In between writing Nine Tolls for Murder, I wrote Waltzing with Ghosts inspired by a true event experienced by three of my friends.

All the characters in this novel are fictitious. Any resemblance to those living or deceased is purely coincidental. Also fictitious are the names of the shops, streets, sports centre, pubs and bakeries. Again any resemblance to those mentioned is a coincidence.

Thanks

Once again I must thank my sister Lesley for her help and support whilst writing this novel. I would also like to thank Sarah Morgan and the members of Cardiff Writers' Circle for their feedback and support.

Text me from your grave

Chapter One.

Rachel hovered at the edge of the broken stone wall that circled the abbey cemetery. She was waiting for her mother to come away from the funeral. She glanced around her. No-one had noticed her hanging about. Only once, at a burial, had someone perceived her presence. When Rachel had realised that, she had spirited herself very quickly to another spot.

Some of her friends advised her not to linger too close at funerals but she was fascinated observing the behaviour of the bereaved. She liked listening to the snippets of gossip shared amongst those who attended. It was a good way of finding out what was happening on the 'other side'.

Rachel's mother was taking her time getting away. Always gregarious and sociable, Anna Bellis was behaving true to form. She weaved in and out of the mourners; examined the names on the wreaths and silently sympathised with family and friends. Her wistful gaze followed each of the bereaved as they left her grave side to get to their cars. Finally Anna drifted across to join Rachel.

"Hello darling. I would love to give you a hug." Anna gesticulated a greeting. Her raised arms, swathed in the blue silk sleeves of her cocktail dress, fanned thin air.

Rachel nodded. "Me too. Her eyes roved over Anna's clothes. I see you have come out in style mum. Did you choose that get up?"

"Yes. Your father followed my instructions to the letter." She gazed down at her outfit taking joy in her white nylon tights and blue shoes that matched her dress. "I hoped you liked those clothes I chose for you. It was such a horrible, terrible time. Planning your unexpected funeral was not easy. It isn't nice for anybody in those circumstances, I know. But you were young. You shouldn't have gone so soon."

Looking down at her ripped jeans and her 'Save the Orangutan' T shirt Rachel grinned. "I was chuffed with your choice. Thank you. But mum, why did you put my mobile phone in the coffin? Surely you didn't think you could contact me in the grave?"

"I did ring you. I could hear it calling you."

Rachel stifled a grin. "I didn't hear it, but I saw the 'phone vibrate and the light flashing telling me there was a call coming through. Not bad considering I was buried six feet under. But obviously I couldn't respond! There was nothing I could do about it. I was unable to touch it let alone answer or make a call."

Anna pursed her lips. "Well I instructed your dad to put my own mobile in my coffin just to see if I could communicate with him. Anyway I wanted him to make sure I was dead. I had a fear of being buried alive."

This time Rachel burst out laughing. "Oh mum, I'm so sorry, but that wasn't going to happen. I'm sure dad would have checked everything. There is no way he was going to let you be buried alive." She softened her voice then added, "I don't think he will try to use the mobile."

"If he follows my instructions he will. He promised!" Anna retorted assuredly.

Rachel smiled at her mother. She let that comment pass. "Mum I am pleased to see you even though I'm sure you would have preferred to be on the 'other side' a bit longer. You aren't that old. God, fifty five. I wasn't expecting to see you again so soon!"

"I know. I thought I would have had at least another twenty years, but that heart attack left me very weak. However, I had time to make some plans and leave instructions. I have left unfinished business."

"Have you asked dad to carry on investigating my murder? I heard him swear to me at my own funeral that he would get justice for what they did to me. He visits me a lot. Gavin comes too."

"Yes of course! He will. It was my dying wish." Anna hesitated. "Please tell me. Did you know the brutes who killed you?"

Rachel shook her head. "No. They were complete strangers."

"Well that's some relief. I always dreaded that it might have been someone you knew. Anyway Gavin will help your father to try to find your killer, as soon as he flies back from Budapest. He will be leaving shortly after the wake."

"Budapest! What is Gavin going to do there?"

Anna smiled. "He is going to see if any of your friends can help. They will be endowed with some power just like you. He knows someone who is a psychic. His name is Phil. Do you remember him? They were in college together a few years ago. Apparently he and his then girlfriend went on a ski-ing trip there and fell in love with the place. They're married now living in Transylvania of all places! They keep in touch with Gavin by email and face book.

Rachel frowned. "Yes I remember Phil vaguely. But I don't have any friends in Transylvania nor anywhere in Romania. And I don't have any power."

"Your *special* friends. You know like you are now. In fact like me too." Anna chortled somewhat nervously.

"Oh I see. Just because we are all dead doesn't mean we are all 'universal friends' you know. And in any case I don't think those dead people in Romania or Transylvania have any more power than us either. All that vampire stuff is just a myth. Besides that, I can't get there to find out for myself. You need special agreements to go there. It is a very complicated system to get permission. In fact it is also very complicated to get permission even to venture outside your relevant zone."

"Zone? What do you mean by zone? I thought ghosts could go anywhere they like."

"That's just it. We aren't ghosts. We are spirits. We are only ghosts when we get the powers to re-visit a place and, in rare cases, be seen by someone living."

"I'll soon get the powers. I'm quick to learn."

"It doesn't work like that."

"What do you mean? Now I'm dead, I can do what I like."

"Sorry mum but you can't."

"I don't see why not." Anna looked earnestly at her daughter.

"You need permission to be a ghost."

Anna frowned. "So do you mean to tell me that even though I am dead, I need some kind of agreement to allow me to go wherever I want?"

"Sort of. It depends on your death. I qualified to be a temporary ghost because I was murdered.

You wouldn't be able to be a ghost because you died naturally."

"That's a shame." Anna sighed. "I was planning on haunting a few people I don't like."

Printed in Great Britain
by Amazon